Other FAWCETT BOOKS
by John D. MacDonald

All These Condemned
April Evil
Area of Suspicion
The Beach Girls
Border Town Girl
The Brass Cupcake
A Bullet for Cinderella
Cancel All Our Vows
Clemmie
Condominium
Contrary Pleasure
The Crossroads
Cry Hard, Cry Fast
The Damned
Dead Low Tide
Deadly Welcome
Death Trap
The Deceivers
The Drowner
The Empty Trap
The End of the Night
End of the Tiger and Other
  Stories
The Executioners
A Flash of Green
The Girl, the Gold Watch and
  Everything
The Good Old Stuff
Judge Me Not
A Key to the Suite
The Last One Left
A Man of Affairs
More Good Old Stuff
Murder for the Bride
Murder in the Wind
The Neon Jungle
Nothing Can Go Wrong
One Monday We Killed
  Them All

One More Sunday
On The Run
The Only Girl in the Game
Please Write For Details
The Price of Murder
Seven
Slam the Big Door
Soft Touch
Where is Janice Gantry?
You Live Once

TRAVIS McGEE SERIES

Bright Orange for the Shroud
Cinnamon Skin
Darker Than Amber
A Deadly Shade of Gold
The Deep Blue Good-By
The Dreadful Lemon Sky
Dress Her in Indigo
The Empty Copper Sea
Free Fall in Crimson
The Girl in the Plain Brown
  Wrapper
The Green Ripper
The Lonely Silver Rain
The Long Lavender Look
Nightmare in Pink
Official Travis McGee Quiz-
  book
One Fearful Yellow Eye
Pale Gray for Guilt
A Purple Place for Dying
The Quick Red Fox
The Scarlet Ruse
A Tan and Sandy Silence
The Turquoise Lament

JOHN D. MacDONALD

THE END OF THE NIGHT

An execution is a very serious thing, and around here we do our level best to have it go smooth and quick, and we try to do it with some dignity too.
—Warden Durkin G. Shires

FAWCETT GOLD MEDAL • NEW YORK

To Roger and Geoffrey,
who left their marks on the manuscript

A Fawcett Gold Medal Book
Published by Ballantine Books
Copyright © 1960 by John D. MacDonald

A substantial portion of this book has appeared in Cosmopolitan Magazine. Copyright © 1960 by The Hearst Corporation.

ISBN: 0-449-13195-5

This edition published by arrangement with
Simon and Schuster, Inc.

Manufactured in the United States of America

First Fawcett Gold Medal Edition: February 1966
First Ballantine Books Edition: February 1984
Second Printing: March 1987

Dear Ed,

Well, we had the big day here, and we sent the four of them off to their reward with what Satchel-Butt Shires, our lovable Warden called "splendid efficiency." Honest to God, if you'd still been here, you would have split a gut watching Shires sweat blood around here as burning day got closer and closer.

I admit it was a pretty big deal all right, four in one day when the most we ever had before was three, and this time one of them was a she. Did you know she was the third female ever executed in this state? I didn't. It just goes to show how fast women can talk, Eddie boy. Do I need to tell you?

Anyhow, Big-Butt Shires knows he's going to have a full house, and he like to drove everybody crazy with this idea he got about rehearsals. He borrowed a stop watch someplace, and half the time it wasn't right because he didn't know how to work it, and then he'd chew us out. Remember how red his face gets? How could you forget? He chewed on you most of anybody.

I can't count how the hell many times he run us through it. Eight of us, and a damn stuffed dummy. He had old Creepy Staples over on the switch as usual. Bongo and me were on the electrodes, straps and hood. Christy and Brewer were on the cart. He couldn't get the Doc to mess around with that kind of nonsense, so he had old Mitch make like the Doc. Marano and Sid were escorts, and he'd say "Go" and they'd walk the dummy in, grinning like fools, with Shires yelling "Take it serious, men!" and they'd sit in on the throne and Bongo and me would make a full latchup like it was for real, and step back to our places. Staples would fake the switch with Shires giving us a slow count, then old Mitch would step in and hold a beatup

1

stethoscope on the dummy and pronounce it dead, and then Christy and Brewer would come wheeling the cart in as we did the unlatching. We'd do it four straight times and then Shires would give us a pep talk and we'd do it again.

Honest to Pete, Eddie boy, you'd think Shires was going to get married.

I'll tell you, we did get us a full house. They were packed behind that glass shoulder to shoulder. I don't have to tell you the types. We had the cops and politicians you see every time on account of they get some kind of boot out of it. One way it's better than auto races on account of when you come here you know somebody is going to get it. Then there were the official witnesses appointed for this one, most of them hating the hell out of every minute, and then there was the reporters. You could tell about the few who'd seen this kind of thing before. They weren't making any smart cracks and trying to play tough. They just looked sick. Shires, by the way, managed to pass the buck upstairs about who could get in, so he didn't have a thing to do with it, and that made him real happy. They were shook down thorough for cameras and little tape recorders and little transmitters, and I hear they got a pretty good haul off those boys.

Shires was scared sick they wouldn't get the woman here on time, but it was timed right, and they brought her in through that little back death-house gate where the stiffs go out. I guess all those guys behind the glass were thinking about all the sexy pictures that got printed of the Koslov woman, and if they were, they had a hell of a disappointment. She put on maybe twenty pounds, and she had her hair in braids, and she'd got religion. She walked in steady, her hands together in front of her, her lips moving every minute, following right along with the Father who was with her, looking down toward the floor. She had on a white dress like a confirmation dress, I swear, but real plain. She didn't even flick an eye at the throne until she come to the step up onto the little platform, and then she stepped up and turned and sat down, not missing a word. She crossed herself before we strapped her arms, and she kept right on with the praying. She was shaved good under those braids, and the plates went on neat and tight. The only thing was just before the hood went on, it was like she saw all those guys behind the glass there watching her for the first time. She said a few words, not loud, but loud enough for Bongo and me to hear them, and I can tell you, Eddie boy, I can't put them in no letter going through the U. S. Mails. She picked up the praying when the hood went on, and we stepped back, and all I have to say to you is that it was a good one. You know how bad even the good ones are. The first time was enough, and when they were running her out on the cart, I looked over and saw our audience had shrunk some, which is always to be expected, and there were a few bottles out, and some of them didn't look like they'd last much longer.

We got Golden next, the scrawny guy that talked so funny and made you so sore that time. He had nothing left at all, that boy. They'd taken his glasses. He had that empty foolish look, and Marano and Sid were carrying all but about two pounds of him. He was trying to make his legs go in that flappy stilt walk they get, and he had ruined his pants before they even got him to the door to bring him in. When that bird spotted the throne, he went stiff as a board and set his heels and tried to thrash around. And he started to make a hell of a noise like I never heard before. For a guy with so many words, he didn't have one left in English. He just went, "Gaw, gaw, gaw, gaw," with the strings in his neck standing out, and he couldn't take his eyes off the throne. Marano and Sid slid him right along, lifted him and spun him and plunked him down and held him a second until we could make the first latch. He was thrashing, but there wasn't much strength in him. He was still going "Gaw, gaw" under the hood when Staples threw it to him. And that was a good one too, and that one cleaned out a few more behind the glass so those boys left had some nice standing room.

We got the big one next. All brute. He didn't take it bad. He had a silly grin on his face and he kept trying to move in any direction except toward the throne, but he handled easy. It could have been a lot tougher, but Shires got scared

of what a guy so powerful might do, so he fixed it with the
Doc to sneak a shot to that boy that would have stunned a
horse. So he hardly knew where he was, and that's why he
acted like a punchy fighter.

I had a hunch that everything was going too good, and I
was sure right. It looked all right at first. But after Doc
checked, he stepped back and gave the sign to Staples for
another bang. He got rattled and didn't give us our chance
to check the plates, so it was the Doc's fault. There was
clearance at the leg and you know what that will do. You
want to know how powerful that boy was? He busted the
right armstraps like wet string, and nobody thought
anybody would ever bust those! I found out later he busted
his right arm in three places, thrashing it. Of course it
didn't work the second time, but Doc gave us our chance to
reset the electrode firm, but then we didn't know what the
hell to do about that arm. We all looked at Shires. He was
like paste, and he gave us the go-ahead. Let it thrash.
Staples made sure on that third run. You know, that one
even made me feel a little funny.

There was a delay while we had to jury-rig something for
the right arm. It was fifteen minutes before we could get
heavy canvas straps from the shop, and I guess the waiting
was hell on that Stassen boy. He was good as the girl, I'd
say. Bongo says better. He came in dead-white and his
mouth a little bit open, moving so fast they had to trot to
stay with him. He hopped up onto the platform and
hesitated such a little time you could hardly notice it, and
sat down and put his arms right where they belonged. He
saw them through the glass then, and I can tell you we had
damn few customers left, and he turned red in the face and
closed his eyes tight. And when Bongo slid the hood on, he
said, "Thanks." Isn't that a hell of a thing? Bongo, he
jumps a little and says, "You're welcome." We step back
then, and that one went good too.

I knew you would want to know how it was, pal, because
you were here in the fun house so long. As you can expect, I
am sitting here writing this to you in an empty house. Like
always, Mabel has gone to her sister's place for a while.

She agrees about the extra money and all, and God knows we can use it, but it makes me sore as hell the way she gets it in her head she don't want to be anywhere around me afterwards, like I had some kind of disease.

All I can say is, I'm damn glad they didn't spread those four out, say about two weeks apart. A man would hardly have no love life at all. Ha Ha. From the way it looks around here, we won't get the next one until July, and he's had two stays already and his lawyers are fighting for another one, so it might stay quiet right into fall, which would suit me just fine. Four of them like that, it takes something out of you, I guess.

Write me a note when you got time, Eddie boy, and tell me how it feels to be retired after a long useless life. And don't forget the bet. You got the Yankees and I got news for you. They're not going to make it this year either.

Yours in friendship
Willy

ONE

IT is not astonishing that the memoranda written by Riker Deems Owen, the defense attorney, regarding what came to be known as the Wolf Pack Murders, have been preserved by Leah Slayter, a softly adoring member of Mr. Owen's staff.

Though Riker Deems Owen had long had the habit of writing windy and rambling memoranda for the files, to "clarify my concepts," his output in this instance is of more than normal interest.

It was his first—and most probably his last—case conducted under the hot glare and distorting lens of national publicity. Perhaps no one could have won the case. And "won," within this particular framework, can be translated to mean any penalty less than death. Riker Owen, at forty, had a solid record of success. Once it had been determined, on a jurisdictional basis, that the four co-defendants would be tried in Monroe—which calls itself The Friendly City—the stunned parents of Kirby Stassen, the only defendant with family resources, made a logical choice when they retained Riker Deems Owen in their attempt to save the mortal existence of Kirby Stassen, their only son, their only child, their only chick, their only illusion of immortality.

Owen had not only his comforting record of success, but also a persuasive plausibility that lessened, to some small and necessary extent, their horrid fear. They could not know that they had retained not a savior, not a hero, but an assiduously processed imitation, the hollow result of boyhood dreams distorted by the biographies of Fallon, Rogers, Darrow and other greats.

This does not indicate a special gullibility on the part of the Stassens. In fact, in the early days of the long trial, most of the correspondents in the courtroom believed themselves privileged to watch the birth of a new legend. But as Riker Deems Owen tired, he could not sustain his own illusion. The gloss crackled. The strings became visible. What had been considered quickness of mind was shown to be dreary gambits, well rehearsed. Originality dwindled to a contrived eccentricity. By the time it was over he had suffered a total exposure; he had been revealed as a dull-witted and pretentious poseur, irrevocably small-bore, a midget magician who strutted and puffed under the cruel appraisal of his audience, lifting long-dead rabbits out of his provincial hat.

Yet it cannot be said that he lost the case, because it can never be proven that anyone could have won it.

The notoriety of the case—the State versus Nanette Koslov, Kirby Stassen, Robert Hernandez and Sander Golden on a charge of murder in the first degree—gives a special interest to Owen's memoranda.

The student of law can read the actual transcript of the trial to his professional profit. Those more interested in the irony of the human condition can read the Owen memoranda instead, and see there the reaction of a rather pedestrian mind to the four souls he was committed to defend.

The confidential memoranda were dictated to Miss Leah Slayter, the newest addition to his staff, who not only took down many of the verbatim conversations between Riker Owen and the defendants, but also acted as his secretarial assistant during the trial itself.

Should the discerning reader detect in the Owen memoranda a certain striking of attitudes which seems inconsistent with the legal approach, it can be blamed not only upon Miss Slayter's physical attractiveness and her tendency toward hero worship, but also upon the confirmed tendency of Owen's wife, Miriam, to treat him and all his works, after twenty years of marriage, with an attitude best described as patronizing boredom. A man must have someone before whom he can strut. Also, any excessive imagery in the memoranda can perhaps be blamed upon a wistful desire to publish those memoranda as memoirs at some future date, a conceit not unusual in all professions.

Miss Leah Slayter's attitude toward her employer kept her from sharing the general disillusionment with the talents of the attorney for the defense. For her he burned as bright as morning. When he sought tears from a stony jury, it was Leah's eyes which misted. When the verdict was returned, her ripe, shocked mouth gaped open, her brown eyes went wide and round and her fingers snapped the yellow pencil in her hand.

Riker Deems Owen's reaction to defeat can only be guessed. He wrote no final memorandum after the verdict was returned. It is safe to guess that he knew what the verdict would be, that he sensed his own cumulative ineffectuality, and saw it confirmed by the very shortness of the jury's deliberations. They were out only fifty minutes—a typical time span when the verdict is to be guilty of murder in the first degree, with no recommendation for mercy. Perhaps Mr. Owen did write a memorandum heavy with blame for every factor except himself. If so, he recognized it in time as an unproductive example of unprofessional flatulence composed as balm for his own ego, and destroyed it.

Nor can Miss Slayter's total emotional reaction to the defeat of her hero be assessed. One can assume, with reasonable safety, that she was able to rationalize the traditional gift of self to ease the agony of the fallen one. Her warm charms, only very slightly overabundant, awarded with worshipful humility, would have properly reinflated the ego of many men less trivial than Riker Owen.

One could say that while he was in the process of tumbling off the merry-go-round, he caught the brass ring.

The first memo in the Wolf Pack file was written after his first few conferences with the parents of Kirby Stassen:

I have experienced a partial failure of communication with Kirby's parents. I understand why this must be, as I have seen it before. Everyone who works with criminals in any capacity is familiar with this phenomenon. It is, I suspect, a classification error. All their lives, they have been conscious of a great gulf between the mass of decent folk and that sick, savage, dangerous minority known as criminals. Thus they cannot comprehend that their son, their decent young heir, has leaped the unbridgeable gulf. They believe such a feat impossible and thus the accusation of society must be an error. A boyish prank has been misunderstood. People have lied about him. Or he has fallen under the temporary influence of evil companions.

Their error lies in their inability to see how easy it is to step across the gulf. Perhaps, in maturity, when ethical patterns are firmly established, one cannot cross that gulf. But in youth, in the traditional years of rebellion, it is not a gulf. It is an almost imperceptible scratch in the dust. To the youth it is arbitrary and meaningless. To society it is a life and death division.

Their son has aided and abetted and participated in the commission of illegal acts. And so he is a criminal. These acts have been of such a serious nature that he can never again lead a normal life and, in fact, is in very grave danger of having life itself taken from him as a barbaric penalty.

They cannot comprehend this. They have the pathetic faith that somehow this will all be "ironed out," with suitable apologies, and they will take their son home with them where he can sleep in his boyhood bed, eat well, and forget all this unfortunate nastiness.

The father, Walter Stassen, is a big, meaty man, positive, driving, aggressive, accustomed to take charge of any situation. He is about forty-eight. In twenty-five years he built one produce truck into a tidy, thriving, one-man empire. He has lived hard, worked hard, played hard. I suspect he has neither patience nor imagination. Now, for possibly the first time in his life, he faces a situation he cannot control. He continues to make loud and positive noises, but he is a sorely troubled and uncertain man.

The mother, Ernestine, is a year or two younger, a handsome, stylish woman with an eroded face, a body gaunted by diet, a mind made trivial by the routines of a country-club existence. She is highly nervous, a possible by-product of the menopause. I suspect that she is a borderline alcoholic. At our two morning meetings she was perceptibly fuzzy. If so, this situation will most probably push her over the edge.

I can detect no real warmth between these two people. They have measured their lives by their possessions. Most probably their emotional wells have been polluted by a long history of casual infidelities. From the way they speak of Kirby, I believe that they have considered him to be, up until now, another possession, a symbol of their status. It pleased them to have a tall, strong son, athletic, bright, socially poised. They were amused at his scrapes, and bought him out of them. Such incidents provided cocktail conversation. They were an evidence of high spirits. For Kirby there was never any system of reward or punishment. This is not only one reason, perhaps, for his current grave situation, but also the reason why they find it so impossible to think of him, at twenty-three, as a person rather than a possession, an adult accountable to society for the evil he has done.

As I had suspected, I met with strong opposition when I stated my intention to defend all four simultaneously. They did not want their invaluable Kirby Stassen linked so directly to horrid trash like Hernandez, Koslov and Golden. They did not see why my services, for which they are paying well, should be extended to cover those people who have had such a dreadful influence on their only son. Let the court appoint defense counsel for them. Kirby would travel first class, as usual.

To convince them, I had to resort to an analogy to explain why this state had been able to extradite them, and why they were being tried for the particular crime committed approximately ten miles from where we were sitting.

I explained that there were several major crimes involved and, of course, many minor ones which we need not consider. The problem was jurisdictional, meaning who would get them first.

Addressing myself to Walter Stassen, I said, "Think of each crime as a poker hand. They spread them face up. Then they selected the strongest hand, the one most likely to win the game. That's why they were delivered into the hands of this state. We have the death penalty here. And this crime is more airtight than the others. And the prosecutor is dangerously able."

"What makes this one so strong?" he asked.

I shrugged. "You've certainly followed the case in the papers. Witnesses, opportunity, sound police work, clear evidence of significant participation in the crime by each one of them."

Ernestine broke in. "I read where it said that Kirby actually . . . He couldn't do a thing like that! What has this got to do with your defending Kirby separately anyway?"

"The state will not entertain a motion for a separate trial for any defendant, Mrs. Stassen. They shared in the commission of the crime. They will be tried together. I can *represent* Kirby separately. Someone will be appointed to defend the other three when they are arraigned on Monday. Maybe that person will approve of the line of defense I am developing. Maybe not. It is a good way to guarantee that all four will be—electrocuted."

"What is your line of defense?" Walter Stassen asked in a husky voice.

It took a long time to explain it to them. On the basis of preliminary investigations, I did not feel that I would find any significant holes in the State's case, any room for reasonable doubt. I told them I would admit the commission of the crime. At that point Ernestine Stassen tried to walk out, weeping. Her husband grasped her roughly by the arm, whirled her back and pushed her into the chair, and snarled at her to be quiet.

I went on, saying I intended to show that the four defendants came together in the first place by pure accident, that due to the personalities, compounded by the indiscriminate use of stimulants, alcohol and narcotics, they had embarked on their cross-country career of violence. I meant to stress that the group, as a group, had performed acts which would have been outside the desires and capacities of any individual member of the group. I explained how I meant to stress the randomness and lack of logic of their acts, the meagerness of their gain, the flavor of accident throughout the entire series of incidents. I explained the legal-historical precedents for this line of defense.

"And if it works, Mr. Owen," he asked, "what's the verdict you're shooting for?"

"I hope to get them off with life imprisonment."

Mrs. Stassen jumped to her feet again at that moment, her eyes wide, mad and glaring. "Life!" she shouted. "Life in prison? What the hell kind of choice is that? I want Kirby free! That's what we're paying you for! You're on *their* side! We'll find somebody else!"

He managed to silence her. He said he would give me their decision later. I had arranged for them to visit Kirby in his cell, for much longer than the usual time allotted. When Mr. Stassen came back to my office I could see for the first time, just what he would look like when he became very old. His wife was not with him. He told me they would go along with my wishes in the matter. He said he had put all his business affairs in the hands of a competent associate, and that he and his wife would locate an apartment and take up residence in Monroe until the trial, so as to be near their boy. I assured him that I would do my best.

I was then free to visit each of the defendants in turn, taking along Miss Slayter to transcribe pertinent comments which I might find useful in my preparation of the case.

I do not know if I can put the precise flavor of the presence and personality of Robert Hernandez down on paper. He is almost a caricature of the brutishness in man. Cartoonists give him a spiked club and draw him as the god of war. He is about five ten, and weighs maybe two hundred and thirty pounds. He is excessively hirsute, thick and heavy in every dimension, with a meager shelving brow, deep-set eyes, a battered face. It is a shocking thing to realize he is not quite twenty-one years old.

His intelligence is at the lowest serviceable level. But unlike the majority of people with a dim mind, he has no childishness or amiability about him. He gives the impression of an unreasoning ferocity, barely held under control. His eyes are quick to catch every movement, and he holds himself with an unnatural stillness. It was curiously unnerving to be in a cell with him. There was a musky tang in the air, like that near a cage of lions.

The only surprising thing about his history is that this is his first arrest for a major offense. The rest of it is what you would expect. Foster homes. Three years of schooling. At twelve he looked like a man, and began to live like a man. Trucker's helper, stevedore, farm hand, warehouse work, road work, pipelines. A drifter, with arrests for drunkenness, assault and the like.

His voice is thin, and pitched rather high. He has only the most vague idea of his own personal history, where he has been and what he has done. He has a low level of verbal communication. Such a creature is wasted in our culture. Attila could have found good use for him.

The interesting and significant aspect of his relation to the group in his attachment to Sander Golden. Apparently he had fallen in with Golden a month or so before Kirby Stassen, the final member of the group, joined them and the Koslov girl in Del Rio, Texas. He had met Golden in Tucson and from then on they had lived by Golden's wits. It was, I believe, similar to but less wholesome than the relationship of Lennie and what's-his-name in *Of Mice and Men*.

My question about Golden brought the best response from Hernandez—best in that for a few moments the wariness was lessened. "Sandy's a great guy. Only good buddy I ever had. Keep you laughing *all* the time, man." I

did not care to inquire what would give this creature cause
for apelike laughter.

His attitude was stolidly pessimistic. They'd been
caught. When you killed people and got caught, they turned
around and killed you. That was the rule. And it was worth
it, because they'd had a "ball" before they were caught. He
was indifferent as to who defended him. If it was all right
with Sandy, it was all right with him.

I knew he would make a terrifying bad impression in
court, but I did not see what I could do about it. He had to
be there.

During most of the time we were in the cell, Hernandez
kept staring at Miss Slayter with a focused intensity that, in
time, made her visibly uncomfortable. She kept licking her
lips and turning her head from side to side like a cornered
animal. I saw the shininess of perspiration on her upper lip,
and heard her sigh of relief when we were at last able to
terminate the interview and leave him alone.

Sander Golden is twenty-seven, but he looks much
younger. He is five foot eight, with sharp sallow features,
mousy, thinning hair, bright eyes of an intense blue behind
bulky, loose-fitting spectacles which are mended, on the left
bow, with a soiled winding of adhesive tape. He gives a
deceptive impression of physical fragility, but there is a
wiry, electrical tirelessness about him. He is a darting man,
endlessly in motion, hopelessly talkative. He can apparently
sustain a condition of manic frenzy indefintely. I hasten to
add that this frenzy is pseudo-intellectual and pseudo-
philosophical rather than personal and emotional.

He has a high order of intelligence, a restless, raging
curiosity and a retentive memory. These attributes are
crippled by his unstable emotional pattern, his lack of
formal education and his childishly short attention span. He
does not seem to appreciate the extent of his personal
danger. He is enormously stimulated by the more subjective
implications of his situation. His mind moves so quickly
speech cannot keep up. During the time I was with him he
lectured me in his pyrotechnic, disorderly fashion on the
nature of reality as it applies to murder, on the entertainment

value of criminal cases, on the special rights of the creative individual, on violence as a creative outlet.

I cannot attempt to reproduce his manner of speech, but I must report that it causes a curious condition of exhaustion and exasperation in the listener. After we left Miss Slayter covered it quite aptly, I thought, by saying that talking to Sandy Golden was like trying to swat a roomful of flies with a diving board.

It is difficult to reconstruct Golden's past. He veers away from all objective discussion, registering impatience with such trivia. He says he has no family. I do not believe Golden is his original name, but there seems to be no way to check it out easily, or any special reason for so doing. He has a record of two arrests, both on narcotics charges. He claims ten thousand close friends, most of them in San Francisco, New Orleans and Greenwich Village. His speech is a curious mixture of beatnik, psychiatric jargon and curious, sometimes striking, similes.

He seems unable to explain why, after staying out of serious trouble for so long, he and these relatively new companions embarked on what the papers have termed "a cross-country reign of terror." He seems to feel that it started with the incident of the salesman near Uvalde, and just went on from there, as though some waiting mechanism had been triggered by that flash of violence.

He darted, whirled, paced, all the time we talked, pausing in a jerky way to fix us with his bright-blue eyes and speak of Zen and love, making such violent washing motions with his soiled hands that his knuckles cracked loudly.

It is too easy, I am afraid, to look upon this Sander Golden as a ridiculous being, an inadvertent comedian. After we left his cell, Miss Slayter categorized him as "spooky." There is an aptness to her word. Under the clown exterior there is a crawling, restless, undirected evil.

It is far too trite to say that life is a series of accidents and coincidences. It would take the largest electric calculator at M.I.T. to estimate the probability not only of these four disturbed people joining forces, but then driving through

Monroe on their route from the southwest to the northwest in a stolen car at exactly the right time, the right instant in eternity, to intersect the path of Helen Wister's life.

I have known the Wister family all my life. And so I knew that nothing in Helen's past could have prepared her for that unholy quartet which came upon her and took her out of the summer night. By then they had nothing more to lose. They were aware of the widening police search. They were out of control. One has only to summon up the image of her, a captive of Hernandez, Golden, Koslov and Stassen, to begin to imagine the totality of her terror and her despair.

She was taken on Saturday night, the twenty-fifth day of July, just a few days after her pending marriage to Dallas Kemp had been announced. We can assume that up until the moment when her life was struck by this ugly lightning, it was, for her, a normal day in the life of a young woman, spiced undoubtedly by her excited anticipation of the wedding. . . .

TWO

HELEN Wister, at mid-morning on the twenty-fifth day of July, drifted slowly, warmly, up through the final mists of sleep, emerging without haste into wakefulness, until an anticipatory tingle of excitement, like kitten-feet along her spine, brought her quickly to a focused awareness of time and place.

She sat up in her bed, stretched until she creaked, yawned vastly, knuckled her eyes, then combed a tousled blond mop back with her fingertips and looked sidelong at the slant of sun on the floor. She checked the sun against the clock. Ten-thirty. Eight hours and a bit. Save your energies, girl. Stay in training. Nineteen days to wedlock. Why did they call it lock? Sounds like chains and things. Ball and chain.

She swung smooth, brown legs out of the bed and stood up in her pale-blue shortie nightgown, padded to the nearest window, turned one slat of the blinds and looked out at the day. The sky was an empty, misty blue. Sprinklers turned on the green lawn that sloped down to the fish pool and the rock garden. Far beyond the roof peak of the Evans house, just visible above the line of maples, she could see a little red airplane heading south. She yawned again, hiked up the right side of the nightgown and slowly scratched her hip, her nails making a whispery sound against smooth flesh.

As she turned back toward the bathroom she pulled the nightgown off over her head and flung it toward the rumpled bed. She angled the bathroom door so that she could see herself in the full-length mirror, and then stepped back, feeling a familiar guilt at this recently instituted ceremony of self-appraisal. The shadowy light in her bedroom deepened her tan and exaggerated the pallor of the bands of white across her breasts and pelvis. Mealy white, she thought. It makes nakedness look more naked. Go on, girl. Stare at yourself. Criticize. What do you want? Reassurance? Took myself for granted for so damn long, and suddenly turn into a nervous exhibitionist, wondering if it's all exactly what Mr. Dallas Kemp wants for his very own. Shoulders back, girl. That's a little better. Dal, honey, you better keep on liking it just as much as you seem to right now, because it's all there is. And it's all—forgive the expression—girl.

She was too healthy-minded to endure this fleshy appraisal without its awakening her sense of comedy. She smirked at herself and struck a pose that parodied the contrived bawdiness of the girls on questionable calendars, and laughed at how silly she looked, and went on into the bathroom.

While she stood under her hot shower, she knew that no deep sleep and no prolonged shower could completely relax her. There was a greedy little knot of sexual tension within her, which, at nineteen days before marriage, was, she suspected, a desirable thing.

For a moment she felt darkly envious of the brides of bygone years who were virgin right up until the first night of honeymoon. They too could have this itch of yearning and wanting, but it would be dampened by their fears. But she knew just how good it would be with Dal Kemp, because there had been that brief, intense, carefully rationalized affair with him back when they had been antagonistic toward each other, before they had, to their mutual surprise, fallen deeply in love.

And last night had not been calculated to relieve anybody's tensions. They had parked on the way home for the usual talk and the usual kissings, under a partial moon. But the kissings had carried her away into a buttery, swarming, underwatery place, puffing like a small frantic bellows, twisting under his hands to make everything readily accessible to him—and had not somebody somehow touched the horn ring, blasting the quiet night with an electonic bray that set nearby dogs to barking and froze both of them in a moment of induced terror, they would have had to part with wry confessions of mutual weakness, and wistful words about the pact they had broken.

After the howl of the car horn had substituted for character and they sat carefully apart with their breathing slowing, Dal was inclined to be grumpy, saying, "It's a pretty artificial arrangement, isn't it? After all, we've . . ."

"But that was two other people, darling. That was the worldly young architect sneaking that silly blonde in and out of his bachelor quarters. Not us. Silly people having a silly affair. But along came love. Remember?"

"Somehow the logic of this escapes me, dearest."

"But it isn't logic, Dal darling! It's sentiment. I love you. I'm going to marry the man I love. And I just want to be as much of a traditional bride-type bride as I can. I just want to be—shy and coy and apprehensive. I'm certainly not so cynical I'm trying to nail you down by locking the cookie cupboard. Do you think that?"

"No, no. I do know what you mean. But at times like this my nerves go bad. Give me a couple of minutes and I'll be ready to joke and sing and do card tricks."

After he had dropped her at her home, Helen realized that she had not risked telling Dal about her impending Saturday night date with Arnold Crown. The narrowness of their escape from breaking the pact had kept it from ever being the right time or place. It would have to be done today, and he would have to be made to understand why she had to see Arnold.

After her shower she packed fresh tennis clothing and a

swim suit in her zipper bag and, wearing a summer skirt, blouse and sandals, went downstairs. Her mother was on the phone, talking about appointing some kind of a committee. They exchanged morning smiles. Helen fixed juice, toast and coffee, and took her tray out onto the kitchen patio.

Jane Wister brought her own cup of coffee out and sat at the round redwood table with her daughter and said, "The bride-to-be was positively radiant."

"Glowing with tremulous anticipation," Helen said. "Why don't you appoint a committee to run this wedding?"

"Would that I could, child. And how does it feel to be one of the unemployed?"

"I can't really tell yet. I wouldn't be working today anyway. Ask me on Monday, Mom. They had a sort of a farewell party for me at the office yesterday. I had to make a speech, even."

"Baby, your father and I think you're getting a pretty nice guy."

"I know I am."

"After some of those clowns you ran around with . . ."

"You hush!"

"What's the schedule for today?"

"Dal and I are meeting Francie and Joe at the club at noon for lunch. Then tennis. Then a swim. And then a drink."

"You may run into twelve-year-old Martians posing as your twin brothers. I think they plan to spend the day making the pool unbearable for the general public. What are you and Dal doing tonight?"

"I'm going to see Arnold Crown tonight, Mom."

"You're what? What does Dal say about this?"

"I haven't told him yet."

"You're doing a very stupid thing, Helen."

"I can't help it. I feel responsible. I was nice to Arnold because I felt sorry for him. I had no idea he was going to— get so carried away. I can't help it if he got the wrong idea. But it was my fault for going out with him in the first place. And I've got to put a stop to all this—constant heckling, all these notes and phone calls, and his driving by the house all the time, and following Dal and me whenever he can. It's a kind of persecution. I hope I don't have to be cruel, but I've got to make him understand he has absolutely no chance at all."

Jane Wister smiled at her daughter. "Ever since you were eleven there's been some smitten Arnold hanging around. You attract the lame ducks, dear. You've always been too kind to them." The smile disappeared. "But this is a grown man and I think he's an unstable man. You see him in a public place and you be careful. Don't go anywhere alone with him, you understand?"

"Oh, he's perfectly harmless! He's just terribly upset."

"Let your father handle it. Or Dal."

"I promised him I'd see him tonight, Mom. I can settle him down. Don't fret about it. It'll be wonderful not to have him popping up from behind every bush. And I can stop flinching every time the phone rings."

"I'd just like to know where a person like Arnold Crown got the idea he'd have the ghost of a chance with a girl like you. The Wisters have been . . ."

"Knock it off, Mrs. Wister. Snobbery doesn't become you."

"But you've had every advantage, and he . . ."

"Owns and operates a gas station, a good one."

"And Dallas Kemp is one of the finest young architects in the state. So I'm a snob. So be it."

Helen Wister did not find a good opportunity to tell Dal Kemp about Arnold Crown until a little after four that afternoon. They had swum in the crowded pool, and then Dal had pulled one of the poolside pads over onto the grass away from the heavy traffic. They were stretched out, prone, side by side, the late afternoon sun biting their backs.

"You get bossy when we play doubles," Dal said lazily.

"We won, didn't we?"

"In spite of all your bad advice."

"Pooh!"

"How about a picnic tomorrow, woman? You bring the food. I have to go look at the Judlund site again."

"That's a lovely place for a picnic. Too bad you're going to ruin it putting a house on it. Sure, I'll bring food."

"We'll make it an early night tonight, hey?"

"Dal, honey, I'm going to see Arnold Crown tonight."

"Give him my best wishes for a pleasant evening."

"I am. Really."

He sat up abruptly. "Are you out of your mind? I—I forbid you to see that meathead."

She sat up and glared at him. "You what?"

"I forbid you!"

"Why the hell do you think I want to see him?"

"To tell him to leave you alone, I would hope."

"So what's wrong with that?"

"Everything's wrong with it. He's got hallucinations about you. He isn't rational. He ought to be locked up. And you want to go hold his hand! The answer it no!"

She narrowed her hazel eyes. "I'm twenty-three, Dallas. I've been away to school. I can earn my own living. Up until now I've done what I've thought best about my own emotional problems. I intend to keep on that way. If you can give me any rational reasons why I shouldn't see Arnold, I'll listen. But I won't be shouted at and ordered around. I'm not a . . . chattel. You don't own me!"

It was a quarrel, and it was unexpectedly bitter. He took her home earlier than had been planned. She gave his car door a hefty slam. He squealed the rear tires as he drove away. No one was home. She showered again and changed, got into her MG and went to a drive-in to ease the healthy hunger that was only partically blunted by her anger.

At eight-thirty as the street lights and car lights were coming on, she turned into Arnold Crown's service station and parked beside the building. Arnold appeared immediately, silhouetted against the floodlights, bulking large, shadowing her.

"I knew you'd come, Helen."

"I said I would. We have to have a talk."

"I know. We got to have a talk, Helen. That's for sure. Your car'll be okay here. Go over and get in the Olds. I'll be right with you, soon as I get a jacket."

"Where will we talk?"

"I thought we could just ride around and talk, the way we used to."

She walked over and got into his car. He seemed more relaxed than she had expected. Poor Arnold. You can almost hear the wheels in his head going around as he adjusts himself to any new idea. I didn't ask him to fall in love with me. He drove me home that time because my car wasn't finished, and we stopped and had a coffee. He seemed so terribly alone.

He got in beside her and drove out of the station and turned left on Jackson.

"Notice how good it sounds now?"

"What? Oh, yes, it does sound good."

"It was the valve lifters making that racket."

"Oh."

A few moments later he said, "A guy with a station over on Division wants to sell. It's a good location. I talked to the bank."

"That's good, Arnold."

"I figure this way. One station won't bring in enough. You're used to things nice."

"I don't want you to talk like that!"

"That's the way I got to talk. Honest to God, I never been so happy, Helen, you coming to your senses and stopping this kidding around. I read that thing in the paper, I nearly lost my mind, I'm telling you. I guess I've really been . . . kicking up a storm."

"Let's just say you kept me aware of your existence, Arnold."

He made a flat, hard sound of laughter. "You kill me, the way you say things. Honest to God."

"Arnold, I'm afraid you're getting the wrong idea, about my agreeing to see you tonight."

"It's the best thing ever happened to me. I mean you go through month after month of hell, and all of a sudden it's over and the sun comes out. I got a surprise for you, Helen, honey."

"Can we stop somewhere and . . ."

"I found out one thing. Without you I'm nothing. I'm dead. There's nothing left to me at all. That's why this is like coming back to life, having you right here beside me again."

She looked out to see where they were. He had followed the pike and then turned off onto Route 813, heading east. It had been a heavily traveled route until the pike was built. Now it was a secondary road, serving the widely scattered farms.

"Please find a place to stop so I can really talk to you, Arnold, and make you understand."

He slowed the car, but it was several miles before he found a place that suited him. He pulled over and stopped. She could see a tumbledown barn with its roof making a sagging line against the stars.

She turned to him, her back against the door on her side, and pulled her knees up onto the seat.

"Please don't say anything until I'm finished, Arnold. Somewhere, somehow, you got the wrong idea about us. I don't know whose fault it was. We've never even kissed. But you've got to get over it. You've got to stop dreaming, because the dreams aren't going to come true. You've got to stop bothering me. I'm in love with Dal, and I'm going to marry him."

She could not see his shadowed face. There was a long silence. She heard his deep, harsh laugh. "You got a couple things wrong there, Helen. It was you and me right from that first day."

"It *never* was! You were lonely. I thought you should have somebody to talk to. That's all."

"You have to keep on playing those games, don't you, right up to the end?"

"I'm going to marry Dal. Nothing can change that. And you must stop phoning me and writing me and following me."

"You got it all wrong. You're talking about the way it was, Helen. For all these weeks and weeks. Right up to tonight. It isn't that way any more. You have to understand that. It's different now. From now on, it's you and me."

Something in his voice gave her a chilly, uneasy feeling.

"Arnold, you have to try to understand."

"I understand that you're the only thing that can happen to me, Helen. The only possible way out. So it has to happen. It can't happen any other way. That's what *you've* got to understand. It's like they say—a destiny."

"I guess you'd better take me . . ."

"Now it's time to tell you about the surprise I got."

"Surprise?"

"I planned it all out careful, honey, just the way you'd like it. This crate is all tuned and gassed. Smitty is going to run the station. I got a thousand bucks cash on me. First time in my life I ever carried that much. In the trunk is two brand-new suitcases, yours and mine. Both full of brand-new stuff. I know I got pretty things you'll like, and they'll fit. So you don't even have to go home again. We're going to drive on through to Maryland and get married there and go on up to Canada for the honeymoon. How's that for a surprise?"

She heard her own nervous laughter. "But I'm going to marry Dal . . ."

His big leathery hand closed suddenly on her wrist, so strongly that she hissed with pain. "That joke is over and I'm sick of it, Helen. I can't get no more laughs out of that old joke. So drop it from now on. We're taking off from here, right now. We'll wire your folks. We're going to drive right on through, so you see if you can go to sleep and rest up for getting married."

He released her and started the car. She heard the high, hard whine of a car coming along the road behind them, coming the way they had come. As the Olds jumped forward she turned and opened the door and plunged out.

She made four or five giant running steps, fighting for balance, hearing a hoarse yell and scream of brakes, and then she tripped and dived headlong into a tumbled blackness where a sudden white light burst like a bomb inside her head, behind her eyes. . . .

T H R E E

DEATH HOUSE DIARY

I, Kirby Palmer Stassen, stood last February—sixteen thousand years ago?—at a window on the second floor of a fraternity house, looking out at the curiously warm, mild rain that misted Woodland Avenue. I was wearing a dark-gray cashmere cardigan and gray flannel Daks. I was smoking a cigar. The window was open a few inches. I felt the damp breath of the day against the back of my hand. It was the best layout in the house, a two-bedroom suite, handy to the shower room. I shared it with Pete McHue. We were both seniors. It was a Tuesday afternoon. Pete was spread out on the couch behind me, wearing an old terry robe, plodding his way through an assigned book, spooning all that dead dry stuff into his head where it would remain forever.

I remember that I'd put some Chavez on the machine. I can't remember the name of the symphony, but it's the one Clare Boothe Luce commissioned him to write as a memorial to her daughter who got killed in an automobile

thing, in California, I believe. If I'd put on the Chavez
Toccata for Percussion it would have fitted my mood better,
but Pete wouldn't have gone along with that. On the far
sidewalk, headed east, was a dumpy little girl in a red
sweater, walking in slow defiance of the rain, hugging
books with both arms, her rump jutting, damp brown hair
bouncing. I wondered what she was thinking about.

When you look back on the moments that change your
life, you get good recall. I was thinking about that good
Spanish word Hemingway used a lot. *Nada*. Nothing.
Pronounced with accent on first syllable. First syllable is
dragged out, sneered, with a lift of the lips. The *d* is soft—
halfway between a *d* and the *th* sound. *Naaaada*. Truly,
Mother, it is nothing. *En su leche*. And that day, that week,
that month of my twenty-second year, the word could have
been suitably embroidered across my groin.

My college career made a nice, neat chart. I'd come
busting onto the scene as a hotshot from Hill, ready to slay
the university, but nobody seemed to appreciate my significance and importance. So I went after them, buckety-
buckety. So draw the chart in a nice upward curve from the
base line, right up to a peak that comes about the middle of
the junior year. Kirby Stassen, large man on campus.
Background sounds of continuous applause.

Then sag it off. No more honors. No athletic participation. Maximum cuts, and then some. And, for the first time,
I found myself on academic probation. And it was raining.
And in the rain was a ghostly whiff of spring. Chavez
rounded off the coda and the player clacked off, and let
some of the sounds of the world come into the room. Traffic
on the avenue. Underclassmen horsing around downstairs.

"It's all crap," I said.

"What?" Pete asked vaguely.

"*Nada*. Zero times zero equals square root of minus
zero."

"For Chrissake, Stass, stop standing around here fingering yourself. Go get drunk. Go get banged. You've been a
drag for weeks."

"I bother you?" I asked him politely.

"You bother everybody," he said, and plunged back into his book.

And exactly at that moment is when it happened. For the first time in a long gray time there was a little queasy wriggle of excitement way down there on the floor of my soul. What the hell was keeping me there? What was the Christ name good of coasting through to a degree, which I could manage to do, and then signing up for that Executive Training Program the old man had all lined up for me?

It is like something going click in your head. I had been part of it—part of Pete, part of the guys horsing around downstairs, part of the traffic on Woodland, part of the strange girl in the red sweater. And all of a sudden, without having made a move, I was on my way. I had peeled myself loose from my environment. Once it was done, in that instant, I knew I couldn't ever go back. I even had a feeling of nostalgia. Good old Pete. It was as if I'd come back to visit one of the places where I had grown up. I stood like a stranger in the middle of my own life, with that excitement coiling and uncoiling way down inside me, making my breath a little short.

I went up into the storage place in the attic and located my foot locker and suitcases and brought them down to the room.

"*Now* what the hell are you doing?" Pete asked.

"Taking off."

"You look like you're planning one hell of a long weekend, old buddy."

"As long as they come. I'm off for good."

"With only four months to go? You're nuts!"

"I'm off to seek my fortune, sir."

He went back into his book, but I was aware of him pausing from time to time to stare at me. I was very neat. I would take one suitcase. I tagged the locker and the other suitcase for express shipment to 18 Burgess Lane, Huntstown. I sorted books, clothes, records, and made a discard pile. Four years of frivolous accretion.

"Pete? Come here and pay attention." He ambled over and saluted. "Please have Railway Express pick these up and ship collect. Take first choice of anything you want in this pile, and distribute the balance among the needy brothers."

He squatted and pulled out a white cablestitch sweater. "We po' folk are humbly grateful, squire."

I shook hands with him. When I left the room he was once again squatting, prodding at the pile. It was my intention to go from room to room and exchange the fraternity grip and bid a sturdy masculine farewell to the brotherhood in residence. But instead I went right down the stairs and out the back of the house, got into the Impala and drove away from there. My checking account was down to about eighty dollars. So, on a slow circuit of the commercial strip next to the campus, I cashed three twenty-five-dollar checks at places where I was known and, ninety minutes after the moment of decision I was clear of the city, singing right along with Doris Day on the car radio as I made a hundred and ten feet a second on the way to New York.

That's what the newspaper types have kept asking me—how did this all start? How did such a clean-cut, privileged, American youth embark upon such a career of violence? The women—do they call them sob sisters still?—are the worst. They are getting a sexual whee out of it. You can tell from their eyes. To the very best of my knowledge, sob sisters, it started that February day, with rain and Chavez and *nada*.

It is strange that while I am trying to fit my mind around the enormity of what they are going to do to me—strap me down and turn out all my lights—precious, unique, irreplaceable little ole me—I can still feel intense indignation toward whatever newspaper clown invented that Wolf Pack designation. How banal and tiresome and inaccurate can you get?

It is as though I expected more dignity out of electrocution, which is in itself a drab and tragicomic thing. It is the suitable terminal incident in the lives of people named Muggsy Spinoza—or Robert "Shack" Hernandez?—but seems unsuitable for a Kirby Palmer Stassen. I resent my pending abrupt demise being labeled a Wolf Pack Execution.

Perhaps any attempt to comprehend what they are going to do to me is as footless as a chipmunk trying to tuck a coconut into his cheek. Objectively I know it is going to happen. But subjectively I know the cavalry will ride over the hill, the redskins will skulk off into the brush, the warden will give me a new suit, a train ticket and a handshake, and I will stride off into the sunset as noble music swells and rises on the sound track.

Another sore point in the newspaper coverage—should I have hired a public relations specialist?—has been the half-ass attempts at amateur psychoanalysis. The favorite conclusion has been to label me a constitutional psychopath. Obviously this takes society off the hook. If I can be labeled as something different—a deviation from the norm—then it is evident that the culture is not at fault. I am sick, they say. I have been sick from the beginning. I hid all my wicked violence behind the bland mask of conformity. I was an imposter. That is the implication. And so all the schools and group adjustment programs and cultural advantages are blameless.

I never felt like an imposter.

I have tried to go all the way back through my years, and down into myself, to see if I can find any stray morsel of proof of the correctness of their classification. I find no thirst for blood. I have nearly racked up an automobile trying to avoid a chipmunk, and once I drove behind a car which swerved deliberately to hit a farm dog, and it filled me with a sick, helpless anger.

I can find but one incident I do not clearly understand, and it was buried deeper than it perhaps should have been.

I am twelve. It is late summer. Ever since my birthday I have owned a 22-caliber rifle, but it has been taken away from me by my father because I lied to him. He is angry at me this year. I lost a fight and came home weeping and so he whipped me and ordered me to stay in the house for a week. My mother hugs me and says he is too hard on me. I think I hate him this year. He seems to be cruel to both of us, to my mother and to me. My friends are out somewhere in the sunshine. I am alone in the house. I am restless. I do not know what I was pretending, but I hid in my mother's closet, and I fell asleep on the closet floor, with one of the sliding doors open a few inches.

I am awakened by nearby sounds. I know at once that it is late afternoon. The blinds are closed. The bedroom is filled with a strange golden light. I know I should not be where I am. I get up onto my knees. I look through the crack where the door is open, and look across into the mirror of her dressing table and see reflected there the two of them, and see that they are making the sound which awakened me and which I could not identify. At first I am stunned with horror, believing that he is killing her in some horrible way, that she is fighting for her life, that they are gasping and writhing in mortal struggle. She makes a long, sighing moan, and I come dangerously close to screaming in panic, believing that she is resigning herself to death.

But the dirt-talk of the playground and the boys' room is forcing itself into my mind. As my eyes become more accustomed to the golden light, and the mists of sleep burn off my brain, I see how they match the sniggering descriptions I have been given. They told me that my mother and father did it, but I could not believe they could secretly indulge in such a nastiness.

They are still. I can sense her horrible shame. She is the most beautiful woman in the world and, being his wife, she must submit to his vileness, to this naked degradation. I vow that when I get my rifle back I will kill him and she will be forever free of the pain that made her cry out.

To my astonishment she gets up from the bed and bends to kiss him lightly and tells him in a teasing way that she loves him. She is smiling. She gets cigarettes and gives him one, and lights his and her own, and then comes toward the closet. In silent panic I move back into the farthest corner, beyond the silk and scent of her dresses. She slides the door open, takes a dressing gown from a hanger and closes the door. I cannot hear them as clearly but I hear casual talk— about a party, about repairs the car needs and about me—

about my disobeying by leaving the house. Later I hear them calling me outside, calling my name into the dusk, and so I go downstairs, pretending great sleepiness, telling them I fell asleep under my bed while pretending I was in a cave. I cannot look directly at either of them. My face burns with their shame. My father gives me back the confiscated gun and rubs my head with his knuckles.

The next afternoon I go into the woods behind the house with my rifle. I stretch out, face down, in an open place, and I try to stop thinking about It, but it is there, golden pictures in my head, a dirty, naked plunging. The grass is a jungle. Ants are the size of lions. I look at the box of shells. Dangerous up to one mile. The Club is less than a mile away. The pool will be full. I know the exact direction of the invisible Club. I aim the gun at a high angle. I empty the clip, reload, fire, reload, fire—panting, my hands trembling, until the last bullet is gone. I see them falling, screaming, drowning, turning the blue water to bright-red. I hurl the new gun into the brush. I am crying. I bruise my fists on a tree, then fall to my knees and vomit.

I am sick when I go home. She puts me to bed. I wait for them to come after me. Nothing happened. The next day I talk to a boy who was at the pool. Nothing happened there. Two weeks later I look for the rifle and find it, ruined by rust. I bury it. When he asks what happened to it, I tell him I loaned it to somebody. By the time school starts, he has stopped asking. For a long time I dream about him. He is standing naked on the high board, his back to the pool. Little black holes appear in his back. He shudders as each one appears. I wait for him to fall. But he turns slowly and laughs at me, and makes a gesture, and I see that where his penis should be, there is a big bullet, the brass case shining in the sun, ready to kill anybody.

The memory was far down, covered by the careless debris of eleven years, but I excavated it intact, using all the care of an archeologist, the lens, the soft brush, the ancient writings. I do not know that strange small boy. He moves through his own world, playing his secret games. The Freudian dream is ludicrously obvious. I understand all of it. But I do not understand the attempt to kill. I wonder where the small bullets went . . . a whole half box of .22 long rifle arcing across an August afternoon.

The light in this cell is never extinguished. It is countersunk in the ceiling, shielded by heavy wire mesh. I have been told by one of the guards—a curiously clerical-looking fellow who spoke with professional pride—that in the event of power failure a standby generator cuts in automatically, and should that fail to kick over, a second generator will assume the load.

A death cell should be a dungeon, with black sweating walls and phrases of despair carved by those who have waited for execution. But this is a bright, clean, sterile place, functional, efficient. One could assume it has never been used before, but the clerkly guard assures me that it has, many times.

Under past administrations, prisoners under sentence of death lived under much the same conditions as the prisoners in the other cell blocks, except for living one to a cell and having no work assignments. But since the completion of the new execution area we, the condemned, inhabit—at the expense of the taxpayers—these special cells. We have soft bunks, books, writing materials, television, radio, good food from a special kitchen, regular medical and dental examinations. I have gained eleven pounds since I have been in this place. We live under continual light, without contact with each other, with a guard always on watch. There are eleven of us here, filling one more than half of the twenty special cells.

It amuses me to imagine a Martian sociologist studying this place, reaching erroneous but plausible conclusions. He might well imagine that we are individuals of great value and importance. He might assume we are being conserved for some superstitious and barbaric sacrifice. For one full year the Aztecs fattened and pampered their sacrificial virgins before taking them one by one to the top of a pyramid and cutting out their pulsing hearts with the obsidian knife at sunrise. I believe these maidens were selected by chance. I cannot avoid feeling that I have been selected in some random irrational manner for this questionable honor.

I have learned what they will do with Nan Koslov. She is being held in isolation in a women's prison a hundred miles away. All the rituals of preparation will be performed there. When it it time to destroy the four of us, she will be brought to this place and, if the scheduling is efficient, will arrive minutes before her important appointment. My clerkly guard smirks and says, "Ladies first."

I now return to the February day when I left the university. I drove into New York at about six o'clock in a heavier rain that was just beginning to turn to sleet. I put the car in a garage on 44th Street and started phoning hotels. There were conventions and the city was loaded. I gave up after a dollar's worth of dimes, and phoned Gabe Shevlan.

Gabe sounded cordial but preoccupied. I told him the hotel problem. He said I had caught him on the way out, but come on over. I could bunk on the couch. He'd phone the apartment later on, and I should wait there for the call.

It was on 77th, near Second Avenue. I pushed random buttons until somebody buzzed the front door open. I went up to 3B and Gabe had left it unlocked as he said he would. It was a smaller, dingier place than I expected.

Gabe had been a fraternity brother. He had graduated a year ago last June, and had worked with CBS for a while and then gone with an advertising agency. He looks like an underfed Lincoln without the beard. He is highly nervous and ambitious, and always has a dozen projects going at once.

After I'd gotten organized and built a drink, I called home long distance and got hold of Ernie. I could tell from the background noise they were having a big cocktail party. She sounded slightly loaded.

"What are you doing in New York? Darling, I can't understand a word you're saying. Hang on while I go take this in the bedroom." I heard her ordering somebody to take the phone and hang up after she got on the other extension.

"Kirby? Now what's this all about, dear?"

I told her I'd quit. She didn't like it. It didn't fit her

maternal ideas of how my life should be regimented. She kept pounding at me to get at some reason that would make sense to her. Was it because of a girl? I kept telling her I was tired of it, and so I'd quit. What was I going to do? Look around and find something to do. She said the old man could line up people for me to see in New York. I said the hell with that. I didn't want any part of that routine, thanks. She asked me about money. I said a check would help, and I gave her Gabe's address. She had me hang on while she went and got the old man. From the time it took, I guessed she was briefing him.

I was right. He came on big and ugly. "What kind of goddamn childish nonsense is this, son?"

"I felt like quitting so I quit."

"You *felt* like it. That's great!"

All I could do was let him rave. I was spoiling the big plans he had for me. I was letting him down. I was letting the Executive Training Program down. I was going to be a bum. Well, by God, no more gravy for me. No more featherbed. I wasn't going to get one dime from him. A fool who quits four months before his degree doesn't deserve any kind of a break. Now what did I have to say for myself?

"Goodbye," I said, and hung up.

Incidentally, the check came from Ernie two days later, on Thursday. Airmail. Five hundred, accompanied by a rambling letter in her angular backhand, telling me how hard this was on the old man. They didn't know what to tell people, and so on, and so on. One reading was all I could give it.

Gabe phoned at eighty-thirty and asked me to come right along and join them at an Italian restaurant in the sixties. When I got there he was pacing back and forth in front of the hat check booth.

After we shook hands I started to thank him and brief him on why I was in New York, but he broke in and said, "Time for that later, Stass. I can use you. There's three at the table. The guy is John Pinelli. The blonde is Kathy Keats, an actress—Pinelli's wife. The little brunette is Betsy Kipp. She's a special friend of mine. I had to stab Pinelli in the heart tonight. He'll want to cling to me like a Bandaid. I want to peel off alone with Betsy, so when any chance comes, you help out."

I agreed. He gave me an extra key to the apartment and said we could talk later, maybe tomorrow. We went to the table. It was a corner table, not far from the bar. A place had been made ready for me. Gabe introduced me around. Pinelli was a big, soft, pink-and-white man who looked more like a Swede than an Italian or a Spaniard or whatever he was. The two women were gorgeous. Betsy was younger and had a special glow. I knew I'd seen Kathy Keats before and heard her name before. I knew I'd seen her in the movies and on television. Her hair was dyed a beautiful silverblond, and done up in a regal and intricate way. She was on my left. Her shoulders were smooth and bare.

She has a Dietrich face, long, slightly Slavic, a long throat, erect carriage, so that at a distance she looks tall. But close up you realize she is a small woman, about five four, a hundred and ten. I never found out how old she is. On that first night I would have guessed twenty-five. Since then I have guessed as high as thirty-seven. She gives an impression of terrible control. Every movement is slow and graceful. When her smiles comes, it is slow in coming, and it flowers to great brilliance, but you feel she is back there behind that smile, watching you, watching everybody.

John Pinelli was stupidly drunk, and drinking steadily. But there was more than that wrong with him. He was like an ox who had been clubbed on the head. He kept shaking his big head in a bewildered way. Two conversations went on at once. One was between Gabe, Betsy and Kathy, bright talk about people I didn't know, none of whom seemed to have last names. John Pinelli carried on a monologue, most of it so slurred you couldn't understand it, all of it ignored by the other three, as thoroughly as they ignored me. From the little I heard of Pinelli's ramblings, he was telling himself about the great, important, sensitive, significant things he had directed.

The food that came was wonderful. Betsy Kipp and I were the only ones who ate it. Pinelli ignored his. Kathy

Keats ate a few small bites with slow precision. Gabe has always been too jittery to eat much.

The whole evening was unreal. At about eleven Gabe said, "I'm sorry, but we have to be running along."

Pinelli fixed him with a heavy, bleared eye and said, "Got to talk to you, my boy. Got to explain why you need me . . ."

I felt a touch on my right knee. I reached down and took folded bills from Gabe.

Gabe stood up and took hold of Betsy's chair and said, "Settle with you later, Stass. Have fun, kids." And they were gone.

I paid the check. It was over sixty dollars. Gabe had passed me two fifties.

I said to the Pinellis, feeling awkwardly out of my depth, "I guess I'll say good night and . . ."

"Stay with us," she said. It was an order.

"Flamenco guitars," Pinelli rumbled. "Flamenco guitars, darling."

She knew where he wanted to go. She gave the name to the cab driver. It was a dark place. The three of us sat at one side of a round table, and looked at the small stage where a man sat in a kitchen chair under a very bright spotlight and played intricate Spanish music on the gaudiest guitar I have ever seen. He had fingernails longer than any woman's. Under the music I could hear Pinelli muttering to his wife. We drank white wine there, a lot of it.

At two-thirty, when there was no more guitar, and Pinelli was slumped with his eyes closed, she worked his wallet out of his pocket, took two twenties out if it, wedged the wallet into her small gold evening bag, handed me the forty dollars and said, "I'll have the cab wait for you."

I helped her get him up. Once he was on his feet he walked well enough. The cab was waiting. We went back up to the seventies, this time off Fifth. The little elevator was just big enough for the three of us. It climbed very slowly. Just as it stopped at their floor, Pinelli slid slowly down the elevator wall and sat on the floor like a fat child, his chin on his chest. We couldn't waken him. She held his head up and slapped his face until the corner of his mouth started to bleed. He was too big to carry. I took him by the wrists and dragged him. She went ahead and opened the door, shut it when I had dragged him inside, and then went ahead, leading the way to the bedroom.

She turned the bed down. We undressed him on the floor, down to his shorts. He breathed little pink bubbles of blood out of the corner of his mouth. I sat him up against the side of the bed and then, kneeling, got my shoulder under his flexed knees and with one great heave, got him up onto the bed.

"I'll do the rest," she said. I went out to the living room. It was a spacious apartment, high enough so that the big windows looked toward the lights of downtown. The apartment had a hotel flavor about it, as though nobody ever lived in it very long.

I was looking at the lights when she said, "Oh, I'd thought you'd left."

I turned. She looked exactly the same as when I had first met her. Glamorous, chic, controlled. Nobody could have guessed she had just put a drunk to bed. "I've got your change, Kathy."

"Put it on the table."

"You've got a beautiful place here."

"Have we? It's borrowed, for Chrissake. Every goddam place we live is borrowed. What's your name, anyway?"

"Kirby Stassen."

She gave me a tilted look of a special insolence. "All this courtesy, motivated by guilt. Get used to it, Stassen. You did well tonight. You might even be human enough to feel sorry for John. But I didn't know that son of a bitch Shevlan ever hired anybody human."

"I don't work for Gabe."

"So did he borrow you from Stud Browning? Don't crap me about a technicality, darling. It doesn't make you any cleaner."

"I don't know what this is all about, Mrs. Pinelli. Yesterday I was a senior in college. Today—I guess I should say yesterday—I quit. I drove to New York. I knew Gabe in school. The hotels are full. I'm staying with him. I've hardly had a chance to say hello to him."

She stared at me. "For the love of God, he's telling the truth!"

"I haven't understood very much of what's been going on this evening. I'm sorry, but nobody has explained anything."

"Sit down, darling, and hear the facts of life." She took my hand and led me to a long, low couch. "Gabe is on leave of absence from the agency. He's been assembling a package for a great big television series. Stud Browning is the producer. Gabe calls himself the unit manager. Gabe came after John to direct. I told John not to trust the mealy little bastard, but John went ahead with it on spec, getting everything lined up for the two pilots they're going to shoot. My God, he's been in on the casting and the story editing, everything. It's a big deal for John. He's had bad luck. I was going to be in it. They claim they still want me. Tonight, Gabe, after using John all these months for free, kicked him off the team. Stud is going to be producer-director and Gabe Shevlan is going to be assistant director. That cuts the nut. And Gabe has milked John for all the ideas he'll need. You're in bad company, Stassen. You have a reasonably clean look. Do you want to be an actor?"

"God, no!"

"You don't know how refreshing that is, sweetie!"

She smiled at me. She was close to me. I was full of wine. I felt very loose and sophisticated. So I took hold of her and kissed her. Her back felt lean and fragile under my hands. It was like kissing a corpse. When I released her she yawned and said, "Go the hell home, will you, before you really begin to bore me, Stassen."

I walked home. It was a clear night. There was a light on. The bedroom door was closed. The daybed had been made up for me. I was touched. I hadn't thought Gabe would go to the trouble.

I heard him leave in the morning. I looked at my watch. Twenty to ten. When I opened my eyes again it was noon. I padded, naked, through the bedroom and stopped with a grunt of shock and surprise in the doorway. Betsy Kipp, in bra and panties, was leaning toward the mirror over the basin, painting herself a new mouth with a small brush.

"I'll be out in one minute, Kirby," she said sweetly. "Gabe has some robes in the closet there."

I put on a robe and sat on the double bed. She had a fresh outfit laid out on the bed, a pale blouse and a tweedy green suit.

"Sleep well?" she called to me.

"Pretty good."

"That couch is lumpy. I've slept there a few times. I made it up for you."

"Thanks."

She came out of the bathroom. "All yours. Eggs, toast and coffee okay by you?"

"Fine."

"They'll be ready in a hurry because I've got a rehearsal at two, so don't stay in there forever."

When I came out, breakfast was ready. From the tiny table for two you could reach the small sink, stove and icebox.

"Sit down, Kirby. There's sugar but no milk for the coffee. How did you like Kathy? Isn't she a miraculous old broad?"

"She's unusual, I guess."

"Oh, I don't know as she's unusual. She's got a nice little talent. And, of course, those marvelous looks. She's fading now, of course. But I'd say she's done as much as she can with what she's got. People wonder why she didn't dump John ages ago. There's a word he has a hold over her or something. But Kathy never says much about herself. And when she does live it up, she never gets conspicuous."

"She's pretty sore at Gabe, apparently."

"That's stupid! Gabe does what he has to do. His job isn't easy. He takes horrible abuse. And they give him the dirty jobs to do, like last night. Lord, I've got to run! Kirby, dear, would you mind cleaning the joint up? No maid service. We're all meeting at the Absinthe on West 48th at six-thirty tonight. I'm bringing a girl for you. Doxie Weese. She's lovely, and she's a very sensitive little actress, and she's been terribly hurt, and she hasn't been out with anyone in ages. So be tender with her, will you? Thank you, darling."

After she left, the apartment seemed exceptionally empty. I cleaned the place. Some of her clothes hung in the closet. I killed what was left of the afternoon. I got to the Absinthe early and was on my second drink when the three of them came in. Gabe looked weary. Doxie had brown hair, sleep-walking mannerisms, and looked about thirteen years old. Betsy was in a bad mood, something about the stupidity of some new choreographer.

Late that evening I got a chance to ask Gabe about John Pinelli.

"We tried to give him a break," he said. "Old John just hasn't got it any more. Too bad. He was eager, but we couldn't take the risk. We're playing with other people's money."

"What will he do?"

"Are you in a sweat about John, or about Kathy?"

"Just curious."

"Maybe he'll find something and maybe he won't. Don't mess with them, Stass. Kathy is a thousand years older and a thousand times rougher than you are."

"I keep wondering how they'll make out."

"And I keep wondering if you had any change left from last night, buddy. Come up with it."

Three days later I got a job, through Gabe. Office boy at the agency. I sorted and delivered mail and memos, and ran errands. Because of Gabe's relationship with Betsy, I got stuck with the chore of squiring Doxie Weese around. She was a zombie. She could cry oftener and harder and for less reason than any girl I ever met. Betsy was very concerned about her. Betsy suggested to me that it might help Doxie if I slept with her. I said I was willing, but I couldn't even take her arm to cross a street without she started crying her heart out. Betsy said try, so I tried, and I did. It didn't help Doxie, and it wasn't worth it.

I began to get restless again, so restless that I said the wrong thing to the wrong man at the agency, and was out on the street ten minutes later, with a pay check in my pocket. I looked for work in a halfhearted way. All of a sudden Gabe went off to Portugal with the unit to shoot the pilots. Doxie went along with the unit. Betsy, two days later, went out to the Coast. Gabe said I could use his apartment while he was gone.

And I kept thinking of Kathy Keats and how her back had felt under my hands, as if I could snap it like a stick. I looked in the phone book. They weren't listed. I found the apartment house. The card under the right button had Pinelli written on it. I didn't have the guts to push the button. She came out at four o'clock the next day, and she was trying to look through me and beyond me, trying to spot a cab.

"Hello!" I said.

She focused on me, and frowned. "Oh, it's the school-boy. What's your name again, dear?"

"Kirby Stassen."

"Get me a cab, dear."

I hailed one and got into it with her. She looked slightly startled. "What in the world are you doing?"

"Nothing at the moment. I want to know how . . . your husband is doing."

"That's sweet of you, Stassen," she said, "but I'm going to have my hair done." She gave the driver the address.

"I'll go along and buy you a drink afterward," I said.

"I won't be out until six anyway."

"I can wait."

"Suit yourself, dear."

We both got out at the hairdresser's. She pointed out a hotel diagonally across the street and told me to wait there, in the lobby or the bar. I waited in the bar and then in the lobby. I wanted courage but not too much. When she came in, she spotted me and gave me that smile when she was forty feet away. She came, walking tall, giving me that smile, and I knew as she did it that it wasn't for me. It was for the people watching her come to me.

The bar didn't get much trade. We had a banquette table, very alone.

"Why do you give a goddam about John?" she asked me.

"I don't really know. But I do."

"Are you working for Gabe now?"

"He left for Portugal. I'm living in his aparptment. I'm looking for work. I had a job for a while. It wasn't something I'd want to do forever, but I shouldn't have gotten fired. Is John working?"

"No. I've been doing some commercials, for some nasty goo that takes hair off your legs. My legs are still good, thank God."

"All of you is good, Kathy."

"You're a brave child, Stassen, aren't you?"

"I'm dauntless. Do you have any plans?"

"Oh, we always have plans."

"Your eyes are just the color of violents."

"A deathless line, indeed! We're going to Mexico, Stassen. To another borrowed place to live. A beach place at Acapulco. John has some old friends who are setting up a company to make movies down there. He thinks he can get into the act."

"I'd like to go to Mexico."

"Why do you keep reminding me of a cocker spaniel?"

"When are you going?"

"It will have to be soon. The Burmans are coming back from Italy this month. They'll want the apartment. And I think it's time to get John out of this town. All the goddam doors are closed. All the secretaries have the word to give him the brush job. Show biz, darling. Kick the wounded. Direct forty pictures that pay off, and you can crush people under your wheels. Add two turkeys and you're dead."

"It's time for me to get out of this town too."

She started to say something, stopped, and looked intently at me. I had the odd feeling that it was the first time she had looked directly at me and seen me. "Of course you can drive a car, Stassen."

"Yes."

"John is a horrible driver. I despise driving. We were going to fly. But this way . . . I could take everything. Would you drive us down? It would be a business deal,

Stassen. We'll pay all your expenses plus . . . oh, a hundred dollars at the end of the trip."

"I'll do it for nothing."

"Thank you, no. We don't need a pal, Stassen. We need a driver. Then everybody will know where everybody stands."

I agreed to do it. Their car was in dead storage. It was a lot of car, a two-year-old Chrysler Imperial, black, loaded with every power gadget there is, plus air conditioning. It had six thousand miles on it. The California tags had run out. I found out that a friend had driven it east for them.

I had it checked over for the trip, and I arranged for new tags. I took my Chev over to Jersey and peddled it for thirteen hundred. It was a horrible whipping, but the best I could do. So I was able to start off with about sixteen hundred bucks, all but two hundred in traveler's checks.

They had a lot of stuff. Most of it was hers. I took it over to the apartment and loaded it the day before we left, a snowy day in mid-March. I packed the big rear trunk right to the eaves, and packed the rear seat to the roof, leaving space for one person back there. She had a lot of ideas about what should go where, and she kept changing her mind.

Finally I said, "Kathy, maybe I should get a chauffeur hat and uniform. To go with all the orders."

She straightened and gave me as cold and flat a look as I have ever received from anybody. "Just do your job, Stassen, without bickering about it, and we'll all get along a lot better."

We stood beside the car with the snow coming down, big wet flakes that caught in her hair. I was close to walking away. I didn't have to take abuse from a little broken-down actress. It was a showdown. She was establishing the relationship right there. A flake caught in her eyelashes. It didn't melt. I wanted to take her by her childish shoulders and kiss that eye and feel the ice of the snowflake against my lips, and the warm round violet eye.

"Yes, sir, Mrs. Pinelli, sir," I said.

There was a slight lift of the corners of her mouth. "Take that big blue one off the bottom and put this leather one there, please. I'll have to get into the blue one when we get into warmer weather."

So I unloaded and reloaded again. "What time should I bring it around in the morning, Kathy?"

"Let's get an early start. Ten o'clock."

So I drove the brute away. It was crouched on its haunches because of the weight. I garaged it and locked it myself, and spent my last night in Gabe's apartment, laying out the route. I figured it for a seven-day trip. I didn't know how naïve my guess was. I thought of sending them a card at home to let them know what I was doing, but I decided it would be more interesting to send the card from Acapulco. It would do more wondrous things for the old man's blood pressure.

By quarter of eleven the next morning, we were through the tunnel and heading down the Jersey Pike. It was a clear, metallic morning, with a dry road and light traffic. I kept the needle locked on seventy. Kathy was beside me, John Pinelli in the back. They both acted morose about the whole thing. There wasn't any excitement or anticipation in them. But I felt like singing.

I felt I should report on the route. "I decided the best thing to do is go right down 301, then cut west on 80 until we . . ."

"That will be fine," Pinelli said.

"I don't know how many miles you want to make a day."

"Every day at four o'clock, Stassen," she said, "start looking for a nice place. We'll stop between four and five. I won't ride beyond five o'clock. Lunch between one and two, please. Try to find nice places for lunch."

And that's the way it went. When you're lucky to get on the road before eleven, and you have to get off the highway a little after four, even in a brute like that Chrysler, it's a good trick to do two hundred and fifty miles a day. At each motel stop she would hand me the money, and I would go in and register, a single for me, and a twin-bed double for them. Then I would drive to their unit and carry their baggage in. I was privileged to eat with them at lunch, but not dinner. They had a fitted liquor case, and each night he would get smashed, and they would eat as late as the nearest restaurant would serve them. They never changed seats. She stayed up front beside me. About once an hour she would turn the radio on and hunt the whole length of the dial and turn it off. I could never figure out what sort of program she was looking for. Every day she spent at least an hour working on her nails. When she had a chance, she would buy a half dozen magazines. She would leaf through them very quickly, like an illiterate looking at the pictures, and drop them out the window one at a time as she finished them. Sometimes she would sleep, but for not more than ten or fifteen minutes at a time. John Pinelli slept oftener, longer and heavier—slumped against the luggage, snoring resonantly.

As far as they were concerned, I was a part of the machine. It irritated me, but there wasn't a damn thing I could do about it. I kept trying to figure out their relationship. Sometimes they would have savage arguments. She would turn around and kneel on the seat. They acted as if I were stone-deaf. Those two would say anything to each other. Some of the arguments were about money. I'd wondered how they were fixed. They weren't hurting as much as I had thought. He'd owned a piece of a couple of profitable movies, and he owned a piece of the producer's end of a television show that had been running for three years and looked as if it would run forever. And he had stashed some into an annuity back in his fat days. I estimated they had thirty thousand a year coming in. They schemed to live in borrowed houses, but in a motel he'd give the boy who brought the ice a five-dollar bill. Some of those kids looked like they'd been hit on the head. There was a flossy gift shop connected with one motel where we stayed. She bought two skirts of handwoven fabric, sixty bucks each.

The biggest money fight was about whether he should sell his piece of the television show and reinvest it in the Mexican movie venture. Every time they argued about it, they switched sides. And they would say things to each other I wouldn't say to a weasel. She, in particular, had the

foulest mouth I've ever heard on a woman. She said things
to him worth killing her for, and fifteen minutes later they'd
both be napping.

Sometimes they fought about how talented they were. He
told her once that if she had fifty times the acting ability, he
wouldn't use her in a mob scene. She told him if he had a
chance to direct the rape of the Sabine women, he'd turn it
into a box-office dog. He told her the mares in Westerns had
more talent. She told him he was the joke of the industry.
Twenty minutes later they'd be telling each other how great
they were. She had more than Hayes and he had more than
Huston.

But the worst scraps were about cheating. Then the
language was so choice I wondered why I didn't run the car
off the road. He'd tell her she made any honest tramp look
like Joan of Arc, that if she'd kept score, her diary would
look like a phone book. She'd tell him that he'd spent forty
years proving he had no discrimination. If it was warm and
wore a skirt, that was all he needed. Then they would start
throwing names, dates and places at each other, but what it
always came down to was that neither of them had any real
proof. He'd call her an ice-cold scrawny, ridiculous bitch.
She'd call him a fat, impotent old man. Once, when they
were going it so hot and heavy I thought he was coming
over the seat after her, a spark from her cigarette stung her
wrist. From the way she carried on, you would have sworn
she had just lost the arm. He cooed at her and petted her,
and she whimpered and yowled until I located a drugstore.
He hurried in and came out with four different kinds of burn
remedies, and fixed her up with a bandage big enough for a
fractured wrist.

It was a weird marriage.

A strange thing happened at a motel just west of
Montgomery, Alabama. It was unseasonably warm. The
pool was drained, but there were chairs around it. I sat out
in the warm dusk, thinking about going and getting
something to eat. She came up behind me, touched me on
the shoulder in a friendly way, and sat in the chair next to
mine. She said John was taking a nap. She called me Kirby

for the first time. She turned on so much warmth and charm, it was like standing in a hot-chocolate shower. We sat there for a least two hours. She drew me out. She made me feel like the most interesting man in the world. I gave her the full report on Kirby Palmer Stassen, from high chair to office boy.

"What do you want, Kirby? Where are you heading?"

"I don't know, Kathy. There's all the pressure to conform. I'm not ready to play on the team."

"Kicks? Is that what you want?"

"That's a word for it, maybe. I want to . . . do everything there is to do. I don't want to go down a tunnel."

Like a damn fool I thought we'd gotten onto a new basis. But the next day I was Stassen, part of the Chrysler. It gave me the feeling she'd used me for some kind of practice session, like a hell of a wing shot getting his eye ready for the season by trap shooting.

We went down 79 and 81 and crossed at Laredo. We stayed at Laredo one night and a half a day. Something happened to them there. Something private and significant and deadly. I don't know what it was, what they did to each other. But it was the end of something between them. You could sense that. I didn't see how it could be anything they said to each other. Nothing could have been more unforgivable than all the things they'd already said.

The change was abrupt. All of a sudden they were painfully polite to each other. They made comments on the road and the weather. No more battles. Something started to end right there in Laredo. And I was in at the finish. Some unknown incident gutted the relationship, and suddenly they had begun to be strangers.

I am treating my relationship with John and Kathryn Pinelli in such great detail because I suspect that it bears a significant relationship to all that came later. I know that on the basis of timing it was significant, because if I hadn't gone to Mexico with them, I'd never have met Sandy, Nan and Shack at that beer joint on the outskirts of Del Rio. On another level, if it hadn't been for the Pinellis and what happened, I wouldn't have been *ready* to meet Golden,

Koslov and Hernandez. I wouldn't have had that special attitude which helped the four of us fit together like the fingers on a glove.

Once you have destroyed somebody, and there's no way to put the pieces together, and you know you're going to live with a funny kind of remorse the rest of your life anyway, you can maybe dilute remorse through more destruction.

So maybe what happened to me is suicide.

I wish that Kathy could have a chance to read this. I wouldn't expect her to understand it, or make any attempt to try. If I could write it as a play, and if she could be given the chance to read it, then she would come alive, frowning in pretty concentration, fitting her mouth silently around her lines. But I know what would happen to this kind of a journal. She would riffle it, see there was no art work, and drop it out the car window and go to work on her nails, or pick a fight with John, or curl into a tiny and fragrant cat nap.

FOUR

RIKER Deems Owen devoted one whole memorandum to a rather rambling analysis of the Stassen boy:

On what now appears to be superficial reasoning, I felt in the beginning that Kirby Stassen would be the one I could communicate with most readily. Now I realize I was misled by the similarity of our backgrounds. We are from the same approximate social and financial level. He has poise and good manners, and treats me with a respect only infrequently marred by a strange attitude of derision.

In appearance he is what might be called a typical American. He is large, as are most young people nowadays. Almost six foot two and about a hundred and ninety-five pounds. He has the look of a man who—if permitted to live on into his middle years—would become quite heavy. His father is a burly man of the same physical type, though about two inches shorter. Though the very deep tan he acquired in Acapulco is bleaching out, there is enough of it left to make a handsome and pleasing contrast with his healthy white teeth, his rather pale gray-green eyes, and his hair and eyebrows which have been sun-faded to a lighter hue than their normal shade.

His eyes are set wide. His nose is slightly flattened at the bridge as the result of an automobile accident when he was seventeen. This gives him a little bit of the look of a roughneck. His features are rather heavy. One could say he is relatively more attractive as a young man than he will be ten years from now, should his life be spared.

There has been much comment in the press about the incongruity of his wholesome appearance contrasted with the savage crimes in which he participated. Some have used the expression "baby-faced." This seems to me quite inaccurate. I would call it a poster face. It could be used to advertise ski resorts or cruises or enlistment in the service. There is nothing sinister about the appearance of this young man. He looks wholesome and rugged.

As I have said, he has a considerable amount of poise. And he has a habit of looking at you very directly. It is a directness almost disconcerting. He is as immaculate about his person as a cat. He moves easily and well. He listens with flattering respect and attention, and scrupulously calls me "sir."

In the beginning, when I began to pay my periodic visits to each of the four defendants, I felt much more at ease with Stassen than with the others. Over these weeks, this situation has become reversed. I can communicate with Kirby Stassen to an astonishingly limited degree. It is like driving a nail through soft pine into tool steel. The first few strokes are easy. Further penetration is impossible.

Some of this, of course, may be no more than the usual lack of contact between generations. It sometimes seems to me that the Great Depression marked the beginning of a special change in our culture. All young people born during or after those years seem to act toward the rest of us with a great deal more tolerant disrespect than can be accounted for merely by the difference in ages. New standards of behavior have infected the world. The divergence seems to be growing more acute rather than diminishing.

I have discussed this observation with my closest friends. They seem aware of it, but the reasons they give do not satisfy me. Proctor Johnson, a practicing psychiatrist, said that in his opinion this new generation has been subjected to such a bewildering, contradictory series of social and cultural stresses and strains that they have ceased trying to establish any sequence of relative importance of ideas and objects. They've had the blissful reassurance that no matter what they do, society will nurture them, and so they have no compulsion to consider a career more important than an ability to water ski. He says we have deprived them of an appreciation of reality by depriving them of challenge.

On the other hand, George Tibault, a professor of sociology at Monroe College says that we cannot communicate with our young because they have no inner direction, no code of behavior based on an ingrained ethical structure. He says they will adjust their own codes over and over, depending on the accepted behavior patterns of each group within which they find themselves. This, he claims, is a splendid mechanism which enables the young to meet the survival requirements of our society better than we older ones, with our inner burden of rightness and wrongness. I told him I thought this rather cynical. He smiled and quoted a dictionary definition of cynical. I wrote it down. "Given to or marked by sneering at evidences of virtue and disinterested motives; inclined to moral skepticism."

I had to confess that it seemed to fit the tenor of our times, as reflected in the public press.

But all that does not solve the mystery of Kirby Stassen. Here is a transcription from Mrs. Slayter's notes:

"To take just one example, Kirby, I would like to ask you this. Do you feel that you would have killed or helped kill Horace Becher if you'd been alone, or with a different group?"

"The question doesn't make much sense, sir."

"In what way?"

"I'd never have seen the man unless it happened just the way it did. So how can I tell you what I would have done?"

"Surely you've got enough imagination to make up a situation where you would have come in contact with Horace Becher in some other way?"

"What kind of way, sir?"

"Say you were hitchhiking alone and he picked you up. Would have have killed him?"

"There wouldn't be much sense in that, would there?"

"You imply that there was sense in the way he was killed?"

"No, sir. That was just the way it happened. It wouldn't have happened that same way again in a thousand years. That's why I can't see the sense in these hypothetical questions, sir."

"Just as a game, then, can you devise a situation where you would feel called upon to kill that man?"

"I guess so. You mean all alone, don't you? I guess if I escaped from this place and hitched a ride with him and he turned the car radio on and figured out who I was. And if we were in the right sort of place. I guess I could do it. I'm not sure, but I think I could do it all right."

"Would you feel you were doing wrong?"

"Oh, I know it would be wrong, sir. Anything against the law is wrong, isn't it?"

"But would you feel guilt? Remorse? Shame?"

"That would depend on who he was, I'd say."

"I don't follow you."

"I mean if he was a valuable person, I mean that would be a waste. But if he was just . . . you know . . . a real drag, ignorant, stupid, a loudmouth type. Why should anybody feel a big load of guilt about that?"

"He was a human being, Kirby."

"I know, sir. With desires and aspirations and an immortal soul. But in the scheme of things, that joker was just about as significant as a gob of spit on a wet sidewalk, and just about as attractive."

"Oh, then you admit the existence of some scheme of things?"

"Don't you, sir?"

"Of course I do! Describe to me what you'd call a valuable person."

"Well . . . somebody who's willing to live way out, sir. Somebody who doesn't go along with the whole cruddy regime. Somebody who's willing to try to bust the race out of this big trap we've gotten ourselves into. Like Sandy says, somebody who can give love without keeping a set of records on it."

"Do you consider the four of you to be valuable people, Kirby?"

"I don't want to sound disrespectful, sir, but that's a pretty stupid question."

"I take it you don't call yourself valuable?"

"We're all just as nothing as that Becher."

"But you felt capable of judging him?"

"Who judged him? He was all creep. He wasn't a rare specimen. There's twenty million of him, all so alike you can't tell them apart."

"Kirby, what I'm trying to do is reach you—find some common area of agreement, so we can talk."

"I understand, sir, but we never will."

"What do you mean?"

"The pipes are clogged. The semantics are bad. Take an object—pencil, automobile, bank vault—we can agree fine. But when you get onto love and guilt and hate, we just can't follow each other. The words don't mean the same things to me they do to you. I went through that whole Mexican thing twice, and you can't get with it."

"I can't see any pertinence to it."

"If you could understand the significance of that, you could understand how all the rest of it happened."

"Yes, I . . ."

"I've explained to you the way I plan to defend you."

"Yes, sir. This business of working on each other . . . intoxicating each other. You want to make us sound like an accident that just got together and happened. Do you think it will work, sir?"

"I don't think anything else will."

"Okay, if I was alone maybe I couldn't have killed that salesman. That's a stupid answer to a stupid question, sir, but maybe it will help you out."

"My purpose is to help you out, Kirby."

"I'm co-operating, sir. I'm with you all the way."

And that is the way it goes. In the beginning I had hoped to be able to put the Stassen boy on the stand. But the prosecutor would shred him. He wouldn't upset Kirby. I don't think he could dent that poise. But he would make Kirby expose himself, in his own words, as a monster.

I used that word without thought. A monster? If he is indeed a monster, we have created him. He is our son. We have been told by our educators and psyhologists to be permissive with him, to let him express himself freely. If he throws all the sand out of the nursery-school sandbox, he is releasing hidden tensions. We deprived him of the security of knowing right and wrong. We debauched him with half-chewed morsels of Freud, in whose teachings there is no right and wrong—only error and understanding. We let sleek men in high places go unpunished for amoral behavior, and the boy heard us snicker. We labeled the pursuit of pleasure a valid goal, and insisted that his teachers turn schooling into fun. We preached group adjustment, security rather than challenge, protection rather than effort. We discarded the social and sexual taboos of centuries, and mislabeled the result freedom rather than license. Finally we poisoned his bone arrow with Strontium 90, told him to live it up while he had the chance, and sat back in ludicrous confidence expecting him to suddenly become a man. Why are we so shocked and horrified to find a child's emotions in a man's body—savage, selfish, cruel, compulsive and shallow?

Walter and Ernestine Stassen can never equate their love-image of their son with this imprisoned, unreachable thing. The contradiction will kill them both.

One can imagine that Helen Wister made a somewhat similar error when she fell into the hands of this dangerous foursome. As an intelligent and perceptive young woman, she must have seen how great was her danger from Koslov, Hernandez and Golden. In this extremity of her terror she would have turned, quite naturally, to Kirby Stassen, sensing a kinship, hoping for protection. To her he would be the only reassuring factor in a nightmare situation, a boy like the boys she had dated.

One wonders how long it took her to learn that this was the gravest mistake of her life.

It seems a pity that Dallas Kemp missed Arnold Crown and Helen Wister by such a narrow margin . . .

FIVE

AFTER Dallas Kemp dropped Helen off at her house on that late Saturday afternoon in July, he drove directly to the small building which housed his bachelor apartment and his office. He felt swollen with righteous anger. He knew he had handled her clumsily, but that did not give her the right to be such a damn fool about that crackpot Arnold Crown.

He was twenty-six, a tall, slender man, swarthy, with a bristling black brushcut, premature pouches under his eyes, large clever hands, great architectural ability, and an enduring capacity for painstaking work. Upon graduation, aided by a small inheritance, he had taken the calculated risk of opening his own office in his home city. His father was retired, and his parents had moved to Venice, Florida. An elder sister lived in Denver with a husband and two small children.

His first year had been bitter and anxious. The first half of the second year had been touch and go. Now, in his third year in practice, he knew he had made it. He employed one draftsman and a part-time secretary. Though he had become the fashionable young architect, he knew his work was sound and good. Two recent residences had received awards. He had that precious flexibility and understanding from which comes houses to fit the owners, not houses to which the owners must dubiously adjust themselves.

Until a few months ago, marriage had been something to consider in the misty future. He had been so completely engrossed in his work that he could readily sublimate his sexual drive, and could thus skillfully avoid the often shockingly overt suggestions of the sillier wives of his clients. When the need was upon him, too pressing for sublimation, he took his pleasure far from Monroe, in the casual, capable, affectionate arms of a girl he had known at school, who was at the beginning of an impressive career as an industrial designer.

He had told himself that when he became thirty-two, he would begin the search for a wife. He had no idea why he had selected thirty-two as the proper age, nor could he foresee how Helen Wister would upset that scheduling.

He met her at a cocktail party at a client's house. He would not have gone had he known it would be a large party. A large cocktail party inevitably produced a small contingent of drunks who felt oddly competent to criticize modern architecture. He supposed the other prefessions had their own problems with drunks. But at any large cocktail party it was a dreary certainty that he would be concerned by tipsy laymen who felt that they were being keen and challenging when they told him that they, by God, didn't want to live in anything built of pieces of bowling alleys and department-store windows. He was supposed to be enchanted and intrigued by their perception and taste. He was supposed to argue defensively. But he was more bored than appalled by the excruciating banality of their statements about a creative field in which they enjoyed almost total ignorance.

He learned that Helen Wister was distantly related to his hostess, and that she was a Smith graduate now doing office work at City Hall. He knew that her father, Dr. Paul Wister, was a dedicated, highly competent and successful ortho-

pedic surgeon, with a socialite do-gooder wife, wealthy in
her own right.

She came over to him, over to where he stood in a corner
of the long living room, smiling with warm and total
confidence as she came. It was the winter season. She wore
a knit suit, in a dull, heathery green. The light behind her
haloed the silky texture of her fine, blond hair. Beautiful
women made him feel uncomfortable and suspicious. Helen
Wister was tallish, slender, poised, luminous and beautiful.
His drawbridges clanked shut, and archers stood ready
behind the walls.

"Marg says you're going to do them a new house, Mr.
Kemp."

"That's right."

"They're both very excited about it."

"Clients usually are."

She had stared at him then, looking a little less certain of
herself. "Are you cross about something?"

"Cross? No. Don't you want to tell me what kind of a
house I should design for them?"

She laughed. Her voice was a clear contralto, melodic.
Her laugh was husky and earthy. "Why should I? Don't you
have any ideas?"

"Certainly."

"Then you don't need my help."

"I had the impression I'd get it, whether I needed it or
not."

"Mr. Kemp, maybe rudeness is becoming to shaggy,
famous old architects. I can't say it improves you any."

She spun away and joined a small group, leaving him
stung and angry. He had not planned to stay until the end of
the party, but he did. Finally he and Helen were the only
guests left. He talked to Willie Layton about the house-to-
be while the women cleaned up after the party. They all
went out to a late dinner together. He and Helen Wister
sniped at each other.

In his bed that night he told himself what an impossible
person she was. Beautiful, spoiled, arrogant, bossy, vain. A
fragrant trap, destined to emasculate her mate.

But he phoned her, dated her, telling himself that it was in the interest of research. Her inevitable monstrous flaw would soon be revealed to him. There was a continual tension between them, emotional and sexual. They exhausted each other with bickering and pointless argument. And as the evenings began to turn warm with spring, with a suddenness that startled them both, it became a physical affair. He knew that she was not promiscuous, and he had told himself that any woman so lovely would be basically frigid, capable only of simulating healthy passion. But her response left no room for doubt of her intensity, her ability to intoxicate herself with the demands of the flesh. Their lovemaking was like an extension of the tension between them—a combat between strangers, juvenile, pseudo-sophisticated, brazen.

And finally it all turned into love. He had to admit that what had seemed to be paragon was in truth paragon. She was precious and valuable beyond belief. Her basic sweetness and decency were genuine. She was aware of and quietly pleased by her own beauty, and glad it was something she could bring to him, like a gift wrapped with love.

They had sidled obliquely, rancorously, into love, and were astounded by this great and sudden gift. It was a strong love that made of marriage a fussy but necessary technicality. They were intensely proud of each other and delighted with the magic of themselves.

He knew her flaws. Stubborness, too much casual generosity with her time and efforts, too much empathy for dreary people. This Arnold Crown thing was perfect example of that.

Dallas Kemp knew exactly how to kill his own anger and indignation. He went directly to the drawing board. The hard, white fluorescence was a bright island in the blue-gray light of dusk. He worked on a scale drawing of the fireplace wall for the Judland house, breaking the lines off neatly, focusing his concentration until, unwatched, the anger drained away.

At eight o'clock he stood up and stretched, working the stiffness out of his shoulders. He thought about Helen and about Arnold Crown, and began to realize, with a certain uneasiness, that he hadn't been very bright about the whole thing. His objection had been that Arnold Crown was irrational about Helen, and possibly dangerous. It would have made more sense to follow them.

He phoned the Wister home. The line was busy. He tried again at ten after eight. Helen's mother answered. "Jane, this is Dal. Is Helen there?"

"No, she isn't, Dal. I just got home a little while ago. Her car's gone. Did she . . . ah . . . tell you her program for this evening?"

"She told me she was going to see Arnold Crown. We had a hell of a blowup about it. I think it's a stupid idea."

"So do I, dear. But you know our Helen. When she was little I had a terrible time with her at zoos. She wanted to climb in and pat the lions. But I do think she'll handle it all right."

"I . . . I hope so. Where was she going to meet him?"

"I haven't any idea."

"At the station?"

"I really don't know, Dal."

"I shouldn't have gotten so sore. I should have stuck with her."

"I'd feel a little better if you had, actually. This Crown person isn't exactly a young boy with a crush on her."

After he hung up he got into his station wagon and drove to Arnold Crown's service station. As he pulled in to park beyond the pumps, he saw Helen's little black MG parked beside the station in the shadows, lights out. The man who had started to come out of the station stopped in the doorway as Dal got out and walked toward him. He was a small man in his forties with a pallid, knotty face, a smear of grease at the corner of his mouth. The name *Smitty* was embroidered over the breast pocket of his twill uniform.

"Is Crown here?"

"You missed him by five, ten minutes. Anything I can do for you?"

"No . . . I guess not. That's Miss Wister's car, isn't it?"

"The little car? Yeah. That's hers."

A car pulled up to the pumps. Smitty went out to service it. Dal moved restlessly into the station. He was staring blankly at a display of windshield wipers when Smitty came in.

Dal turned and said, "Miss Wister was with him when he left here?"

"That's right, mister."

"Well, if her car's here, I guess it means they're coming back here."

The small man looked at Dal with a rather strange grin and said, "I wouldn't count too much on that, mister. I mean they're probably coming back here, but it won't be right soon. I mean I got my orders about that car. The keys are in it, and I'm to roll it in when I close up, and tomorrow I'm to get it washed and serviced and have one of the boys run it over to Arn's place and put it in his garage."

Dal stared at him. "Why? I don't understand."

"She's got no need for it for a while, that's all."

"Why not?"

"The last thing you'd take on a honeymoon is two cars, mister. They took off in Arn's Olds."

"Honeymoon!" Dal said blankly.

Another customer arrived. Smitty hurried out. It took an exasperating length of time before he came back.

"What's this about a honeymoon?" Dal demanded.

Smitty sat on the corner of the desk and grinned amiably. "I tell you, mister, it hasn't been easy around here lately, working for a guy in love. That Helen like to give him fits. They were going together regular and then she broke off and started going with some other guy. Arn was like out of his mind for a couple months and more. He'd chew you out for nothing at all, like a crazy man. I was about to quite forty times, honest. But all of a sudden, thank God, they got it all ironed out. You never see a guy so happy as him today. I bet a dozen times he bust out laughing, over nothing at all. I guess if you get to run off with a girl like that, it's worth feeling good about. Their suitcases were all ready in the back of the Olds since yesterday. And he showed me a wad of bills big as a ham sandwich he's got for the trip. So she showed up like he said she would . . . oh, about a half hour ago, pretty as a picture, and shy like. You know. Like a bride. I'm in charge until he gets back. He told me she'd marry him. You know, I never really believed it until I saw them take off together. She's from a big-shot family. If you know her car, I guess you know Helen. She looked shy and happy when they took off. Arn, he'll make a good husband. He's a worker, and there isn't anything he won't do for that girl." Smitty stopped smiling and stared at Dallas Kemp. "You sick or anything?"

"No. Thank you . . . thank you very much."

He drove down to police headquarters. He announced to a desk sergeant in a firm, loud voice that he wanted to report a kidnapping. He expected bells to ring and people to gather around, asking a hundred questions. The sergeant told him to take a seat. He could hear the monotonous hammering of a teletype in some room nearby. A drunk was brought in and booked and led away. The sergeant carried on several low-voiced phone calls.

Ten minutes later a man about thirty came into the room. He was slope-shouldered, long-headed, with a bitter, turned-down mouth, sleepy eyes. He was in his shirt-sleeves. He smelled strongly of perspiration. He wore dark-red suspenders over his white shirt, a green tie with small yellow polka dots.

Dal jumped up as he came toward him.

"I'm Lieutenant Razoner. You want to report a kidnapping?"

"What's your name and occupation?"

"Dallas Kemp, registered architect."

"Who's kidnapped?"

"Helen Wister."

"Who's she?"

"We're to be married . . . in less than three weeks."

The lieutenant looked at him and sighed and turned, saying, "Come on with me."

He took Dal upstairs to a large bullpen office, where three out of a dozen desks were in use. He sat at one of the empty desks and had Dal sit beside the desk. He asked questions in a bored voice. He made notes. Dal told him the whole story.

When he had all the information he threw the pencil onto the desk and leaned back, clasping his fingers at the nape of his neck.

"What do you expect us to do, buddy? Loan you a crying towel?"

"I—I think you should find them!"

"The lady changed her mind. They do that, you know."

"It isn't like that, Lieutenant. This is serious! That man is dangerous."

"I've known Arn Crown for ten years, buddy. Solid guy, I'd say."

"He's acted irrational about Miss Wister."

"Like following you and phoning you and all that?"

"Yes."

"Man in love, he'll do a lot of stirring around. Arn break any laws?"

"No, but . . ."

"There's no law about running off and getting married, Kemp."

"Believe me, that's the last thing she'd do—marry Arn Crown."

"I guess it must seem that way to you, you being the one she left behind. Believe me, it happens all the time. And other guys have just as much trouble believing it as you're having right now."

"Lieutenant, will you talk to Helen's mother?"

"Why should I? She lied to you. She could lie to her mother. Now, if she was under age, maybe we could do something about it . . ."

A heavy-set man came striding into the office. He looked around, spotted Lieutenant Razoner and said, "Lew! On the double!" He turned and hurried out.

Razoner stood up. "We can't help you, buddy."

"I'd like to talk to you some more about . . ."

Razoner shrugged. "Stick around then, but you may have a hell of a long wait." He hurried out of the room.

Dallas Kemp sat there on the hard chair. It was five of

ten. He was trying not to think about Helen too specifically. It made him feel cold and sick to think of her with Crown. He knew he should call Jane Wister. He wondered if it would be all right to use the phone on Lieutenant Lew Razoner's desk. Just as he had decided to attempt it, the lieutenant came to the doorway and said, "Kemp! Come here!"

He was taken to a smaller office. There were four men there, two of them talking over phones.

To the elderly man behind the desk, Lew Razoner said, "Barney, this is the guy reported him for kidnapping."

The man called Barney stood up. "Bring him along, Lew. We'll talk on the way out there."

They went down to the courtyard. A driver was waiting behind the wheel of a police sedan. The three of them got into the back, Dallas Kemp in the middle.

"What's happened?" he asked. "Is Helen all right?"

The car sped out through the gates, elbowing its way into traffic. "Give me this kidnapping thing," the elderly man ordered.

Lew Razoner gave it to him, compacting it neatly and tightly, a professional résumé, uncolored by personal opinion.

"Can't you tell me what's going on?" Dal asked.

"Captain Tauss is head of Homicide," Razoner said gently. "The sheriff's got a body tentatively identified as Arnold Crown."

"An accident! Is Helen hurt?"

"What happened to this Crown," Captain Tauss said, "sounds like on purpose. No accident. I don't know anything about the girl."

Dallas Kemp realized that they had turned out of the main traffic arteries and were headed east on Route 813 at a high rate of speed.

"Looks like over the next ridge, sir," the driver said and began to reduce speed.

They swept over the ridge and Kemp saw the shallow valley ahead of them filled with a confusion of lights and vehicles. State Police were posted to prevent the curious from stopping. Summer bugs wheeled in front of the floodlight and headlights. The generator on an emergency truck throbbed. As they got out, Razoner said, "Stick close to me, Kemp. Don't wander around."

"I want to know what happened to . . ."

"So let's find out."

Kemp saw an abandoned barn on the left. On the right, a hundred feet beyond the barn, an Oldsmobile was snugged down into a deep ditch, tilted far over onto its right side, lights still on, turning the weeds in the ditch to a vivid artifical green. Technicians knelt, studying the road surface, making careful scrapings. A man in coveralls stood patiently by a red tow-truck, hands in his pockets, cigar stub in the corner of his mouth. An ambulance was parked parallel to the ditched Olds, rear end open.

Kemp followed Tauss and Razoner as they approached a small group of men who were examining something that lay near the rear of the Olds, half in the ditch. Hard, white light was focused on the body. Cameras flared.

Kemp got close enough to see the face. He swallowed and took a half step back. The heavy features of Arnold Crown were barely recognizable.

A wide man in khaki was squatting heavily on his heels. He wore a blue baseball cap and a sheriff's badge. He glanced up and said, "Hello, Barney, Lew," and came lithely to his feet.

"That's Arn Crown," Lew said. "He didn't do all that going into the ditch."

"Did maybe none of it at all. He got banged around some, and then there was a knife."

A tidy little man got up off his knees and said tartly, "That's all I can do with it here. You might as well load it."

"When can you do a complete job, Doctor?" the sheriff asked.

"Tomorrow, tomorrow," the little man said. "Tonight we're entertaining." He gave a barking laugh, snapped his case shut, and walked quickly away into the night.

The ambulance people loaded the body. The sheriff signaled the man standing by the wrecker. He went down into the ditch with the hook, clanged it onto the frame, climbed into his cab and yanked the big car up onto the highway, the big red warning lights on the wrecker blinking off and on.

"We got witnesses, Barney. Nice nervous witnesses," the sheriff said. "Right over there. Come on. We'll play People Are Funny."

He strode away toward the silent group on the other side of the road. Tauss and Razoner lagged behind.

Kemp heard Razoner say in a quiet voice to Barney Tauss, "Out here in front of the newspaper people? He should take them in."

"Usually, yes. Not in an election year. Honest Gus Kurby, the reporter's pal."

Somebody shifted lights until the small group was harshly floodlighted. A young couple squinted apprehensively into the lights. The boy was about eighteen. He wore khaki pants and a T shirt. He had huge, powerful, sun-red forearms, a heavy thatch of brown hair, long sideburns, a big, soft, unformed face. He held the hand of a small girl who wore blue-jean shorts and a striped Basque shirt taut across the unfettered abruptness of juvenile breasts. She had tousled dark hair with two white streaks dyed into it, a narrow face with eyes set close together, a wide, slack, pulpy mouth.

A man reached into the open window of the official sedan and brought out a hand mike on a long cord. He handed it to the sheriff, saying, "It's working good. I checked it twice."

The sheriff thumbed the button and the small red recording light came on. He held it a few inches in front of his mouth and said, "Twenty-fifth of July. Ten-forty P.M. Sheriff Kurby interrogating witnesses at the site of the Arnold Crown murder. Now let me have your name and address, son." He stuck the mike in the boy's face.

"Uh . . . Howard Craft. I live two miles east of here. Star Route, Box 810, Sheriff."

"And you, girl?"

"Ruth Meckler," she said in a thin, childish voice. "Fifty-two Cedar Street, over in Daggsburg."

"Now, Howard, you tell me in your own words how you happened to be here."

"Well, I had a date with Ruthie, and we drove around some and we come out here. We . . . been here before, a lot of times. I pulled around back of the barn there, like always and we . . . went up the ladder into the loft."

One of the newsmen snickered. The girl moved closer to her boy friend. Kurby clicked off the red recording light and turned and said, "These kids could have took off and never said a word, but they phoned in. If you people want a story, keep your mouths shut. Otherwise I'll finish this in my office."

"Anyhow, we're engaged to be married," the girl said.

"Continue, boy," the sheriff said.

"We were just inside that loading window there," Howard Craft said and pointed. They all turned and looked at the barn glowing in reflected light. The high window was a rectangular hole, about five feet long and three feet high. A fringe of hay lapped over the bottom edge.

"Ruthie and me, we were there maybe only fifteen minutes when that Oldsmobile came along, moving real slow, and parked over there right across from us, and turned off the lights and the engine."

"What time was that?"

"I'd guess maybe ten to nine, Sheriff. They sat there and talked. A man and a woman."

"Could you hear what was being said?"

"Not really. It was an argument. It seemed like he was trying to talk her into something she didn't want to do. We could only catch a word here and there."

"Like 'surprise,'" the girl said. "He talked about a surprise and money. I heard him say a thousand dollars. We weren't listening good because we were just hoping they'd go away."

"He said about getting married a couple times," the boy said.

"Then all of a sudden the lights came on and they started up real fast,' the girl said.

"We were looking out," the boy said. "I guess she

jumped out when he started up. But not quick enough. She fell, I guess. And he racked the Olds right into the ditch. Then he came scrambling out and ran back to where she was, there on the edge of the road. He was yelling, 'Helen! Helen! Helen!' It was hard to see them. Then this other car came from the west. It was wound up real good. When the headlights hit them, we could see them good. A big guy in a white jacket kneeling beside a blond woman.''

"She had a white skirt and a green blouse," the girl said.

"The car coming braked real good," the boy said. "It was handled good. It stopped maybe thirty feet from them, where the guy was trying to pick the girl up and get her off the edge of the road. It was a dark Buick, a big one, pretty new, maybe last year's. Dark-green or dark-blue or maybe even black."

"Dark-blue, I think," the girl said.

"Four people got out," the boy said. "One of them was a girl. They left the doors open and the motor running. They acted . . . funny."

"How do you mean, funny?" the sheriff asked.

"Excuse me, Gus," Barney Tauss said.

Kurby turned irritably. "Yes, Barney?"

"I was just wondering if it wouldn't be a smart thing to establish road blocks so . . ."

"That's been done. After the first informal interrogation, I requested the State Police so to do. All right, son. In what way did they act funny?"

"Well, it wasn't like they wanted to help. They were laughing and joking around. It seemed to me they were drunk, the four of them."

"You saw them clearly?"

"When they got out in front of their own headlights, yes. We saw them pretty good."

"Take them one at a time and give me a description."

"One was a big, dark, tough-looking guy. The three guys all wore sports shirts and slacks. The big one had his shirt outside his slacks, and the other two had theirs tucked in. Then there was a skinny guy wearing glasses, maybe getting a little bald. He was hopping around all the time, making cracks and laughing in a funny way. The third guy was pretty well built, a big, blond guy with a good tan."

"He maybe looked a little like Tab Hunter, only bigger and rougher," the girl said.

"The girl wore brown slacks and a yellow blouse and high heels," the boy said. "She had long, brown hair. She was pretty, I'd say."

"She was kinda hippy to be wearing slacks," the girl said.

"What did they do?"

"They gathered around the blond and the guy who had put the Olds in the ditch. We couldn't hear much of what the others were saying, but we could hear the crazy guy with the glasses pretty good. He was saying crazy things, like it was lucky there was a witch doctor in the audience. And he said if people were throwing beautiful blondes away, the country was in worse shape than he thought. Then he got down on his knees and took the blonde's hand and yelled, 'Speak to me, darling! Speak to your old buddy!' That made the guy in the white jacket sore. He pushed the guy in glasses away so hard that he rolled over onto his back, his legs in the air, and he yelled, 'Let her alone!' The next second the big, tough one smacked the guy in the white coat and knocked him down. But he scrambled right up again. The big one went after him. He fought—the one in the white coat—like a crazy man. But then they were circling around behind him."

"Who was?"

"The other three. The girl too. The one with glasses had picked up a rock in each hand. The girl had a knife. There was hardly any sound. Just shoes scrapping on the road, and the way they grunted, and the smacking sound when they'd hit him. And the one with glasses laughed some. The fight moved away from the blonde girl. All of a sudden it was a terrible thing. All of a sudden you knew they were killing him. Ruthie started to cry. I whispered to her not to make a sound. I knew they'd kill us too. I knew they'd kill anybody. They weren't like people you see. I didn't know people could be like that. I saw something like that a long time ago. I was twelve, maybe. A pack of dogs got after a bull calf. It was a long way from the farmhouse. I didn't have a gun or anything. The calf kept bellowing and circling, but if didn't do him any good. The dogs weren't even barking. They kept circling and snapping and they pulled him down and tore this throat open. It was like that."

"Can you give us any kind of a sequence, son?"

"Just how it happened? It got pretty confusing. The blond guy knocked him down a couple of times. They'd let him get up. The skinny guy knocked him down with a rock, and he got up slow. By then he wasn't fighting. He kept yelling, 'Wait! Wait! Don't!' It was a terrible thing. When he could hardly move, the big one got him by the throat and bent him over the back of the Olds. The girl moved in close and I couldn't see the knife, but I could see her elbow going back and forth, real fast. The big guy let go. The skinny guy popped him again with a rock. The blond guy kicked him into the ditch as he slid off the back of the car. Just then the blonde woman sat up. Her face was in the lights. I guess she didn't know where she was. They went to her. They talked low. We couldn't hear what they said. But they helped the blonde up onto her feet. She seemed to sort of let them lead her. The girl and the blond guy helped her. They walked her to the Buick and got her into it. They slammed all the doors. The skinny one with glasses got behind the wheel. They scratched off and they were doing I'd say seventy by the time they got to that next ridge."

"And what did you do then?"

"We got down to my car fast as we could. I drove out and stopped by the ditch. I held my lighter close and looked at his face and I knew he was dead. I didn't want Ruthie to see him. Sometimes a car won't come along for a half hour. I drove home fast and phoned. It was about twenty-five after nine when I phoned. Then we came back here to . . . meet you people and tell you about it."

"You did not see the plate on the Buick?"

"No, I told you, Sheriff. It was out of state, but I don't know from where."

"I want to thank you, Howard, and you, Ruth, for your good citizenship." The little red light went off.

"Can we go now, Sheriff?" the boy asked.

"Yes."

"Will I be in the papers?" the girl asked, smiling.

"You sure will, honey," one of the reporters said. "How about a few more questions before you take off, kids?"

"Sure," the girl said.

Kemp heard one of the other reporters say, "Al, that dog pack thing writes itself. Wolf pack. Hey, I like that better! Wolf Pack Murder."

"This is the third score for that wolf pack, Billy, If they're the same ones."

"What do you mean—if? It all matches up, Al. Uvalde, Nashville. It's the same bunch. By tomorrow, boy, the wire services and the networks will be in here like . . ." The confidential voice faded away on the summer night. Kemp lengthened his stride to catch up with Tauss and Razoner.

Tauss was saying, ". . . might as well strut while he has a chance. The FBI is on this one already. But while he's showing off, old Gus better not slip up on any of it or they'll peel him good. Kemp? Let's get on back to town. Get in."

And he was sitting between them again as the driver turned the car around. Dallas Kemp felt remote and wooden.

"Those people . . . they took Helen."

"And they took the honeymoon money, Kemp."

"But what are you going to *do*? What's going to *happen*?" He heard his voice break.

"Try to stop them. The trick is find them."

"I heard those reporters talking. It sounded as if those people are . . . wanted for other things."

Razoner laughed abruptly, without mirth. "Other murders. Don't you read the papers?"

"I—I remember something recently. In the Southwest though."

"In Texas and then in Tennessee and now here," Captain Tauss said. "If they weren't the hottest thing in the country already, they are now. Three men and a girl. And we haven't made one of them yet. Tonight is the best break yet. Witnesses. Descriptions."

"I don't understand," Kemp said. "What are these people doing? Why? Who are they?"

"They," said Tauss, "are the kind of people who make police work tough. There's no rhyme or reason or pattern. Maybe they're hopped up. They all of a sudden decided to buck society all the way. I don't know why. I'll bet they couldn't tell you why. They're after kicks, not profit. They'll do all the damage they can, and if they're smart it'll be a lot, and they'll be caught. That's one sure thing. The surest thing in the world. It's not knowing where and when that makes it rough. From the pattern, they're heading northeast. Yesterday it was an eight-state alarm."

"I suppose," Kemp said, "I've got to . . . go tell Helen's people."

"Don't worry about that," Lew Razoner said.

"What do you mean?"

"They found her purse in the Olds. It had her identification. Gus is no damn fool. He knows how big the Wisters are. He sent a deputy there first thing, and didn't spill it to the press. Next he'll come on the scene with a flock of reporters, and milk it dry."

"She may be badly hurt," Dallas Kemp said.

"About the only thing you can do and the only thing her people can do is pray."

They went directly to headquarters. Captain Tauss was anxious to alert the Chief of Police and the Commissioner, and give them all pertinent details. They had no more need of Kemp. He got into his station wagon and drove out to the Wister home. On the way he heard the eleven-thirty news over the car radion from local station WROE.

". . . murdered Arnold Crown, owner of a local service station, and abducted his companion, Miss Helen Wister, only daughter of a socially prominent Monroe family. The murder and kidnapping occurred on a deserted stretch of Route 813 about ten miles east of the city limits at approximately nine-fifteen this evening. Three men and a woman are involved. Sheriff Gustaf Kurby has stated that this is unquestionably the work of the same foursome who murdered a salesman near Uvalde, Texas, last Tuesday, and killed again yesterday near Nashville. Road blocks have been established and it is hoped that the foursome is trapped in the area bounded by . . ."

He punched the button that turned the radio off. The flat voice of the announcer could not make it any more real. It was all nightmare. It had the impersonal malevolence of summer lightning. It had struck Helen. Life had no point without her. It was monstrously unfair. People like that belonged in the impersonal newspaper headlines. They had no right coming into your life, destroying things. Life had been neatly planned. Nineteen days before the marriage. He had the plane tickets to Mexico City, the suite reserved at the Continental Hilton. A thing like this *couldn't* happen.

When he got to her home, she would be there.

But he saw the official cars in the drive. And as he walked to the front door he looked in and saw Jane Wister. Her face was twisted. Tears were wet on her cheeks. She looked seventy years old.

S I X

DEATH HOUSE DIARY

IT was March in Laredo, and hot. John and Kathryn
Pinelli were excessively polite to each other, and to me. As
I said, we hung around there a day and a half. It didn't have
to be that long. But it was a stepping-off place. I got the
black Chrysler completely serviced. I had to unload it and
reload it so Kathy could get to her hot-weather wardrobe.

It was a strange thing about her—her taste in clothes. In
New York it was rich and conservative and good. But as she
got more informal, she seemed to lose her judgment. Maybe
it was the Hollywood years coming out. Theatrical. Maybe,
on the other hand, that outfit she wore in Laredo was a way
of punishing John Pinelli in some way that I didn't
understand. Something had suddenly gone dead-wrong
between them. So wrong that I could sense it wouldn't ever
be right again. It changed the reasons for the trip and
everything else. It turned it into a different trip. It was as
though we had all forgotten where we were going.

The outfit she put on to go shopping in, in the heart of

Laredo that full day we were there, I felt funny letting her out of the car. She'd put on tight little pumpkin-colored short shorts, and a full-sleeve yellow silk blouse, with a Chinese type collar. She wore a white straw coolie hat and white gloves and high red heels, and sunglasses with red frames. I tell you, when she walked away from the car, she kept everything working for her. She handled it with a runway strut, and those heads snapped around and the jaws fell open when Kathy went by. I don't know what she was proving, and I don't think she did. Those little legs were wonderful, and no lady ever walked like that.

It got hot in the car. I got out and waited in the shade of a building. She was gone almost an hour, and I saw her coming in the distance, carrying a silver package. She came swinging toward me, a lovely little doll, and I had to grin at her, but her mouth did not move in response. She took off her glasses as I opened the car door for her. Her eyes were ten thousand years old.

"Buy something pretty?" I asked her.

"This is a stinking hot town. Get me home before I die, Stassen."

So there wasn't anything to say on the way back to the motel. We got a fairly decent start in the morning. I'd guess that by nine-thirty we'd had breakfast and we were across the river. At Customs I had to unload the car and carry everything inside, then carry all the sealed suitcases back out and load it again. Neither of them carried a damn thing.

And so I buttoned the big black car up, and turned the air conditioning on, and we went plunging down across the baked brown land into Mexico. The motor made a deep hum. The car rocked and swayed on the road. But we sat in the coolness and silence and it was like a kind of aimless drifting. The needle, at seventy, meant nothing. The world outside was a drab travelogue, without sound track, poorly edited. John Pinelli dozed in the back. She wore lime-green shorts and gold sandals and a green-and-white-striped blouse, and very dark sunglasses with green frames. The air conditioner was cold on her legs, I guess, so she pulled them up into the seat, and sat with her knees turned toward me.

Have I ever described Kathy's hands? They were peasant hands, with short, wide, thick palms, stubby fingers. They were soft and beautifully kept, but the care she gave them could not disguise the basic earthy shape of them. The very long, curved nails helped a little, but if you noticed them particularly, you saw that they were not pretty hands. Her feet were short and wide, with rather puffy insteps.

I do not know what was going on in Kathy's mind that morning. But there was hate in the car. You could feel the hate. And so there was sickness. So there was a sickness in her mind, and she infected me with it. She passed on to me a part of what the world had done to her.

I was driving. My hands were locked on the wheel at ten after ten. And suddenly that small, thick hand came crawling over my right thigh on its stubby fingers, a large soft pale insect . . .

I have stopped this account. I needed time to think about myself. It is a tired irony, I suppose, that I should be removed from this life before I have had any chance to understand it. Yes, I've been to college. In an objective way I've learned the various schools of thought—man's efforts to understand himself. At one end of the scale are those who say we are a long-range result of a chemical accident, and what we call thought is an ultimate refinement of instinct. At the other end, man is in the image of God, and is divine. The individual is the result of heredity, environment—and something else. An X factor?

Yes, I had thought of such things—talked weightily in bull sessions. But until these past few weeks it has never been subjective. What is this thing I—in some process of simplification—call Me? It has a name. Kirby Palmer Stassen. (Say this enough times and it becomes meaningless—a mouthing of nonsense syllables.) The name is an inefficient tagging, a kind of identification. I have existed. I have moved through time and place, without thought. The world has happened to me, not me to it. My hungers and emotions have been primitive.

During this final year of my life I have done things society condemns. And even though they were acts committed by me, they are more like things that have happened to me. I see them on a small stage, brightly lighted—little painted figures moving on awkward strings, making empty sounds. The thing called Me is on that stage in every scene, in every act. I am the lead in a pointless drama.

While I thought, they brought the midday meal. They have just taken the tray away. I was hungry. I ate. In that sense Me is an organism, converting foodstuffs to energy through a process of gobbling, mastication, chemistry. Another Me has slept, renewing itself. Another Me has made love, and spoken with great confidence of eternity. A million million things have gone into my head, and memory is one of those toy cranes which can dig at random and never come up with as much as ten per cent of what must be there, buried under round candies.

Most men give up seeking an answer to the riddle of their own existence. It makes their heads hurt. They give up and go play manly games, dig hard for the buck, get slopped at the country club and chase all available tail, and if forced to think about themselves, they say introspection is unhealthy—a suitable diversion for eggheads.

They aren't giving me enough time to wrestle with the big riddles, but I can amaze myself with the little ones. After my—excuse the expression—Wolf Pack career, it seems entirely strange that I should feel a revulsion about writing down what Kathy Keats did to me, a temptation to skip it. Since they are going to strap me down and put me to death by electricity, what difference would it make if I covered all this paper with obscenities?

But I cannot be explicit. I am in many ways a prude. Murderous, but a prude.

She trained me the way you train an animal, and with less respect than you show a decent animal. When I felt the touch of her hand I reached down automatically and clasped it. She snatched her hand away. Lesson one—the hand must not be touched. Lesson two—do not look at her, even for an instant. Her mouth was level, the Dietrich face expressionless, the eyes invisible behind the darkness of her sunglasses. Lesson three—do not permit the driving to become erratic.

I remember that I looked far ahead to where the road shimmered into mirage, and I tried to divorce my mind from my body. I knew the actions that would stop her, but I was powerless to use them, trapped by my own queasy fascination. I told myself it was a tawdry, silly, childish thing she did. But she was turned so as to stare directly back into the face of her sleeping husband. And I was frightened. I felt too young. I felt like a child being bathed by an evil nursemaid. I felt that some unspeakable thing was coiling and vomiting in her mind. I had fallen among strangers I could never understand, and when next we stopped I would leave them and they would never see me again. God knows I wish my resolve had not weakened.

At a dreamlike seventy the car fell forward into the endless overexposed Kodachrome landscape. And far behind the car a ball of orchid facial tissue spun along the rocky shoulder amid the spin-devils of our swift passage and came to rest under the brass of an Aztec sun. Kathy curled away into the far corner of the front seat and went to sleep with her head on a small crimson cushion. John Pinelli awakened and coughed and asked where we were. Kathy's trained animal answered him in servile tones.

The new motels of Mexico enable the U.S. tourist to leave his country with the assurance he will not have to adapt himself to alien ways. He can be comforted by the same bold and banal architecture, the same wide asphalt parking areas, the innersprings and mixer faucets and spring locks and wall-to-wall carpeting. If he can avoid staring at the world outside his motel he will not be upset by the look of burned mountains, overladen burros and the brown and barefoot *gente*.

Our up-to-date highway guide reported a new motel as being the last one for sixty miles. A desk clerk beamed and bowed at me and said he was full, he could not accommodate us. I went back to the car and told them. Kathy got out quickly, and I followed her into the office. She walked to the desk in her green shorts and her green-and-white blouse and her very dark glasses with the green frames and her golden sandals.

She took her bill clip from her purse, placed a twenty-dollar bill on the counter and said icily, "I have gone far enough today." She placed a second twenty on top of it and said, "I am tired and we will stay here." She added a third bill and said, "We will require a twin-bed double and a single, not connecting, and ice immediately."

"Yes, señorita!" the man said, bowing, beaming. "Yes, of course." He hissed like an adder and a small boy came and helped me with the bags.

As we walked to the car, I said, "If you want me to handle it that way . . ."

"You couldn't possibly," she said. "You wouldn't know what to look for. You wouldn't know how much. I watched his eyes."

And that was the last I said to her on that first day in Mexico. After I was alone in my room I thought about her. I decided I hated her. Perhaps in the same way Pavlov's dogs hated him. I felt dirtied, because she had known how to force my acceptance, how to deny me the male role, how to turn me into her creature. She had spoiled my own picture of myself—the clever, boyish, slightly sinister aggressor—a charming young man who had gone off on this mad adventure on optimistic off-chance of putting horns on the husband-director, puffy, pink-and-white John Pinelli.

The motel had a bar. I got drunk. I told outrageous lies to two girls from the University of Texas on spring vacation. I managed to split them up and get the larger of the two, and a bottle, back to my room. Underneath all the alcohol I told myself she was the obvious cure for what had happened to me with Kathy. The girl was large, alert, muscular and elfin. She would permit only the most meager and innocent intimacies. And then she would begin writhing and laughing like a madwoman, all hard brown outdoor knees and elbows. After I gave up with her, I felt as though I had fallen down several flights of stairs.

We were on the road by ten-thirty. I had a dull headache. John Pinelli had a head cold. Kathy wore white shorts, a black blouse, red sandals, and sunglasses with white frames.

I had sworn I would not let her play her nasty game again. I would be a man, not a trained animal. In that way I rationalized my wish to stay with her. I waited in tension for the chance to repulse her, but nothing happened on that second day in Mexico. We stopped at four-thirty that afternoon, a half day short of Mexico City. The motel was very much like the first one. March flowers were growing, with a sweet spoiled scent, heavy in the air.

At dusk I met Kathy. I was going toward my room. She was headed for the bar. There was a narrow walk, roofed, with open arches on one side, a wall on the other. I saw her coming toward me in a cotton dress with a bold, broad stripe, her hair brushed out to long smooth silver, molten in that half light. I saw her and the sight of her hollowed my belly, hurried my pulse.

"Kathy," I said, and she gave a mild half nod and attempted to walk by me, but I imprisoned her there, bracing my hands on the warm stone wall on either side of her. She put her shoulders against the wall, folded her arms close under her breasts and looked up at me, her head slightly tilted, her expression one of weary patience. She was a small-boned woman, quietly arrogant. I suddenly felt humble and awkward and unsure of myself. All resentment was gone.

"I suppose I gave you the right to make a nuisance of yourself, Kirby," she said. "Could you possibly manage to forget it, dear?"

"Tell me why. I just want to know why."

"There isn't any 'why.' Even if I had all the words, there isn't any why. Once I threw a painting into the fireplace. John had paid ten thousand dollars for it. He didn't ask me why I did it. On impulse I've done things that would make your littleboy face turn green, darling. And I haven't asked myself why. My God, we don't go around checking motives. You brought up the idea of following me down here. You invited yourself. We both know you're all steamed up for a nice romp. Who asks you why? Don't ever bore me asking why."

"What do you think that did to me, Kathy?"

"I couldn't care less. I had no curiosity. Then, or now, dear."

"John is probably taking a nap. Why don't you come to my room right now, Kathy?"

She put her fist to her mouth. I could not guess whether the yawn was real or faked. It hurt as much either way.

"As if I owe it to you or something?" she demanded with a trace of anger. "One of those dull cause and effect things? Follow through? Little man, if you go through life looking for any kind of logic in sexual relationships, you're going to raise lumps all over that boyish head, believe me. You don't have any sort of claim on me, Stassen. I owe you nothing, college boy. Just drive the car. And if you *must* have a reason, just tell yourself the lady gets bored on trips. Stop collecting motivations, or buy a couch and go into the business."

"I'm a person, Kathy. I'm not an object, or an experiment."

She had looked withdrawn. She suddenly used her actress face, and it came alight with tender, theatrical concern. "Oh, have I hurt you, my darling? My God, how thoughtless of me! How cruel and selfish and heartless! I swear, my love, it will never, never happen again."

She ducked under my arm quickly and was gone. I took a hesitant step after her. She looked back, and with a quick expression of malicious mockery, an extra switch of her hips, she disappeared around the corner of the wall.

It did not happen again. I knew it would not have happened at all had not the climate of their marriage changed so abruptly and finally in Laredo, that ugly, shabby, tawdry border city.

We drove to Mexico City. They took a suite in the Continental Hilton. I assumed that he wanted to put on a

look of importance for the people he wanted to get in with. I
didn't meet any of them there. I met some of them later in
Acapulco. I was provided a room in the Francis, across
from the new Sanborn's, near the Embassy. I didn't get
much time in Mexico City. They decided to stay a few days
and then fly down to Acapulco. I would drive down alone. I
had the Chrysler serviced again. I helped Kathy unload the
basic clothes she would need in the city—about a hundred
pounds of them.

I left early the second morning, knowing only that I had
to locate the house of a man named Hillary Charis. There
would be servants there. I had gathered that Hillary had
made his money out of some kind of wide screen lens. He
and his newest wife were away, wintering in Montevideo.
On the afternoon before I left, Kathy, in her most to-the-
manor-born manner and accent, had given me the word.
"Here are two thousand pesos, Stassen. I shall expect you
to keep an accounting of it. Drive on down and unpack the
car and get settled in. I understand there are five bedrooms,
so there's no reason why you shouldn't move in for a little
while. Please don't select the most attractive guest room
because we shall be doing some entertaining. Purchase any
little things you think we'll need to be comfortable there.
You know our schedule, so you can get the household
operating properly. Make sure the utilities are all in working
order. When we're ready to come down, we'll phone you
when to meet us at the airport. Is that all quite clear?"

"Yes, sir, Mrs. Pinelli, sir!"

"Really, Stassen, I did *employ* you to drive us down, did
I not?"

"Yes."

"It's so much easier to be able to give orders than to have
it all on . . . a loose sort of friendship basis, don't you
think?"

"If you say so, Kathy."

"Have a pleasant trip, Kirby."

"Thank you, ma'am."

So faithful, loyal, reliable Stassen went booming up the
auto pisto into the high mountains on the day of April Fool,

and over the highest pass, and then down and down, ridge by ridge, all day long, down through the *tierra colorado*, down to the rich tropic beach.

I found the beach home of Hillary Charis. It was west of the city. It was a pale, faded blue with a red tile roof. It sat about fifty feet above the highway, on a ledge of solid rock. The big garage had been cut out of the solid rock. The garage door could have served a fortress. From the garage level you climbed one hundred wide, flat, curving, concrete stairs up to the house. My first view of the wide blue Pacific at sunset from one of the terraces was like being hit solidly behind the ear. My jaw sagged and I felt as if I would stagger. Fishing boats were headed in. You could see the exotic hotels of Acapulco to the east.

I came to know the house well, its moods and vistas. The biggest and most dramatic terrace was on the south side, overlooking the sea. There were tile floors thoughout the house, and plaster walls in cool shades of green and blue and lavender. Soil had been carried up to make small garden pockets around the house, tended by Armando who seemed to live on his knees. He was a knotted old man, rosewood brown, seamed and eroded, with bad teeth and one milky, sightless eye. His wife was Rosalinda, the cook. She was a timeless Indian woman, square as an up-ended box. Her face had the impassive features of an aging hero of many Westerns. It gave her an almost comic look, as though, through some convolution of the plot, Our Hero had dressed in pink cotton and a horsetail wig the better to make his escape. When she smiled, a slow blooming smile, it was a glorious thing to see.

I had a phrase book and two years of college Spanish. Rosalinda had perhaps fifty words of English, and a striking talent for pantomime. We could understand each other. Armando made no attempt at communication. They both came down when I arrived. By burdening ourselves like burros, we were able to unload the car with but two trips up the hundred stairs. Armando fell immediately in love with the black car. He circled it, hissing softly. He linked hoses together so the water would reach, and washed it lovingly with soft rags and polished it until it was dazzling.

Rosalinda assured me that the *electricidad* and the *agua* and the *teléfono* were all working and in readiness for Señor and Señora Pinelli. It was evident to me that they had been lonely and bored in the house, and welcomed the chance to be busy. She said that there was a girl in readiness, who would begin work as a maid as soon as the Pinellis arrived. The girl's name was Nadina, and she was related to them in some way. I did not have the words to explain to her my relationship to the Pinellis. I said that I was a friend, but that I also worked for them. She smiled and nodded with total lack of comprehension.

The servant quarters were adjacent to the house, on the east side where the crest began to slope down, so that it was about six steps up from their doorway to the kitchen door. I selected the smallest bedroom for myself in the main house, on the northeast corner, with no view of the sea. The Pinelli luggage was placed in the master bedroom, a room about twenty by forty with huge glass doors that opened onto a private terrace overlooking the sea. There were two great double beds there, with massive posts carved of black wood.

After I had unpacked my own things, I went to the master bedroom. Rosalinda was unpacking Kathy's things, hanging her clothing in a vast closet big enough to serve as a dressing room. She gave little cries of pleasure as she examined the dresses and suits, skirts and blouses. *"¡Qué lindo! ¡Qué bonito!"*

By then it was dark, and so I did not see the beach until the next day. It was the most private beach imaginable. Two hard ridges of rock reached from the height down to the level of the sea. They were about eighty feet apart. Only at the lowest tide was it possible to walk around them. They enclosed a crescent of coarse, clean, brown sand. Stone steps reached from the front terrace down to the beach. They were of reinforced concrete and projected out from the concave wall of the cliff, with a hemp railing on the sea side. They made one long sweep, descending, from east to west, to a balcony halfway down, then reversed and slanted down from west to east to a truly massive freeform sun platform six feet above the sand. The platform was about eight by ten, and of reinforced concrete at least ten inches thick. It was anchored in place by steel rods as big around as my wrist. At high tide the sea came up under it, covering all the sand, so that each time the tide ebbed, the beach was new again. When I wondered at the massiveness of the platform, Rosalinda told me, with elaborate use of pantomime that it was the third such platform. Storms had smashed the other two. She made a spinning motion of her hands to show that they had been hurled high in the air. She said this one would be taken by the sea one day. She seemed to think it incomprehensible to try to outwit the sea's fury.

I cannot forget what it was like to awaken there that first morning and hear the sound of the sea, and see the sun against the mint-green wall of my room. I had that feeling of inexplicable and joyous anticipation which had been gone for a long, long time. I felt renewed. All things were possible.

I was served on the terrace, elegantly, with papaya, toasted muffins, strong, black coffee. I went down to the sea and swam out until the blue house was a sandbox toy. The sea sighed and heaved and glittered. I floated there, and yelled for no reason, and went all the way in, using a long racing crawl, spending myself. I baked in the sun. I showered. Rosalinda served lunch. I napped until three, then drove into Acapulco and bought myself an ornate silver lighter and a snakeskin billfold, sat and drank black beer at a sidewalk café and smiled at pretty girls who walked slowly, arm in arm, in the dusk, while the birds made a great clatter over settling down for the night in the big green trees.

Those four days before John and Kathy arrived were good days. They were the last good days of my life. Had I known they were, I could not have enjoyed them more. I did not think of the future in terms of purpose or direction. I just had the unreasonable confidence that everything was going to be fine and golden. It was euphoria. And it could not, of course, last. I sent a card to my folks. I bought a lottery ticket and won two hundred pesos. I worked diligently on my tan, and my Spanish. I waited for the phone call from my employers.

I picked John and Kathy up at the airport at noon on Friday. There were two men with them. August Sonninger and Frank Race. August was a squat, bald, imperious little weasel in a soiled scurfy beret, Bermudas, Indian sandals and a sports shirt emblazoned with pastel fish. He was obviously the dominant, completely in charge, full of power plays and rude contradictions, snapping his fingers for service. The others treated him as if he were king. Frank Race was a towering, languid, storklike man in a cotton cord suit and a tasteful tie. He drawled in an inconsistent Limey accent, and seemed to be trying to give the impression that all this was a sort of grotesque game, and he was playing along for kicks. He was almost amusing, in a withdrawn, ironic way. Kathy was being very windblown and girlish with them. It didn't seem to suit her. The big surprise to me was John Pinelli. The great soft pink-and-white thing had come alive. He was full of snap, glitter and enthusiasm. For the first time I was aware of the quality of his mind—quick, perceptive, agile, imaginative.

They were hopped up, so busy with plans and schemes that they seemed only vaguely aware of being in Acapulco.

August Sonninger and Frank Race stayed through until the following Tuesday afternoon when I drove them and John Pinelli back to the airport. I guess it was not what Rosalinda had expected. She had a sense of order. They would not conform to any schedule. They seemed to take no pleasure in the house. They talked business endlessly. They fought over details. To the four of them I was a part of the background, like the house and the sea and the servants.

I learned that Kathy and John were still being remote and formal and polite with each other. From their arguments I gathered that John Pinelli had bought into the enterprise by signing over, in exchange for a stock interest, his piece of the successful television property.

They had brought a pile of scripts with them. They called

on me for some special service on Saturday night, at about
eleven o'clock. They were all in the big living room. Frank
Race came and got me off the terrace. He had me sit down
with a script in my hand. He and Kathy both had copies.
Sonninger sat scowling at us.

"Read the Wilson lines, old boy, if you will," he told
me, pointing to a speech that started a scene.

"I don't know anything about . . ."

"Just read the lines, old boy."

I started to read the first speech, feeling like a damn fool,
trying to sound the way I thought Wilson should sound from
what little clue I had.

Sonninger broke in. "You!" he said.

"Yes?"

"This is not talent scouts," he said in his slight Mittel
European accent. "It is not Actors' Studio. Just read,
please. Nothing more."

I shrugged and read my lines as if I were reading a market
report. That's what they wanted. That's what they got.
Kathy had the corner on emotion. Frank Race and I read our
lines woodenly. She emoted. I thought she did fine. But I
thought the script was horrible stuff, full of pretentiously
poetic expression. It went on until three in the morning.
They would quarrel viciously, yell at each other, and then
mark up the copies of the script. Sonninger was boss. I
couldn't see how they were improving it in any way. If this
was going to be the first release by Sierra Productions, it
looked like a poor place to stick your money.

The only other time I wasn't totally ignored was on
Monday morning at about eleven. I had swum and I was
baking on the platform above the beach. Frank Race came
gingerly down the steps, his pallid, narrow body gleaming
with oil. He carried a beach towel and a script.

After a casual greeting, he stretched out and worked on
the script for about a half hour. When he put it aside, I said,
"Is that thing really as bad as I think it is?"

He looked at me, slightly startled, and then smiled.
"They can read bad, old boy, and play well. We're all
happy with it. And, forgive me, we have the benefit of

professional judgment. The people who will release it are happy with it too. And they're quite shrewd about these things."

"There seems to be a hell of a lot of talk in it."

"We're taking a little out, here and there."

"Kathy will play the lead?"

"That's the idea. The old dear is a little long in the tooth for the part. But that's a camera and lighting problem. It's worth that gamble to have John."

"John or his money?"

He looked at me intently. "You are a very brash young man. You seem to like to talk about things you know nothing about."

"I'm just asking questions. People haven't been falling over themselves to hire him. So all of a sudden he's wonderful?"

"I'll tell you a little more than you need to know, old boy. John Pinelli is a director of the first grade, sensitive, creative. A director must have one additional talent. He must be able to control his stars, keep them from acting like petulant children, keep them from bluffing him. John used to have that. When he lost some of his confidence, he lost that first. The rest is intact. Sonninger will produce. I will be unit manager. We will work closely with John, and we'll control the talent. He can do the rest. Once we wrap this one up, and it's good, then all the confidence will be back. And he'll be an enormous asset to us on the other pictures we've scheduled. I expect him to make me rich, old boy. The feds cleaned me last year. I miss the money."

"So this first one has to be tops?"

"It will be."

"I hope it is," I said. I didn't see how it could be. The story seemed silly to me. But maybe they knew what they were doing. Then I thought of all the brilliant, confident people who use up a whole year out of their lives to bring something to Broadway which lasts three performances. It seems like a mutual hypnosis deal. They all tell each other the material is great until they finally believe it.

Anyway, I took them to the airport on Tuesday, and Kathy

and I were left alone in the house with the three servants. Nadina, the maid, was a round, brown girl with broad, bare feet. When you addressed her directly, she would put one of her black braids in her mouth, bite down upon it, try to turn her head all the way around on her shoulders, and giggle. When working, she sang softly to herself in a clear, true voice.

There was a sense of isolation about that house. It was as if the concrete steps were a rope ladder, and when you were up there, they were pulled up and you were alone.

I saw more of Kathy than I expected. We ate together. This seemed to please Rosalinda. There were always fresh flowers on the table. Kathy was casual and remote. She spent a lot of time on the beach and on the sun platform. And she spent a lot of time grooming herself, exercising. I did not mention my plans. At the time I made an accounting and gave her the balance from the two thousand pesos, she gave me the hundred dollars I had been promised. But she did not ask me what I would do. It seemed agreeable to her for me to stay on. She gave me errands to do. I drove her to and from town when she wanted to shop. It annoyed me that she preferred to sit in the back.

Things changed between us on the following weekend, late on Sunday afternoon. We were down on the sun platform. Rosalinda called her to the phone. She had been expecting John, and had been growing more irritated when there was no word from him. When she came back down, her face was pale under the new copper-gold tan, and she was so furious her hand shook visibly.

"Was that John?" I asked.

"Be still!" She stretched out with her back toward me. Her hip in gay nylon was mounted high. The nape of her neck looked tender and touching and defenseless, like the neck of a child. The strap of the halter top bit into the slender softness of her back.

She rolled up onto her knees abruptly, turning to face me. "Come on," she said, a whisper almost lost in the sound of the ocean. It had come up under the platform. She looked at me over a gun sight. She got to her feet. "Come on," she said. It was a command that needed no explanation. She went quickly and lightly up the steps without looking back. I followed her.

We went to the master bedroom. She adjusted the heavy wooden shutters so that narrow strands of the late sun lay against the far wall, filling the room with a luminous golden light. As she fixed the shutters I could hear the shallow quickness of her breathing and the whispery sound of her bare feet on the blue-green tiles. She turned, tiny and imperative, and held her arms out toward me, and it was as if reality had merged with my own erotic imaginings, making the present moment dreamlike.

I believe it would be ridiculous for me to waste any of this imprisoned tag end of my life in description of the mechanics of copulation, in the more intimate devices of this particular pair of adulterers. Go to any loan library. Select a novel with a reputation for naughtiness. Open it to the section where the pages are most smudged. Substitute Kathy and Kirby for the names in the text. Our novelists seem to write of physical love as though they were under some obligation either to acquaint a herd of Martians with the fleshy facts, or to compose a handbook for the inexperienced.

Now that I am so far away from it, I can coldly chart the short history of our physical affair. In the beginning, as is always the case, pleasure was handicapped by the awkwardnesses of new lovers. As we learned each other, on the physical level, in the way the tricks of performance of a new sailboat or sports car must be learned through use, pleasure was heightened. As with all lovers since the origins of mankind, as pleasure was heightened, we indulged ourselves more often. Such intensity invariably creates a hypnotic aura which dims all the other aspects of existence.

And now I must account for the change in Kathy, a change which astonished her. She tried to explain it to me many times. When John had phoned her from Mexico City he had taunted her with an account of Sonninger's continual pressure to sign a younger actress for the lead in their first production, and he had tried to make her feel insecure by telling her he might back down and let Sonninger have his way. Kathy, furious at John, had sought the handiest weapon of revenge, to take a boy who meant nothing to her into the bed of her husband. It was to have been a meaningless and destructive act, a service she would require of me which would lead to no emotional involvement.

But to her surprise, and her mixed joy and consternation, she did become emotionally involved, and far more quickly than she would have believed possible. I now know that it was not some uniqueness in me—it was her vulnerable condition.

Her marriage had turned so bad she could not be sure John Pinelli cared whether she lived or died. She had fought the ravages of age to a precarious draw for several years, but now the other side was growing dangerously strong. She had let herself slip into an emotional pattern dangerous to any woman—telling herself she did not need anyone and did not want to be needed by anyone.

She had sought a quick, dirty little revenge, not sensing the depth of her own vulnerability, and suddenly found in the circle of her arms a young man who adored her. There had been too many men who had tried to use her to their own advantage. Here was one whose only humble desire was to be close to her, serve her, love her.

There was, in addition, a physical aspect to her vulnerability. She was a woman with a strong sexual drive, and except for those rare times in her past when she had not been working at her profession, she had sublimated that drive, used the force of it to refine her actress art. She was not working. John had not touched her—she said—since we had left New York. She was strongly ready to be used. And I had a youthful vigor she was soon able to surpass.

It was the small and dubious miracle of my life to watch such a woman slowly, and then more rapidly, turn all her clocks back to eighteen. It must be remembered, and understood, that in all my life I had never given of myself. I knew nothing of the pattern of giving. Those six weeks are as close as I ever came to love. I felt both humble and exultant. I believe that for those six weeks I was a good

man. I struck no poses. I had no devious ideas of gain. I
wanted only to love her and watch the continuous blossom-
ing of her, a special gift that intrigued us both.

A warm spell in autumn will trick a flower into bloom. It
was that way with my Kathy. Her harshness and her
coldness went away. Her eyes were soft for me. The
textures of her body changed with the flowering of her
heart, silky, scented, poised always for acceptance.

We became fools, as do all true lovers. We had our own
language, invented our own ceremonies, created our own
jokes—and in this way made our own shining wall against
the world. I had never heard her laugh aloud until those six
weeks of our love. I learned the meanings of all her kinds of
laughter, from paean of joy to bawdy guffaw, to velvety
chuckle of pleasure. We bought absurd presents for each
other down in the city. She was an actress, and a dozen
women, and I knew that should I ever learn all aspects of
that dozen, I would find a whole second series beyond that,
like those clothing store mirrors, where images stretch off at
an angle to infinity.

We swam, and we baked in the sun, and we went to the
big hotels and sat at their bars and danced to their music,
and we made five hundred plans to go away together, all of
them necessary and impractical, and we knew we would not
go away together, but it was a reality you could not
mention.

She knew how much I enjoyed doing small things for her,
and so she helped me think of things I could do. One special
time was when I would brush that shining hair, a hundred
strokes of the brush while she sat erect at the dressing table
like an obedient child, her eyes watching me in the mirror.
After the hundred strokes, I would wrap the brush in a nylon
stocking and brush her hair thirty times more to bring out a
special gloss, and then take the crackling electricity out of it
with a tortoise shell comb. I was permitted to paint her
toenails with the silver lacquer she used, while she looked
down at me. She sent me to the city on personal errands.
She was a small precious possession, and I cared for her,
and her obvious sparkling happiness made me gloat.

We had one game we played often, and I imagine it is a game played by all lovers with but minor variations. She would announce primly, but with a glint of mischief, that on this day we were going to be "good." And so we would tantalize ourselves with this false pose of noble self-denial as long as possible. But there would come a moment, inevitably, when our eyes would catch and lock, and I would see her mough soften and see the pulse of her throat become more prominent, and see her head sag just a little as it would seem to become too heavy for her slender neck to support. And wherever we were then, on the beach, in town, at the table, we would pick the quickest route to the inevitable bed. "We're horrible types," she would whisper. "No character at all, my darling. No restraint at all, lover. Thank God."

In the beginning we made a few weak efforts to hide our infatuation from the servants. But soon we ceased to give a damn what they thought. The institution of the lovely wife with a fat old husband and a muscular young lover is a cliché of the Latin world. John Pinelli had been brusque and rude to all three of them. Their approval of us was expressed in small ways that delighted us. Flowers from Armando on the table where we dined. Very special dishes prepared by Rosalinda. Giggles and blushings from Nadina. They all seemed part of a delicious conspiracy.

The intense affair suffered four interruptions during the six weeks. Perhaps the fourth one cannot legitimately be called an interruption. John flew down four times, once alone, once with Sonninger, twice with Sonninger and Race. On the second visit, he took Kathy back to Mexico City with him for two days. While she was gone I roamed my empty world like an abandoned dog. She flew back alone. When I picked her up at the airport, the expression on her face wiped away those two days as though I had never lived them.

It worried me that John Pinelli would see the change in her and guess the reason for it. I did not see how he could help it. I did not see how he could be in the same room with the two of us and not sense what we had become to each other. But she was indignant at my fears, saying they were a slur on her professional ability. And when John was there, she could turn off all that vibrant joy—almost all of it—and become, in some frightening way, a stranger. His fourth visit cannot be counted as an interruption to our affair. He came with Sonninger and Race, and they stayed but one night, stayed up late, drank heavily. At dawn she awakened me by coming violently into me bed, chuckling, nestling into my chest and throat, her breath hot, her hair clean-scented, her small body sheathed in whispering silk.

Let me say that this adventure did not have a flavor of evil. It was more like a mischievous conspiracy—like children raiding an orchard. In some way we had cleansed ourselves with love. True evil was the incident in the car on the way down into Mexico. Once she spoke of that and said she was sorry in a voice that broke, and wept and was comforted. She wept easily in our days of love.

Sometimes, usually when she was asleep in my arms, I would remember that I had seen this woman on the big screens of movie houses and drive-ins, and on the flat small world of television, and had felt as had all other men watching her, that little twitch of speculation, that recurrent, unavoidable, egocentric daydream of coupling with that electronic projection of desirability. And when the absurdity of your wish becomes apparent to you, the ego protects itself by saying Aw, she's scrawnier than she looks, and those show biz types are too stuck on themselves to be any damn good in bed, and she's probably lez anyway.

Then it would seem incredible that I could be so lucky as to hold this almost mythical creature in my arms. I would study her sleeping face, the intricacies of her ear, and of her lips softly parted, study the delicate structuring of nose and brow, the incredibly perfect texture of her skin, the tiny perfect hairs of brow and lashes, like little gilded wires. I would wait in love and patience for her eyes to open, knowing they would be blank, unfocused, uncomprehending as she came out of the private jungles of her sleep, knowing that as they focused upon me a gladness would come into them and the corners of her mouth would lift, knowing she would stretch in supple ways within my arms, give a yawn that would expose the upcurling tongue, and then bring her mouth strongly and greedily against mine, and I would then begin to pleasure her in every way she especially liked.

There is always the perfect confidence of lovers that it will all go on forever. There is a timelessness about such things. The world stood still while I focused my life upon her, totally content. At high noon she loved to lie, Bikini-ed, upon a beach pad on the sun platform down above the beach and have me knead the sun oil into her body until her little moans and sighs of luxury were like the purrings of a cat. When the sting of the sun was too much to endure, we would cool ourselves in the sea, and then go up and have lunch in the shade of the patio. After lunch, before siesta, she relished having me cleanse the last of the sun oil from her body. There was a huge tiled shower stall, and a noisy turbulence of hot water. She would turban her hair in a big towel, and I would scrub her with a large soft brush and the mild musky soap she adored, and as she stood solemn and obedient as a child, I would towel her slenderness and ripeness until she glowed. It was traditional that during these chores I would digress from duty to caresses, and it was a part of our pattern that she would chide me and tell me to keep my mind on my work, please. It was love play, of course, and she enjoyed the pleasure I took in watching her, and it readied us to the point of torment for the love hour in the big bed after which, utterly spent, we would join the siesta sleep of all the rest of the world.

The unending, unendable world of love came to an end on the second day of July. I had fallen asleep facing her and the wall beyond her. She awakened me with a frenzied abruptness, making love to me with rapid little violences, biting at my mouth, making an odd little humming sound, digging me with her nails. Her eyes looked around, wild and mad. She laughed in a flat, strange way. Her intensity brought me quickly out of the blur of sleep into an almost immediate response to her. Of all the creatures she had been and had pretended to be, this one was quite new to me. But it was a part of our love, and if she felt like simulating a frenzy close to madness, I would play it her way. She was in such continual writhing motion that it took a surprising amount of strength to catch and cup the frantic chalice of her hips, and pin her long enough to permit a hasty joining.

But the moment I had accomplished that entrapment and that abrupt depth of conquest, I heard directly behind me sounds that seemed to stop my heart. I heard a low ferine grunting, a bestial gasping, a flat, splashing liquidity. I spun away from her to turn and stare at John Pinelli. He was not six feet from me. He held onto the footboard of the other bed. He was doubled over, vomiting on the tile floor. I knew instantly that she had been awake and had seen him come in, and had chosen to use me to hurt him in the most vicious way any man can be hurt. As she had aroused me to her purpose, she had been looking toward him, defying him, flinging him that ultimate challenge. Her frenzy had been built upon hate. It had not been love, but exhibition.

At the moment he was incapable of looking at me. I ran to the chair, took my damp swimming trunks that hung from the back of it, and yanked them on.

"Don't leave me now, darling!" she called, projecting with full dramatic volume and timbre. "Don't leave me like this, lover!" And crouched there on the rumpled bed, her silvery hair in wild disarray, her face venomous, she began to scream with laughter.

As I tried to go by him he straightened up, eyes streaming, and reached a heavy arm toward me. I do not know what he was trying to do or express. In pure panic I swung and hit him, heavily, blindly, I know not where, and heard him fall behind me as I went through the door. Rosalinda was standing at the far end of the corridor, her eyes huge, brown fists pressed to her belly. As I raced by her I saw her cross herself.

There was no place in the world I could go. And I could never go fast enough to run away from memory. In my touching innocence I thought I was the owner of the world's most vivid and most distressing memory. The world is seldom charitable to fools.

I hesitated, then went out through the front of the house, across the the terrace and down the steps to the beach. The tide was almost high, and there was a medium sea rolling in. I lay on the platform. The sea slid under me and smashed the rocks and threw spray high. I rolled over onto my back and the spray fell onto my face. On my lips it tasted as salty as tears. For a long time I thought I was going to be sick. But the feeling finally went away.

I was eye to eye with a contradiction, one many men have faced. If my love was capable of doing what she had done, then I had never known her at all. If I did not know her at all, then our love had been an indelicate farce. Are not all young men incurably romantic? The world cures the uncurable, however. And so in a lonely way, wrapped in the roar of the sea, I celebrated the death of love, or of illusion. Because I still loved the imaginary woman who could not have used me to strike such a deadly blow at the heart of her husband. But she had never existed.

This, I told myself, was no way for a sophisticate to behave. I ordered myself to put it all into proper perspective. A fading actress had dared play an ingénue role because her audience, her naïve intrigant, had been so very uncritical. I had been handy and healthy when she had desired fun and games. I counted her flaws: the almost invisible crescent scars at her temples from the cosmetic operation that had tautened the skin of her face into a semblance of youth; the beautiful teeth—expensively capped; the hair roots that were causing her much less trouble now that they were growing out gray; the crenelations of the flesh on the insides of her thighs; the deflated sag of her small breasts when she forgot to keep her shoulders well back; the ugly toes, crumpled by years of shoes too small; the peasant thickness and stubbiness of her hands and feet; the frank and blatant indelicacy with which she referred to all matters physiological.

But even her flaws were unbearably precious.

I knew exactly what a true sophisticate would do, and by

God, I would do it. I would stay as inconspicuous as possible until they finished their battling and John Pinelli went back to the city. Their fights in the car had ended quickly. Her little hobbies couldn't actually mean very much to him. So I would stick around and we'd continue the same pleasant routine.

Everything, I told myself, would be *exactly* as before. And I wondered why I started to feel sick again. She would sparkle for me, and we would divert each other with all our little games and devices and love words and private jokes. There would be but one small difference. This time I would know it didn't really mean anything—to either of us. I hung my head over the edge of the sun platform and vomited into the sudsy green sea.

When it was over, I wondered how long I had been there. A long time. At least two hours. Possibly more. I squinted at the sun and estimated that it was six of its own diameters above the edge of the sea.

I heard a faint sound over the roaring of the waves. I looked up. A man stood on the cantilevered steps, fifteen feet above the platform, calling my name. I stared up at him, raising my eyebrows, pointing at myself. He made that strange Mexican beckoning gesture which looks as if they are waving you away rather than summoning you. He stood just beyond the reach of the spray.

I went up the steps to him. He was a big man. He wore a pale silk jacket, sharply tailored, a grey bow tie, a cocoa straw hat with a feather. He looked like Don Ameche a little bit.

"Mr. Kirby Stassen?"

"Yes."

"I am of the police. Come with me, please." His English was very clear and deliberate. I followed him up the steps, thinking that John was giving me the roust the hard way. All he had to do was tell me to go.

There were five people in the living room. The three servants were lined up. A fat sleepy-looking policeman in uniform stood behind them. Another big Mexican in a white linen jacket stood facing them. He turned as we came in. He

wore a blue shirt and a maroon bow tie, a straw hat just like
the one who had come to get me. He looked a little bit like
Richard Nixon, but bigger and jowlier. They were two
smooth types. They had those police eyes, direct and
skeptical.

White jacket motioned toward me and projected a flood
of fast Spanish at Rosalinda. Rosalinda answered. I could
not follow the words. But I saw the pantomime that
accompanied them. I saw John Pinelli stalking in. I saw the
embrace that meant love. I saw myself running out, and
going down to the beach. White Jacket tapped his watch and
hammered her with short questions. She answered with
explosive dignity.

Ameche said to me, choosing the words, "The woman
says that you have been down at the beach while this thing
has happened."

"What has happened?"

"You heard no shots?"

"I didn't hear anything! What happened?"

"Come with us, please," Ameche said. He gave an order
to the uniformed man. I went with White Jacket and
Ameche to the master bedroom.

At the doorway, Ameche said, "Kindly do not step into
the blood, Mr. Stassen."

I had no intention of so doing. There was a Fourth of July
smell of cordite in the room, and the bland sick smell of
blood and the sharpness of vomit. John Pinelli lay face
down on the floor by the foot of the bed where his wife and I
had made love. He lay in an ocean of blood. A partial dental
bridge lay three feet from his head, a small ship making sail
across the sea.

I gagged. I looked for Kathy. I did not see her.

Ameche showed me a gun. I had not seen him pick it up.
He held it by a yellow pencil he had inserted in the barrel. It
was a hell of a big gun, a Colt .45-caliber revolver with
walnut grips. He held it so I could read the silver plates set
into each grip, first on one side and then on the other.

One side said, "The John P., fastest gun on location."

The other side said, "From Wade, Joan and Sonny—'Action at Box Canyon.'"

I remembered seeing the movie a few years ago, a pretty good Western. I had not known Pinelli was connected with it in any way.

"Are you familiar with this firearm?" Ameche asked me.

"I've never seen it before."

He laid the gun on the bed, retrieved his pencil. "I shall make a reconstruction for you, Mr. Stassen." He walked to the wall, skirting the blood. He pointed out four widely spaced scars in the plaster, each about four feet off the floor.

"He stood about where my associate is standing, and he fired these four shots at the woman. She was dodging back and forth, screaming. One of them caused the wound upon her arm, here." He touched his left arm just below the shoulder. "This spray of blood is from that minor wound. It is believed that she then sought refuge under the bed, still screaming. He knelt and crawled after her and placed the muzzle of the gun against her body, here." He pressed his finger down against the top of his shoulder, near his neck. "This large slug ranged downward through her body, killing her. The impact slid her halfway out from under the bed. He stood up, walked around the bed, and turned her over onto her back and fired once again into the center of the stomach. He pulled her out from under the bed all the way to look at her face and be sure she was dead. The gun was then empty. He walked to the bureau there and took one more shell. He walked back and stood where he could see her, and shot himself in the throat and fell where you now see him."

Yes, I could see John Pinelli. But as he had explained how it happened, I had grown more and more conscious of what I couldn't see, what I didn't want to see. I knew where it was. I took four slow steps. And I could see her. There had been much blood in her too. She lay naked on the tile, tiny and gray and shrunken, her hair lifeless, her cheeks sucked in, her eyes turned up out of sight, her small teeth showing. Her breasts had sagged flat. She looked like an old, old woman.

I backed until I could no longer see her. I heard voices in

the other part of the house. More officials had arrived. White Jacket hurried out.

"This disturbs you?" Ameche asked. "We will talk on the little terrace."

I was glad to get out of that room, and away from the stink of death. I pulled the outdoor air deep into my lungs.

He perched one tailored hip on a metal table, pulled out a pack of Kents and gave me one. He looked at me shrewdly.

"They employed you?"

"Just to drive them down."

"But that was some months ago. Have you been working for them?"

"Just . . . the odd errand. A little driving. They haven't been paying me. I've been a house guest you could say."

"Yes, of course. A guest. And providing . . . a very personal service for your hostess, no?"

"Is that illegal here?"

"No, of course not. But stupid carelessness should be made illegal. You were caught with her."

"Yes."

"So we have a murder and a suicide. Now I shall tell you some facts of life, Mr. Stassen. This is a resort place. We like . . . rumors of intrigue, but not dirty violence and scandal. Mr. Pinelli was in poor health. He was despondent. You are not in any way in this picture."

"I'm not?"

"Your things will be packed. You will be out of this house in ten minutes. You will be out of Acapulco by the first aircraft. I cannot insist, but I would say it would be wise for you to leave Mexico. Go now and dress and leave here."

I looked at him. I shrugged and turned away. After I had gone a dozen feet he said, "Mr. Stassen!" I looked back at him. "She was much too old for you, *chico*."

Kathy was under a great bed, screaming and screaming, holding her bleeding arm. John Pinelli, crawling, peered under at her, the big, ridiculous gun in his hand.

There was nothing in the world worth arguing about. I

left. I had a thousand dollars when I arrived in Mexico City. I found a cheap hotel. I got blind, stupid drunk. Four days later I had eleven dollars left, and somebody had stolen my suitcase. I wired home for money. Ernie wired me a hundred dollars. I bought the clothes and toilet articles I needed. I fooled around the city for a while, living cheap, trying not to think about Kathy. I drank enough to keep the whole thing a little dulled, a little far back in my mind. When the money was dangerously low, I took a bus to Monterrey. There I ran into a family from Sonora, Texas. A man and wife and two small kids, traveling in a pickup truck.

He had a bad infection in his right hand, and his little Mexican wife couldn't drive a car. So we made a deal.

I came back across the border at Del Rio on Sunday, the nineteenth day of July. He felt he could drive one-handed to Sonora. We parted company there, in Del Rio. I had a little over fifteen dollars left. I didn't give a damn where I went or what I did. It was a blistering afternoon. I decided I might as well hitch-hike east. I walked a way east out of town on Route 90. I had no luck. I kept moving slowly as I tried. I came to a beer joint. I went in. After the glare outside I couldn't see anything.

A high penetrating voice said, "And here is Joe College, seeing America first, having a great big fat adventure before he poops out and joins Rotary."

That's how I met Sander Golden, Nanette Koslov and Shack Hernandez.

SEVEN

IN the fat Wolf Pack file, the first memorandum written by Riker Deems Owen about Nanette Koslov is perhaps the most pretentious one of the lot. As with most men who claim to be unable to understand women, Owen tends to overcomplicate his observations, to see devices and nuances where none exist.

Yet in spite of the somewhat fevered pace of his imagination in his account of this semi-attractive young woman, one cannot say that his observations would in any way impede the sales of the memoirs he plans to write some day.

Like most small-bore, pretentious men, Riker Owen shows the tendency to strike an emotional attitude and then, using that prejudice as a base, draw vast, unreasoned, philosophical conclusions.

One can see this device in action in the very first paragraph of the first Koslov memorandum:

It would be a most unprofessional attitude for a doctor, a psychiatrist or a defense attorney to believe that any individual is evil in the old-fashioned, Biblical meaning of the word. In my conferences with Nanette Koslov I have had to consciously fight to prevent myself from succumbing to this inaccurate oversimplification. I have, in fact, delayed my preparation of this memorandum until I could be certain in my own mind that I have established a completely objective attitude toward her, rather than an emotional or even semi-superstitious attitude.

She is but twenty years of age, but it is extraordinarily easy to overlook the fact she is a young girl.

She is five foot six and weighs a little over a hundred and twenty pounds. Her breasts are smaller than average, her hips rather wide and mature. She has a heavy, glossy mop of chestnut-brown hair, which she customarily wears completely unfettered. It falls below her shoulders. It is rather raggedly cropped in front, cut off at the level of her heavy eyebrows. She seems to look out from under it at you, like an animal safe under a hedge, watching you. Her eyes are a slightly muddy green, and very direct. While talking or listening she has a lot of tics and mannerisms that are all involved with the hair. She is forever fingering it, pulling a sheaf of it across her throat like a furry scarf, or pulling a strand of it across her lips, or across one eye.

Her other mannerisms, the way she sits and stands, are, I have been informed, a conscious imitation of that little French strumpet with the face like Huckleberry Finn. The French call such conscious imitation *bardolatrie*, I believe. Her features are quite plain, the nose snubbed and rather flat, the mouth broad and soft, the skin texture coarse, with the enlarged pores particularly evident on the broad cheekbones. Her only make-up is a dark lipstick, carelessly and lavishly used. On her brows and her strong hands are those small random scars acquired by those lives are spent close to the edge of darkness.

I find in reading over these paragraphs of description that I have not done her justice. The description itself is accurate, but in her case she adds up to more than the sum of the parts. There is a savage, sensuous impact to her appearance. Sander Golden has called her an animal. That word captures some of the essence of her. She exudes an automatic sexual challenge, a knowing, skeptical arrogance that makes a man feel there is something he should prove to her. I do not believe this is a conscious thing with her. It is, perhaps, a matter of glands, hormones. Even the slightly unwashed look of her constitutes, in itself, an inexplicable appeal—possibly an appeal to the base desires shared by all men, though acknowledged by very few of us.

I do know that it has been, and will continue to be, difficult to conduct interviews with her. When she has those direct green eyes on you and pulls that shinning hair across her lips and slowly shifts her round, solid thighs, it is as if you are exploring two channels of communication simultaneously, only one of them verbal. And at times the subterranean communication becomes so strong as to drown out the words you are saying. And then, for a time, you are lost, and must pause and remember what you were trying to say.

Her background is drab. Her people are Polish peasants. They fled to West Germany in 1945 and were one of the fortunate families who spent very little time in a resettlement camp before coming to the United States with their three small children and settling near Bassett, Nebraska, in a tenant-farming situation. Nanette was six at that time. Three more children were born to the Koslovs in Nebraska. Nanette learned English rapidly, attended public school, and worked on the land. Her people were so strict as to border on cruelty. Nanette matured early. At fourteen, after being expelled from junior high school as a result of scandalous behavior involving some senior high school boys, she ran away with a migrant farm laborer who later abandoned her in San Francisco. Her family made no attempt to find her. She looked older than her years. Passing herself off as eighteen, she obtained work as a waitress. When she was sixteen she fell in with a bohemian group in that city. For the next three years she was a fixture in that curious subterranean artistic world of San Francisco which specializes in incomprehensible jazz, foolish painting and hysterical poetry, with their inevitable by-products of mysticism, coffee-house conversation, drug addiction, violence and self-pity. She worked sporadically and was passed back and forth from musician to painter to poet, as a model, an inspiration and a bedmate. During this period she learned the jargon of that milieu without the necessity of having to understand what she was saying—a condition shared, perhaps, by most of her associates.

Last year a painter with whom she was living was killed as a result of a violent argument during an impromptu party. Friends hid Nanette until it became certain the police wanted her for questioning. She fled to Los Angeles and became a member of a smaller group there. It was there she met Sander Golden. When a narcotics raid broke up the group, she left Los Angeles with Golden. Their tentative destination was New Orleans, where Golden had friends. They met Hernandez in Tucson, and the three of them traveled together as far as Del Rio, where Kirby Stassen joined the group.

It is difficult to assess the effect of Nan Koslov on the three men, insofar as their short career of extreme violence is concerned. Each member of the group had, I believe, a catalytic effect on the other three. In one sense perhaps the men felt a necessity to "show off" for the girl, to show her that they were beyond all rules and restrictions. But in order for her to achieve this effect upon them, it would first have been necessary for her to communicate to them her own taste for recklessness.

From the meager clues she has given me, I can perhaps reconstruct her attitude at Del Rio. Here was a girl who, for several years, had lived only for sensation. For kicks, as Sander Golden would say. Highly spiced foods deaden the palate. So ever-increasing quantities of spice must be used. It is the same with physical sensation. Though she denies it, there is, I believe, a good chance that she was directly involved in the killing of the artist in San Francisco. He was stabbed repeatedly in the abdomen with a long skewer used for fireplace cooking, and in the throat and in the nape of the neck with a table fork. There is such a flavor of primitive violence in this woman, of revolt against cruelties inflicted upon her, that she may have found a new and special pleasure in the act of killing. It is, one could say, the ultimate sensation, and she had been increasing the tempo of sensation over her short lifetime.

Also, Sander Golden had put her on his own routine of stimulants, a schedule which he had arrived at through trial and error and which he terms "The biggest thing since the wheel."

It involved a carefully regulated intake of powerful tranquilizers, plus raw dexedrine and barbiturates.

As Nanette described it, "It was the most I'd seen. It kept you out there. Everything, every little thing, like a stone or a bottle, looked bright and important in a funny way, and you could laugh and understand things the squares couldn't. He changed it a little for me, different from the way he took it, and kept asking me, and changing it, until he had it just right for me, and I could float all day and all night. But he couldn't give much to Shack, because Shack went crazy. Sandy said he was going to patent it. You couldn't get hooked on it. But sometimes my heart thumping would scare me a little. And anything you did—it didn't seem to really count. Do you know what I mean? You could step off a building and laugh all the way down. We put Stass on it, and we both kept asking him, and Sandy kept changing it, but we never got it to him just right. We'd have him either all shaky and hopped, or falling asleep."

So the regimen of the stimulants and depressants was another catalytic agent. It was a queasy rapture.

I must make one further point about Nanette Koslov which involves a reappraisal of my own thinking. It is a truism that men do not understand women. But until I met Nan Koslov, I had been content with one generalization which I felt fitted all women, from whore to princess. I had felt that women had a strong drive for stability and security. I believed it was a primitive heritage. They, I thought, were the undiluted conservatives in this world, the apostles of "things as they are." They play safe. They do not gamble. They each want a safe nest somewhere in the world, and when they do not have it, they work and yearn for it.

But Nan Koslov falls completely outside this pattern, thus voiding my comfortable generalization. She is disconcertingly complete within herself. I can detect in her no yen for any kind of security or stability. She was content to wander, to stake no claim on any man, to take what she was given and make do with it.

It is only logical to relate this to her sexual attitude. I realize that every culture has its own violent superstitions about sex. The incestuous practices of the ancient Egyptians appall us. We are sickened when we learn that the dynastic line was maintained through the offspring of father-daughter copulation. We feel utterly superior to primitive races, and call their sex play "dirty habits." Even in our own times, we cannot comprehend the frank, uncomplicated, casual attitude of the Scandinavian countries toward unregulated sexual promiscuity. Even as we condemn their young people, they condemn us for what they term our "obsession" with sex. They think we are the twisted ones. They smile and say it just does not have the importance we give it.

Perhaps we are twisted, but I personally find it a suitable way to live. I respect continence. The sexual act in its purest sense should be a sacred act, an act of devotion, a ceremony of love. A coin passed too often from hand to hand loses its mint-sharpness. The inscription can no longer be read. If it is agreed that life should contain acts or symbols of value, is not the sexual act a suitable thing to be so acclaimed? If nothing in life has great meaning, then life itself is denigrated.

To Nanette Koslov, the act of sex has no emotional significance. It is, to her, a way of achieving a mild, unselective pleasure. For several years she has been, to the men around her, an uncomplicated convenience—like a free lunch in the old-time saloons. If the man who was housing and feeding her preferred that she reserve herself for him, either through some emotional quirk, or through that same fastidiousness that prevents the sharing of a toothbrush, she was agreeable. Should he wish to share her, she was co-operative. Love talk bored her. Jealousy was an emotion she could not comprehend. She wanted men to want her. It was the only sort of reassurance she seemed to need. She could have followed the legions of the Romans on remote campaigns. The life would have suited her.

Thus, to me, she is an uncomplicated evil, and a new thing in the world—a denial of most of what we mean when we say Woman. From what she has told me, I now believe that she is one of a multitude. This is a terrifying thing to contemplate. It is more than a revolt against the puritan aspects of our culture. She does not feel that she is in revolt. She feels that she is honest and natural. If she is legion, what is happening to us all? What is happening to a familiar world? She has reduced the magic of life to a low and dirty denominator, made of herself an idle receptacle, and feels neither shame nor regret. She is, to use a word she could not comprehend, godless.

It is unprofessional of me to feel satisfaction in knowing that she is now very afraid. She is afraid of death, the way an animal is afraid. She does not have the imagination to fear life imprisonment.

She asks me many questions. She bites her thick lip, and then asks if you feel anything when you are electrocuted. I tell her it is very sudden. She asks if I can get them off. I tell her I will try. And she asks me again if it will hurt. She asks the way a child might ask about a whipping.

The four of them, during their brief career, were a strange, interrelated group. She was Sander Golden's from the beginning. I have learned that his use of her was as unimportant to him as to her, and it was infrequent, as might be expected in a man whose vital energies have been depleted by years of abuse. Though she was of no importance to him, he would not let Hernandez have her. This was a game Golden was playing, a cruel and rather dangerous game. Hernandez wanted her badly. Golden apparently wanted to prove to himself that he could control Hernandez even with this additional strain upon their relationship. He flaunted his possession of the Koslov girl, and blocked every effort Hernandez made to possess her. The girl was aware of the game, and idly amused by it, and increased the tension by flirting with Hernandez, teasing him the way one might tease a caged bear. Hernandez was caged by his great regard for Sander Golden. Sander had to learn how stout the bars were.

After Kirby Stassen joined them, Sander Golden was able to increase the pressure on Hernandez by sharing the girl with Stassen. This had the effect of directing all Hernandez' sullen rage at Stassen, rather than Golden. I feel that Hernandez would have murdered Kirby Stassen sooner or later, had not the tension been broken by the acquisition of Helen Wister.

Of course, the first I knew of the invasion of our county by this foursome was when, on Sunday morning, I read the frontpage account of the murder of Arnold Crown and the abduction of Paul Wister's daughter. As a matter of professional interest, I had been following the news stories of their track of violence. Until the murder of Crown the authorities were not certain whether it was two men or three men or four men and a girl involved. It was a stroke of luck that the crown murder had occurred in front of unseen witnesses. As yet no positive identification of any of them had been made. I had expected to read that Sunday morning of their having been trapped and captured. Their luck was incredibly good. Their crimes had the mark of the amateur, plus that curious frenzy of the unbalanced mind. Individuals have run amuck in every society the world has known, and will continue so to do. It is unusual for four crazed ones to join forces.

Back on that twenty-sixth day of July, on that hot still Sunday morning, I had no idea that I would find myself defending them. The authorities were tackling the problem with great energy. . . .

EIGHT

By ten o'clock on Sunday morning, July 26, the provisional headquarters of the FBI team assigned to the Wolf Pack case had been transferred from Nashville to Monroe. The FBI had come into the case as a result of the previous kidnap-murder near Nashville. Several agents remained in the Nashville area locking up the details of that investigation. The Special Agent in Charge was Herbert Dunnigan, a tidy, tailored, rather nondescript-looking man with graying auburn hair and a very slight stammer. He arrived by plane at the Monroe airport along with four agents just twenty minutes before the three more agents he had requested arrived from Washington headquarters.

He took over three offices on the third floor of the Monroe National Bank Building, adjacent to the offices occupied by the small FBI staff resident in Monroe. He called in city, county and state law enforcement officials and made it quietly clear to them that he was in charge of the case. He requested their co-operation, and stated that any information released to the press would be released through him.

Herbert Dunnigan, as a roving specialist in kidnap cases,

111

was the first to admit that this case was far outside the usual pattern of such crimes. No one was taking a cold risk for fat profit. This was like trying to shoot mad dogs.

And, in talking to the local officials, he had felt considerably less brisk and confident than he had sounded. Of late he had begun to feel that his public personality was like one of those movie sets where only the fronts of the buildings are erected. But the two-dimensional fronts were tilting and sagging in a high wind, and Herbert Dunnigan was racing back and forth, out of sight of the camera, strengthening the braces, tightening the guy wires.

He had gone into the bureau right from law school, back when it had seemed a bold and satisfying adventure. But over the years he had tired of both bureaucracy and violence. The criminals were always the same—vicious, stupid, subhuman. The victims were uniformly hysterical, or irreparably dead. The newspaper people were tiresome and repetitious. Violence had so little meaning. It was a little area of decay in the great soft body of society, a buildup of pressure, and then a gaseous belch.

By the time he had begun to question the wisdom of what he was doing with his life, there were Ann and the kids and the house in Falls Church and the increasing comfort of seniority, and the prospect of retirement. So he had accepted the nagging feeling of waste and boredom as a part of his life. When he was not on a field assignment, when he was working civil service hours in the Statistical Analysis Division, Domestic Crime Section, he had the time to make fine reproductions of Early American furniture in the tidy workshop in the basement of the brick house in Falls Church. Sometimes, as he worked, he thought of the other life he could have lived. In that life he was a lawyer in a small Southern city, working on civil cases and estate work, ᵛing on boards and committees, taking an active interest ᵃl politics.

ᵉd Sheriff Gustaf Kurby to wait in his temporary ᵗhe made certain that his people were establish- ᵒutines, setting up the communications net, analyzing the obsolete roadblocks, evaluating the police work already accomplished.

He went back and closed his office door and sat at his desk and looked at Sheriff Kurby. Another showboat sheriff, with the displaced ranch hat and the inlaid ivory grips on the inevitable .38 Special, and the big, bland, meaty, political face.

Dunnigan tapped the Sunday paper on his desk and said, "You took the ball and ran with it, Sheriff."

"Murder day," the sheriff rumbled. "Gus Kurby day."

The big man looked indolent, smug, content. Dunnigan felt a sharp twinge of annoyance. "Are you as stupid as you've acted, Sheriff?"

Kurby shifted in his chair to face Dunnigan more directly. "Let's have your professional opinion, mister."

"Let's assume these people can read. We haven't made them yet. Now they read that a pair of hot-pants country kids can pick them out of a lineup, and those kids have given a detailed description. Let's assume they have a little sense left. What do they do, Sheriff?"

"Kill the girl and bury her deep. Ditch the car. Split up and run."

"You surprise me, Sheriff. Will you surprise me some more by admitting you've made a mistake?"

"No," Kurby said. His eyes were unexpectedly shrewd and aware. "You come in with your slide rule and see one side of it, Dunnigan. It's a good safe bet the girl was dead before the papers were on the street this morning. It would fit the pattern. Agreed?"

"I'll go along with that."

"A little over three months from now a hell of a lot of people in Meeker County are going to go behind the green curtains and pull the little levers. Kurby is a name they should remember, but you have to keep reminding them. They've got short memories. This will put me in for four more years, Dunnigan."

"And if it's at the girl's expense?"

"Don't look as if you tasted something bad. This will be a fifth term. I'm not a politician who happened to get to be

sheriff. I'm a law man who has to mess with politics. This is
a big county, Mr. Dunnigan. I've fought like an animal for a
big budget. There isn't a dime of if goes to waste. You
won't find a cleaner county in the state. Monroe has
exploded way beyond the city limits. Satellite communities
all over hell and gone. It's all my baby, and I mean to keep
on taking care of it, keeping the sharpshooters out, keeping
the lid on. So I had to get to be a legend, sort of. Hell, that's
why that Craft kid called me. He feels he knows me. If
some hungry boy beats me at the polls, the orgainzation will
be shot. He won't know law work. I do. I've built up the
finest lab this side of the state capital. This is one murder,
Mr. Dunnigan. One stolen girl. There's almost exactly a
million people in Meeker County. So don't use hard words
unless you know the whole picture."

"My job is to . . ."

"Hold it one minute. We aren't so far apart in age. Let's
you hold it one minute and give a little thought to how
you'd handle things if every four years you had to get voted
back into your job by a lot of people who pay your budget
out of taxes. Would that change the way you handle your
job?"

Dunnigan looked at Kurby's knowing grin and found
himself liking the man, liking him very much. He grinned
back. "Okay, Sheriff. It just shouldn't be an elective
office."

"I could do a better job if it wasn't. Now it's your baby. I
got in there, front and center, while I had the chance. Now
anything you want, we'll do our damnedest to do it for you,
and do it right."

Under Dunnigan's direction, the investigation proceeded
swiftly and logically. It was poor country for effective
roadblocks. There were too many secondary and tertiary
roads. It could be assumed that, through luck or cleverness,
the Buick had slipped through one of the holes in the net.
The possibility that they had holed up inside the roadblock
area was not entirely discounted, but the chance was con-

sidered sufficiently remote to permit disbanding the road-blocks.

Scores of tips came in. The Buick, containing people matching the description, had been seen in forty different places, heading in every possible direction. These tips were reassigned to appropriate agencies to be checked out. As it seemed logical that the criminals might travel by night and hole up by day, state police in three states ran a motel and cabin check.

The autopsy on Crown was completed, showing that either the knife wounds or brain injuries were in themselves of sufficient gravity to cause death. Measurement of the abdominal wounds showed that a rather small-bladed knife had been used, a blade about four inches long a half inch wide, with one sharp edge, possibly a switchblade.

Howard Craft and Ruth Meckler were brought in and questioned again by Dunnigan and his people. They had told their story so many times that the facts had begun to be obscured by fantasy. Through adroit questioning the known facts were isolated. Additional fragments of description were pried out of the memories of the young pair. A commercial artist, following the pair's corrections and changes, tried to come up with pictures that would satisfy them. They were quite satisfied with the rendition of the husky one, and a little less satisfied with the drawing of the balding one with glasses. The other two would not come through. The two usable drawings were sent by wire transmission to thirty cities in the Southwest, with an urgent request for help in identification.

Of the dozens of photographs of Helen Wister available, Dunnigan selected the one he thought most satisfactory. The pictures were spread out on his desk.

"She *is* a beautiful girl," Dunnigan said.

"A one-time queen of the Dartmouth Winter Carnival, I understand," the agent standing at his elbow said. "A blond doll. With a faintly chilly look. A lady."

"A lady in bad company. Use this one," Dunnigan said. "Ask the wire services to use this one exclusively. Feature it. Get TV coverage. I don't think anybody will ever see the lady alive again, but there is a ten thousand-to-one chance."

When the Buick had braked hard, one tire had stubbed and chattered on the road, leaving, in black rubber, the distinctive tread pattern of a Goodyear Double Eagle, sharp enough to indicate low wear. It was not a tire that would come on the car, so either the owner had had the tires installed before taking delivery, or he had worn out the original set and replaced them. In any case, it was a potentially valuable clue.

In mid-afternoon the car was identified, almost beyond doubt. It had been stolen on Friday evening in Glasgow, Kentucky, from a bowling alley parking lot. It was a dark-blue '59 Buick with low mileage, owned by a plumbing contractor. He had Goodyear tires installed before delivery. The car had been left unlocked, with the keys behind the sun visor. The plate number was put on the teletype circuits immediately, plus the more positive description of the vehicle.

Acting on emergency instructions, the Glasgow police made a street by street search of the area adjacent to the bowling alley, expanding the area until they found an abandoned red-and-white Chevrolet with Arkansas plates, the car which matched the description of the one involved in the Nashville killing.

Specialists went over the car with great care. The steering wheel and door handles had evidently been hastily wiped clean. The car had been driven hard and far and fast, with the oil at too low a level. The bearing surfaces were badly scored, the car sluggish and noisy. There was half a fresh thumbprint on the rear-vision mirror. In the rear ash tray were several cigarette butts clotted with a heavy, dark-red lipstick. There was an empty tequilla bottle under the front seat with many prints smeared and overlapping, and a few relatively distinct ones. A small smear of lipstick on the neck of the bottle matched the lipstick on the cigarette butts. Wedged in the front ash tray was an empty folder of book matches from a motel in Tupelo, Mississippi. An agent was sent immediately to Tupelo.

By eight o'clock on Sunday night, Herbert Dunnigan went to the Grill Room of the Hotel Riggs for dinner, accompanied by a young agent named Graybo.

Dunnigan felt weary but reasonably content. "It's beginning to unravel," he said.

"There's still no identification."

"There will be. We'll find out where the Arkansas Chev was stolen, and we'll find the Ford wagon they took from that tile salesman, and that's give us a little more, just like the Chev did. And the motel in Tupelo will give us a little more, I hope. And when we make one of them, we'll get a lead to the others, and then we'll know all of them."

"Do you think they've split up, sir?"

"Perhaps. But I don't think it will make any difference in the long run. Somehow I don't think they have."

"Why not?"

"They've taken crazy chances. They think they're invulnerable. Maybe one will get nervous and drop off. I think we'll take them in a package."

"It's all so . . . pointless."

"It's for kicks, Graybo. Four misfits. Unbalanced people, full of hostility. Something tipped the lid off. Maybe an accident. Maybe the tile salesman was an accident. And that set them off. From then on, what could they lose?"

"That was back last Tuesday, sir. And they're still out there. It's funny to think of them out there tonight. I wonder what they're like. I wonder what they're saying to each other. Unless we can get them—they'll do something else."

"Probably."

"So that means there's somebody walking around not knowing he's gong to run into those four."

"You've got an active imagination, Graybo."

The young agent colored. "I was just thinking out loud."

"Don't apologize. Imagination can be valuable. Police work can take you only so far. Then a good guess can be worth all the rest of it."

"Sir, are you going to be able to talk to Kemp?"

"Who? Oh, the boy friend."

"He's been hanging around all day."

" It won't do any good. I . . . I guess I can spare the time."

An agent named Stark came swiftly toward the table. Both men looked alertly at him as he sat down. "Bert, I think we've made the burly boy. Phoenix came through. We've got a good correlation on two print classifications, but it'll take visual comparison to check it out. They're wiring a mug shot we can check with the kids. He's small-time. Ninety days last year for assault. Robert Hernandez. Unskilled laborer. The only thing that doesn't seem to match up is the age. He's only twenty, but Phoenix says he looks older. No address of record. No record of other convictions."

"It sounds good enough so I think we should go ahead right now and check it out with the regional Social Security office and get . . ."

"I started that ball rolling, Bert."

"Good enough."

An hour passed before Dunnigan remembered Dallas Kemp. He checked and found out that Kemp was still waiting, so he had him brought in.

When Dallas Kemp finally met Herbert Dunnigan, he felt a sharp sense of disappointment which he hoped was not apparent to Dunnigan. Kemp was shrewd enough to realize that—perhaps through the conditioning of television and its all-wise, all-powerful heroes—he had expected to met some sort of father image, some idealized, personalized version of law and order radiating supreme confidence.

But this was a rather clerical-looking man, not large, obviously weary, obviously troubled. He had an indoor pallor, nicotine stains on his fingers. The slight suggestion of a stammer contributed to the impression of ineffectualness.

"Sit down, Mr. Kemp, I c-can't give you much time. I suppose you want reassurance. About the only assurance I can give you is that we'll take them. Sooner or later. I don't know what that's worth to you."

Dallas Kemp sat in the chair beside the desk. He sat down slowly. Ever since it had happened he was aware of performing all physical acts slowly and carefully. He felt as though any hasty movement would destroy his control, and he would fly into small pieces, or begin yelling and be unable to stop.

"You see," he said, "we quarreled. The last time I saw her, we were scrapping." He paused. "That isn't what I meant to say to you."

"I can see how that makes it worse for you."

Kemp felt grateful to the man. He hoped the tears would not flood his eyes again. They were always there, a slight stinging sensation—always in readiness.

"I'm an architect."

"I know. A good one, I've been told."

"I like form and order. Grace and dignity." He looked at his large hands, flexing the long fingers. "I can't fit what happened into any frame of reference—into anything I know, Mr. Dunnigan. I guess I wanted to see you because I want to be told eveything is going to be all right. I guess you can't tell me that."

"I could, but what would it mean?"

"I want to do something. It's been twenty-four hours. I can't just wait and wait. I want to be given something to do. Something that will help."

"This isn't a movie, Kemp. No chance for the hero to outwit the bad guys and rescue the girl. You have to wait. We all have to wait."

"Do you know anything at all? Is there anything you know that you can tell me?"

Dunnigan hesitated, then handed Kemp a picture. It was on unusual paper, limp, glossy, yellowish.

"This is one of them," Dunnigan said. "The two kids made a positive identification."

The photograph was composed of tiny lines, as on a television screen. Some of the lines had not printed properly, but the face was clear enough, two shots, full face and profile.

It was a beast face, empty, unreachable, merciless.

Kemp tasted the sickness in his throat as he swallowed. "This—is one of them?"

"They beat and kicked and stabbed a stranger to death, Kemp. For no reason. What would you expect one of them to look like?"

"I—don't know. Like this, I guess." He handed the picture back. He smiled. It was a grimace of tension, not a smile. "There isn't much Helen . . . or anybody could say to that kind of a person. She's so outgoing. I'd thought that . . . if she had a chance to talk to them . . . but . . ."

"Get hold of yourself!"

"I . . . thanks."

"It's been twenty-four hours, Kemp. There's no point in trying to kid you. Pray she's alive. Pray they've kept her alive. They might do that. But if we get her back alive, she won't be in good shape. Face that at least."

"All right. But . . . damn it, it's such a jungle thing. It's out of the dark ages. A thing like that shouldn't happen to her."

"In this day and age? Because we've got plastics and television and tailfins and charity drives? Human nature doesn't change, Mr. Kemp. There'll always be animals around, walking on their hind legs, looking just like you and me. You could have gone your whole life understanding that. But now you've had your nose rubbed in it."

The phone rang. Dunningan picked it up and put his palm over the mouthpiece. "All we can do is wait," he said. "Try to get some sleep."

As Kemp closed the door behind him, he heard Dunnigan say, "Too bad, George. That lead sounded good to me too."

It was a hot weekend over most of the country, with no news of any special interest to compete with the Wolf Pack story. Routine drownings and taffic deaths and drab political announcements, national and international.

There had been mounting interest and coverage of the story prior to the Crown murder and the Wister kidnapping. The pump was primed. The Monroe violence had the proper ingredients—a slain, unsuccessful suitor, a wealthy and beautiful blonde abducted, a woman in slacks wielding a knife, a country road, eyewitnesses.

And so, suddenly, it was BIG. There was a lot of Page One space to fill. A lot of air time. A lot of television time. A lot of people aching to get into the act.

Any fool could look at a map of the country and trace a line from Uvalde to Tupelo to Nashville at Glasgow to Monroe. Tuesday through Saturday. And any fool could project that line into the densely populated Northest and make a guess—as good as anybody's—as to where they were going. Newspapers featured that map—and pictures of Helen Wister.

Look out for the Wolf Pack. Keep your eyes open. Look for the car.

In summer the crazies are in full bloom. Helen Wister was seen in Caribou, Mainc, tied to a tree, being whipped by three burly men. A motorist, too frightened to stop, reported this. Helen Wister was seen in Miami, being forced, weeping, into a motel on the beach.

Three boys in Danville, Virginia, taking a short cut to a swimming hole, did find a dead blonde. But she was two weeks dead, and she had been half again as old as Helen Wister. It was a local problem.

Over thirty neurotic, semi-psychotic women presented themselves to police authorites across the country, claiming earnestly to be Helen Wister. The eldest was in her seventies. Once upon a time she had claimed to be Amelia Earhart.

The insane avalanche of false clues made the isolation and investigation of the potentially valid ones almost impossible. Hysterical types demanded police protection. Mystics and visonaries knew exactly where to find the Wolf Pack.

In the city of Monroe, all day Sunday, the idle boobs rode around in their cars, gawking. They gawked at Arnold Crown's service station, and bought until the underground tanks were empty. A police guard kept them from turning into the driveway of the Wister house, or parking in front. They would park as close as permitted and get out and stare at the house. Some worked their way around to the lawn behind the house, trampling the flowers. A few parked and stared with endless, empty, idiot patience at Dallas Kemp's office and living quarters. But by far the favorite spot was the place on Route 813 where Crown had been killed. Two accidents occurred, one serious, where you turned off the pike onto 813. They parked up and down the road for two hundred yards in both directions. They climbed up into the sagging barn and looked out. They took hay as souvenirs, and grease-streaked grass out of the ditch, and fist-sized stones. "Hey, Mary Jane, maybe this was one of the rocks they clunked him with, hey?"

Finally one too many climbed into the loft, The barn sighed and sagged, slowly at first, as the women went shrill with terror, and with a gentle rending sound and a thumping of timbers, it collapsed. A three-year-old named Walter James Lokey III was crushed to death. There was one broken back, eight broken legs, three broken arms, several less important fractures, and dozens of sprains, bruises and abrasions. Ambulances howled through the noonday heat. A police guard was posted to keep people away. But throughout the afternoon they kept coming and trying to steal splintered pieces of the barn.

At midnight on Sunday, Dr. Paul Wister sat alone in the kitchen of the silent house. His mind moved slowly, aimlessly, heavy with misery. He asked the eternal, unreasonable *Why*—and there could be no answer. He had given his wife sedation. He envied her the loss of awareness.

The kettle boiled. It boiled for some time before he became aware of it and got up and fixed himself the cup of instant coffee. Paul Wister did not look at all like the public conception of a fine surgeon. He was a big man, with a heavy torso, a large head, big reddish, chapped-looking hands. He moved ponderously, somewhat awkwardly. His eyes were a clear, impenetrable porcelain blue. He had a clipped way of speaking, a rusty, abrupt, shocking guffaw of a laugh. Those who did not know him thought they

detected something comical about him, a Colonel Blimpish-
ness, a slowness of mind. Those who knew him well—and
there were very few—knew of the sensitivity and the
dedication and the subtle, ranging mind. They knew that the
pseudo-military brusqueness was his wall against a trivial
world. He had to be a strong and tireless man to be able—
for example—to work steadily for eight hours, repairing all
the miraculous intricacies of a human hand, making it
useful again, something that could hold, grasp and turn. He
was a devout man, respecting the living materials that
yielded to his skills. The big red hands, clumsy with cups
and keys and neckties, were steady and quick and certain
under the bright, hot lights of the operating room. His
hobbies—for which he had too little time—illustrated the
textures of his mind. He collected jade, and his knowledge
of it was encyclopedic. This had led him into a study of the
history of China and the Chinese peoples. He had learned
the twenty thousand basic, symbolic ideographs of the
printing style, used from the third century until the
Communist revision of the language in 1956, and he had
translated early poetry into English, two volumes of which
had been published by a university press under a nom de
plume. And he had kept abreast of the literature and
technical advances in his profession. His energies were
vast.

He sat in the kitchen of his home and thought about his
daughter. He was a realist, a man of sentiment without
sentimentality. He saw how easy it was to abuse himself for
not giving her more of his time, yet it would have been
artificial and unsatisfying to have done so. The relationship
had been loving and good. He knew that genetically and
emotionally they had had good luck with her, and he knew
that luck is a factor with children. The twin boys were going
to present far more serious problems.

Yet, realist that he was, he could not completely ignore
the superstitious feeling that in some way he was at fault.
This was his small ship, and he was captain, and someone
had been lost, so it was his fault. Paul Wister knew that life
is an almost excessively random affair. Health and love and

safety are not earned. They are not rewards for behavior. They are part of the luck that you have or you don't have. When you have it, in your blind human innocence you think you have earned it. And when it is gone, you feel you have offended your gods.

He sipped the steaming coffee and he thought of the things that had happened to others— so abrupt, so cruel, so meaningless. The Stallings family. Ard Stallings had been head of surgery at Monroe General. A lovely wife named Bess. Two teen-age children, a boy and a girl, bright and popular. For them it was as though a wall had suddenly been breached, releasing disaster. Ard had been walking in the woods with Bess. A stray bullet, never traced, had struck his right hand at a devilish angle, inflicting maximum damage. Paul Wister had operated three times, nerve grafts, muscle transplants. But he could not put the cleverness back. That had been the beginning. The boy was driving back from a dance with his date. A truck driver fell alseep. The boy and his date were killed. The truck driver suffered a sprained wrist and superficial lacerations. Bess had a cervical biopsy, a diagnosis of malignancy. Radical surgery was too late. It had spread. The only good thing about it was its speed. She died in a hard, dirty way, but it was quicker than most. Father and daughter went away. They were fleeing from disaster, but it was their appointment in Samarra. Their *turismo* left the highway in the mountains east of Mexico City. Ard Stallings was thrown clear. The girl died with the other passengers. Three months later, in the basement of the house in Monroe which was listed with the real-estate people, Ard injected himself with a lethal dose of morphine. He left no note. There was no one to leave a note for. From the time the bullet struck his hand until the night of his suicide, it was only thirteen months. It was as though there had been a magic circle around them, protecting them. And when the bullet struck, the circle was gone, and the blackness came in upon them. They were gone as though they had never existed. People clucked and shook their heads. Terrible bad luck for those folks.

You could ask a man of God about it, Paul Wister

thought. You could ask *Why*. He would say it is God's will. He would speak of a pattern we cannot see or understand. So do not try to understand. Just accept.

This, he told himself, is the ultimate sophistry. Life is random. Luck is the factor. The good and the evil are struck down, and there is no cause to look for reasons. There is a divine plan, but it is not so minute and selective that it deals with individuals on the basis of their merit. Were that so, all men would be good, out of fear if nothing else. Those unholy four could have gathered up a tart in front of a bar. They happened to take Helen. It was chance. No blame can be assessed. And any living thing is the product of a series of intricate accidents—46 chromosomes in each living cell—the stupendous roulette wheel of fertilization. So even as a man cannot accept the cold knowledge that all his uniqueness, all his magical identity, is the product of chance, he will not accept disaster as the other side of the casual coin. He must look for a pattern. The Lord giveth and the Lord taketh away. He gave Helen her special identity, her soul, her heart, the shape of her mouth, in a random genetic pattern. And He can take it away through another accident, and in that sense it is an offense against Him to demand in a puny and indignant way that any pattern be made clear, or even to demand that there be a pattern, discernible or not.

He thought about his daughter as the coffee grew tepid. Obviously she had jumped or fallen from the moving vehicle. Laymen believe serious injury comes only when the brittle integrity of the skull is cracked. But far more deaths occur when the skull is intact. The brain is a jelly, massively supplied with blood. A hard blow, as against an asphalt road, can do many fatal things. A few small subdural bridging veins can be torn by the abrupt movement of the mass of the brain within its bony carapace. The small subdural hemorrhage can grow slowly, exerting increasing pressure until in turn that pressure closes off other small veins by compressing the thin walls. When the dwindling supply is stopped, those starved portions of the brain die, and slowly death comes to that portion which controls the heart or the lungs.

Perhaps, he thought, if it happened that way, that would be the best thing for her. As the slow pressure built, she would be like a person drugged. She could not know what was happening to her.

He had thought of her as the Golden Girl, and he had been able to reach beyond the demands of his parental pride to see that she was a special thing in the world, a prideful, honest girl, with faults that time would cure—such as her sometimes infuriating stubbornness, and her rather obvious rudeness toward pretentious people, and her extreme patience with those empty ones who demand of you your time and your attention, and waste it, thus wasting and spending the only truly valuable thing in life.

Though his emotions recoiled from the thought with an almost explosive anguish, he could accept the cold supposition that she was already dead. It was a hellish waste. But life had a habit of wasting the best of itself.

He rinsed the cup and turned out the lights and walked slowly to the bedroom, unknotting his tie as he went. He paused, quite surprised, just inside the bedroom door and said, "What are you doing up, honey?"

Jane Wister, in a pale-blue robe, sat in the chaise longue near her dressing table. It was a big room, a bedroom-sitting room, with space for her desk, comfortable chairs, a shelf of his books, a big glass door that opened onto a miniature terrace.

"I guess you didn't give me enough."

"How long have you been awake?" he asked, walking over to her.

"I don't know. A half hour. Maybe more." Her voice was listless.

"What are you doing? What's that you're looking at, Jane?"

She made a childish, instinctive effort to cover what she held with her hands, and then handed it to him. It was a folder of photographs, made like a visible file index, with overlapping glassine slots for the pictures. She had several of them, each covering different parts of their lives. This was all of the children.

He sat on the arm of the chaise where the light was better, and flipped it open at random to a picture. It was in color. Helen, a knobby twelve, stood with another girl, grinning and squinting into the camera. They each held tennis rackets and, in prominent display, tiny trophy cups.

"Remember?" Jane said. "They spelled Wister wrong on her cup when they had it engraved later. Wester, they had it. And she was furious."

He closed the folder. "Why do this to yourself, honey?"

"I lay there, remembering everything. So I got up . . . to look at these. That's all. I just wanted to look at them. I haven't looked at them for a long time, dear."

"Don't do this to yourself."

"She's smiling in every one. You never had to tell her to smile for the camera. You never had to tell her."

"Jane, Jane, Jane."

Her face twisted. It was an expression like anger. She closed her hand into a fist and she struck her husband on the thigh as she said, "She was so joyous! So damn joyous! When she was little, even. She'd either be laughing, or so mad she was purple. And always running. No whining, no sulking. She was . . ."

And then she was beyond words. Dr. Wister dropped the folder on the floor and held his wife in his big, strong, clumsy arms. He could not comfort her. He endured the awkwardness of his position until the first storm of her anguish had passed and she had exhausted herself.

He went to the bathroom and brought her back another capsule and a glass of water. Her face looked stained and gray under the light.

She hesitated. "Will this put me so far under you won't be able to tell me if . . . they find out anything?"

"No. I can wake you easily," he lied.

"Are you going to take anything? You should sleep too, darling. You look terribly tired."

"I took one," he said, lying again.

She took the capsule and drank half the water. He put the glass aside and took her hand and helped her up. He took her robe and she got into bed. He bent over and kissed her on the forehead. He prepared slowly for bed. He went over and stood by her. She was breathing slowly and deeply.

"Jane," he said softly. She did not stir. "Jane!" he said in a louder tone. There was no response. He went to his dressing room and put on a robe and went back to the kitchen and turned on the burner under the kettle. It was nearly two o'clock.

WHILE Dr. Wister sat in the kitchen of the house where his wife and his sons slept, Dallas Kemp sat at the drafting table in his studio, working, driving himself. He and Helen had planned that after they returned from the wedding trip, they would live at his place. And then, in a year or two, they would begin to build a place of their own. They had talked about the kind of house they would like, an enclosure for their love.

"I'll make like a difficult client," she had said to him. "Light and space and air, yes. But I don't want to be on display. I don't want people looking in at me. I don't want a huge place, because I'll have to be taking care of it, and I can only mop so many floors before I begin to feel futile. But I want a part of the house to have . . . scope. A big feeling of space. And I want part of it to be . . . cozy. Isn't that a hell of a word? And I want it to be a place where children can romp, but also where they have their own place, shut off but not too much. And it better be sort of flexible, because once I start having kids, I might like it well enough to have scads."

"How about materials?"

"Oh, nice things to touch and look at. Rough, hairy textures. Wood and stone and stuff. I want to be able to hang a pot in the fireplace and sit on the floor. That's what I don't like about a lot of these glossy, new houses, made of miracle plastics and things. They're not sit-on-the-floor houses. See? I'm a difficult client."

"Difficult? You're impossible."

"You're the bright architect. Whip me up a dream, boy."

Ever since they had talked, he had been working out the problems in the back of his mind. He decided that a hillside house would be best. The hill should be abrupt, but not necessarily high, and overlooking an emptiness of vista where nothing could suddenly rise up and stare in at them. Then, with glass, he could give her all the light and sun and space she craved, and with a big cantilevered deck in front of it, nobody could stare up into the house.

After he had left Dunnigan's temporary office, he had gone home and started to work, sketching front and side elevations, balling them up and discarding them until he was close to what he wanted. He had secretly located a two-acre hillside tract south of the city and had paid thirty per cent down and signed a mortgage deed for the balance. It was to be his wedding present to her.

Now he was working on the floor plan. The house would be on three levels. He knew it was good. When he worked on something good he got a special feeling in pit of his stomach. This could be a gem. This could be the best thing he had ever done.

He worked with a special dedication, a unique intensity. Without bothering to clarify it in his mind, he felt that it was an affirmation. If he worked well enough, and hard enough, then they would one day live together in love in this place taking shape and form on his drawing board. If he did not do it well, she was lost forever. It was his incantation, his offering. It was the only thing he could do which would bring her back. She would have to come back to a place so special. Any other outcome was inconceivable.

And so, deep in the fury of concentration, he was not quite sane. But he was using himself utterly, and that was all he could do.

A bright, round, flawless sun came up out of the Atlantic on the twenty-seventh day of July. An enormous and stationary high pressure area covered all of the Northeast and the Middle Atlantic states, and reached as far west as Illinois. Vacationers congratulated themselves on having selected that segment of the summer which included these perfect days. Those whose vacations were over wished they had waited. Those who had not yet gone, hoped the weather would hold.

The newspapers which thudded against front doors and were stuffed in rural tubes, dropped in heavy bundles on street corners, inserted in store-front racks, yelped and thumped and yammered about the Wolf Pack. The early commentators said, with mock regret, that the criminals were still at large. On buses and subways, over breakfast tables and lunch counters, around office water coolers and factory Coke machines, the nation talked about the Wolf Pack and Helen Wister.

"It's a terrible, terrible thing. Her poor parents.—If a guy was going to steal him a blonde, he couldn't do better, hey, Barney?—Mark my words, when they capture those fiends, they'll find they have been drinking alcohol, Mary.—You know, that's the kind of deal Bugsie would pull, he had the nerve.—This is another example of the accelerated decay of public morals, gentlemen.—The broad with the knife, that's the one for me, Al. I go for the mean, gutsy ones.—You can't tell me it wasn't all planned between her and those thugs. I'll bet you she paid them to kill that boy friend of hers on account of he was blackmailing her with that architect. Had enough money, didn't she? Didn't put up any fight, did she? Well?

The sun climbed high and bright toward noon. Four hundred and thirty miles north-northeast of Monroe, up in the western end of the state of Pennsylvania, was the small resort community of Seven Mile Lake. The whole south shore of the lake was a long strip of tawdry honky-tonks—ice-cream stands, boat rentals, shooting galleries, lunch-rooms, cabins, cottages, beer joints. It was the height of the vacation season. Jukes whined and thumped. Boats roared up and down the lake, towing water-skiers. The pebbly beaches were half paved with the baking, shimmering flesh of the sunbathers. Squalling children dropped ice cream in the dust.

In the middle of the commercial area were the Lakeshore Cottages, managed this season by Joe Rendi and his wife, Clara. They handled the rental of the cottages and operated the small ice cream and sundries store at the roadside, on a

percentage basis. Joe got up, surly as usual, at eleven. He
went down the street for breakfast and then walked slowly
back to the store. There were no customers at the moment.
Clara was washing glasses.

"What the hell was the night bell last night?" he
demanded.

"You heard it? You mean you really heard it? Tanked on
beer so bad you snore like a walrus couldn't sleep in there
too, and you heard it?"

"Cut the goddam comedy. What was it?"

"I rented number four, that's all."

He sat down heavily on the stool and stared at her. "Oh,
great! Oh, fine and dandy and nifty! You rented number
four. Bully for you! And tomorrow comes those people for
all the way up to Labor Day and a hunnert twenny-fi dollars
a week and a fifty-dollar deposit we got already and you can
say sorry, we're full up."

"So you're so smart, why didn't you get up?"

"It wasn't so hot, I'd clout you in the mouth one, Clara."

"If you're so smart, how'd you get us stuck in a deal like
this, working like a dog all summer and for what?"

"So the take is little, so you cut it down."

"So I increase it, wise guy. Somebody has to get smart
around here."

"So how do you increase it?"

She straightened up with her hands on her hips. "One
night only. He swore it. I believe him. Just before dawn, he
rang the bell. Two couples, he said. Twenty-five bucks, and
they'll leave tonight, he said. It don't go on the books, Joe.
This one is all ours. I'll clean it up before the Shoelockers
get here tomorrow. Honest to Christ, stop looking so
confused. And don't think you'll get aholt of that money.
You can twist my arm right the hell off, and I won't tell you
where it is."

"Suppose they don't get out?"

"He said they would. A nice-talking fella, he is. I had
him sign a card. He didn't want to look at number four first.
I tore up the card already. So what skin is off you."

"They better get out," Joe said darkly.

"They will! They will! They will!"

"So stop yelling at me, can't you?"

"Go fix the lock on number eight. It's loose. All it needs is a screw driver, and they can't do it themself for some reason."

Joe Rendi walked by number four on his way to fix the lock. A dark-blue Buick was parked close beside the side steps, heading out. The blinds were closed. The place looked very still. What a way to use a vacation, he thought. Drive all night, sleep all day. Twenty-five bucks is twenty-five bucks. She could have got thirty, maybe.

It was one of the big cottages. There were six big ones and eight little ones. The big ones had a sitting room, bathroom, screened porch and two bedrooms and a tiny kitchen in one corner. The little ones had but one bedroom. They were old, flimsy frame cottages, dressed up for summer in new paint—bright yellow with bright-blue trim and red front doors.

Number four was silent throughout the long, hot day. Children yelped in the dusty areas between the cottages. Insects keened in the afternoon heat. The noise of fast boats was unending.

Later, as the dusk deepened, neon came on, up and down the strip, and day noises faded as the night sounds began.

At eight-thirty, when it was dark, Joe Rendi got nervous about number four. He strolled back there, wondering if he would have to remind them of their promise to check out. He stared, turned and hurried back to the store.

"Hey, they're gone!" he said.

"Who's gone, stupid?"

"The people in four."

"They said they'd go, din they?"

"Yes, but . . ."

"Go to Schiller's, see can you buy a box of sugar cones off that robber. I'm almost outa cones here."

"Okay! Okay!"

"Now who's yelling? Here's two dollars. Don't stop for a beer."

NINE

DEATH HOUSE DIARY

THIS morning I have been conjecturing about how long it will take me to be totally gone. By that I mean more than death. I mean the amount of time before no one will give me one single specific thought, no matter how fleeting. In a sense this is a discussion of limited immortality, a very contradictory phrase. Immortality is an absolute, not subject to limitation.

The old man and Ernie will remember me, of course. I think she'll last longer than he will. She's pretty tough. She's forty-seven now, and I'll give her the benefit of the doubt and say she'll live to be ninety. That will take me a little past the year two thousand. That salesman named Horace said his youngest was eighteen months. I can assume his wife will teach his kids to use our names as curse words, and I will assume that the youngest will remember my name, and live to be ninety, so that extends awareness of Kirby Palmer Stassen up to 2050, approximately. I can't stretch it and extend it to the salesman's grandchildren. I suspect it won't mean a damn thing to them. They will know vaguely that their grandfather was murdered, but that's all. Taking it to 2050 takes it well beyond the span of anyone I know, of course.

Now consider physical things. Matter cannot be destroyed. It is a curious thing to realize that there is still in existence, somewhere, every cinder I have ever had in my eye, every paring of fingernail and toenail, every stone that has bruised me. My physical being will continue to exist. It will be tucked out of sight in Memorial Grove at Huntstown. It will be a very, very private funeral, I am sure, with no brave stirring words spoken. There will be a marker, of course. Ernie will insist upon that. Something very small, but it will bear the name Kirby Palmer Stassen. I could cheat on this game and say the marble will last a thousand years, but if the name means nothing to anyone who reads it, then I am truly and totally gone. The scandal will stay alive in Huntstown. I think I can assume that there will always be old ladies who recount the black deeds of past generations, so I will stretch a little and say that in 2100 they will still retain some dry morsel of information about this.

As far as possessions are concerned, I imagine Ernie and the old man will get rid of mine as quickly and quietly as possible, diverting them to the anonymity of the village dump and the Salvation Army. Ernie will save a few things, I imagine. Baby shoes. Pictures. But she won't dare look at them when the old man is around.

The third aspect of this conditional immortality is a chancy thing. The crimes and the way they were done and the trial have, I suppose, some meaning to sociologists. They stimulate themselves with case histories. I shall appear, I am sure, in some laborious texts. I will doubtless be called K.S. or Kirby S. or perhaps simply S. But in this game I can count that, because they will be discussing *me*. This journal I am writing, should it get into the right hands, might possibly cue a very exhaustive study. Yet, in most cases, these books die when the professor who insists his students buy them dies. On that basis I can assume a half-life only until—say—the year 2000. But there is an imponderable here which cannot be measured. It is possible that my case might be written up by someone capable of turning out a classic. If it is very, very good, if it is a work of art, it could well last three hundred years. I would say that would be the outside limit, due to the continuing change in the language. So genius is my only hope of outliving gossip. This could take me up to 2260, a very science-fiction sort of date. And on one day in that year the last man will read of me, of a crime three hundred years old, and discard the last book, and then I will be gone as completely as though I had never lived at all. The final ultimate rest.

Isn't three hundred years a vast span of time? It is one ten millionth of the estimated life span of the planet to date. Or it is the same ratio as is three seconds to one full year. And on the same scale, my life span has been one quarter of one second.

Riker Deems Owen came in at the end of the morning and did his usual splendid job of boring me wretched. At least, this time, he spared me the presence of the nubile, self-conscious Miss Slayter. They took me down to the carefully engineered little conference room to meet with him. We talk into microphones and are separated by two thicknesses or bulletproof glass. He seems quite unaware of having made a thorough ass of himself in court. He is a pompous, pretentious, slack-witted little man. He spoke today of the complexity of appealing this case, of his hopes of obtaining a stay of execution. I suspect constant pressure by my male parent. It is useless, of course. Riker Owen knows it and I know it, but he beams at me in a glassy way in an effort, I suppose, to build up my morale. One can only exist in places like this when all hope is gone. Hope is an ennervating weakness that makes adjustment impossible.

He said again that they would like to see me, Ernie and the old man, and that it could be arranged, but once again I told him that it was not my pleasure to see them. It could not possibly do any of us any good. He asked if I would write, at least. I told him to tell them that I am well and in reasonably good spirits, that I am given anything within reason that I ask for. I told him that I am writing a record of my experiences and that I have been assured that it will be passed along to them after I have been put to death.

Right here is as good a time as any to insert my personal note to you, Ernie and Dad. I do not expect you to understand all this I am writing. I do no expect you to try to understand me. I have very little understanding of myself. You could read it and save it, and one day you might find a very wise man, someone you can trust, who will read it and tell you why all this happened, and tell you that in most basic ways I am no different from the sons of your friends. All of them are, potentially, exactly like me. They have been favored by the enduring of lesser crises.

Let me say also that I am not trying to wound you through frankness. Were I to write only what I suspect you might wish to read, there would be no point in writing at all.

I had carried my account as far as Chubby's Grill on Route 90 on the outskirts of Del Rio. I have devoted a lot of time and space to the Kathy Keats episodes. It is not an episode, or an aside, or a digression. What happened there, to her and the relationship between us, is close to the very heart of all that came after.

It was a Sunday afternoon. Sandy Golden had jeered at me, but not in a way that made me angry. It was in the tone of his voice, a sort of lift of nervous excitement.

I smiled over toward the dingy corner where the voice had come from, then bought a bottle of cold ale at the bar and carried it over, ale in one hand, suitcase in the other.

"Every college boy likes to be recognized *immediately* as a college boy," he said. "It's like scratching a dog behind the ear. Have you been dude ranching, man? You aren't wearing your Marshal Dillon threads."

"It's a new kind of ranch kick, man," I told him. "Nobody wears anything. They kept us on health food. You had to carry your own horse."

"Sit, college boy," he said. "Meet Nan and Shack. What's your name?"

"Kirby Stassen."

"Sit, Kirboo, and we'll talk up a storm. I've fallen among dull comrades. I'm Sander Golden, poet, experimenter, cultural anthropologist. I dig the far pastures of the spirit. Sit and browse."

I sat. My eyes had adjusted to the dimness. Shack was an ugly-looking monster. Sander Golden was a soiled, jumpy and amusing phony, a little older than the rest of us, close to thirty I decided. His heavy glasses were repaired with tape, and sat crooked on his thin nose. His teeth were not good and he was going bald. Nan was a sulky, sultry broad with too much hair and a practiced way of staring directly into your eyes. It was a corner table with four chairs.

In trying to write this down, I find that there is one special problem I cannot solve. I cannot put down the unique flavor of Sandy's conversation. When I try to put down his words, they sound flat. His mind with always racing ahead of his words so that at times he was almost incoherent. And there was a flavor of holiday about him. That's the best word I can find. He was living up every minute, enjoying hell out of it, and he pulled you along with him. You were certain he was a ludicrous type, and you kept wondering what he would say and do next. He was ludicrous, but he was alarming too. He was making up his own rules as he went along.

They had a bottle of tequila *añejo* on the floor. Sandy and the girl were drinking it very sparingly out of little porcelain sake cups which had come out of his beat-up, bulging rucksack, I found out later. Shack was belting it down. I bought a house setup and, on invitation, started belting along with him.

Shack and Nan took no part in the conversation. They stared at me from time to time without approval. I was the outsider. And, way in back of all Sandy's effusiveness, was a disdain which also marked me as one who was not of the group. I was a sample of the outside world, and they were examining me.

The conversation with Sandy spun in a lot of dizzy directions. He was showing off, I knew, and I was waiting for a chance to trap him. I didn't get it until he got onto classical music. Do not ask me how we got onto that. I remember dimly that the conversation went from Brubeck to Mulligan to Jamal and then jumped back a century or so.

"All those old cats borrowed from each other," he said. "They dug each other and snatched what they liked.

Debussy, Wagner, Liszt—hell, they admitted taking stuff off Chopin. Take that Bach character. He lifted from Scarlatti."

"No," I said flatly. The tequilla was getting to me.

"What do you mean—no?"

"Just plain old no, Sandy. You missed the scoop. Vivaldi influenced Bach, if that's who you're thinking of. Antonio Vivaldi. Alessandro Scarlatti was the opera boy. He influenced Mozart, maybe. Not Bach."

He sat as still as a bird on a limb, staring at me, then suddenly snapped his fingers. "Scarlatti, Vivaldi. I switched wops. You're right, Kirboo. What goes with education? I thought all you types learned was Group Adjustment and Bride Selection." He turned to the others. "Hey, maybe I got somebody to talk to, you animals. Shack, hand me the sack."

Shack bent and picked the rucksack off the floor. Sandy held it in his lap and opened it. He tood out a plastic compartmented box. It was about eight inches long, two inches deep, four inches wide, with six compartments in it. The compartments were almost full of pills.

He looked at his watch, took two pills out, two different ones, and pushed them over in front of Nan. She took them without comment. He put two aside for himself. Then he selected three and pushed them over to me. One was a small gray triangle with rounded corners. One was a green-and-white capsule. The third was a small, white, round pill.

"Eat in good health," he said.

I was aware of how intently the three of them were watching me. "What are they?"

"They'll put you way out in front, college boy. They'll get you off the curb and into the parade. They won't hook you. Miracles of modern medical science."

If I had anything left to lose, I couldn't remember what it was. I washed them down with tequilla. "You've got a supply there," I said.

Nan joined the conversation for the very first time. "Chrissake, he had those prescription pads in L.A. and any time anybody goes any place, they got to hit a new drugstore for Doc Golden. He papered the town."

"In old Latin," Sandy said, patting the box. "It gives me this deep sense of security."

"What'll they do to a square?" Nan asked.

"That's what we're checking out, man," Golden told her.

As we talked I waited for something to happen. I didn't have any idea what to expect. It all happened so gradually that I wasn't aware of the change. Suddenly I realized that my awareness of everything around me had been heightened. The golden color of the sun outside, the stale beery smell of the low-ceilinged room, Nan's bitten nails, Shack's thick hairy wrists, Sandy's eyes quick behind the crooked lenses. The edges of everything were sharper. The edge of my mind was sharper. When Sandy talked I seemed to be able to anticipate each word a fraction of a second before he said it, like an echo in reverse. There was a steady tremor in my hands. When I wasn't talking, I clenched my teeth so tightly they hurt. When I turned my head it seemed to be on a rachet, rather than turning smoothly. I had a constant butterfly feeling of anticipation in my gut. And everything in the world *fitted*. Everything went together, and I knew the special philosophical significance of everything. Sometimes I seemed to see the three of them through the wrong end of a telescope, tiny, sharp, clear. Then their faces would swell to the size of bushel baskets. Shack was an amusing monster. Nan was loaded with dusky glamour. Sandy was a genius. They were the finest little group I had ever met.

And the talk. My God, how I could talk! The right words came, the special words, so I could talk like poetry. I didn't need the tequila. I got onto a talking jag. I put my trembling fists on the table and, leaning forward, I told them the Kathy story, all of it, and I knew as I was telling them that it was a pitiful shame there was no tape recorder there so it could all be saved. I told it all, and I finally ran down.

"He's really humming," Sandy said fondly.

"Too much D?" Nan suggested.

"He's big. He can use a heavy charge. So you're headed no place at all, Kirboo?"

"No place, on my own time, free as a fat bird," I said. My ears were ringing. I could hear my heart, like somebody hammering on a tree.

"We'll go to New Orleans," Sandy said firmly. "I've got wild friends and playmates there. It'll be a long ball. We'll scrounge a pad and live fruitfully, man."

"This party gets bigger, we can rent a Greyhound," Nan said sourly.

"Look at all he can learn," Sandy said. "We can take his mind off his problems, Nano. Where's your milk of human kindness?"

"We don't need him," Nan said.

Sandy, quick as light, thumped her so hard on top of the head with his fist that for a moment her eyes didn't track.

"You're a drag," he said, grinning at her.

"So we need him," she said. "You don't have to clop me on the skull, man."

"I can let Shack do it, you like that better, doll."

I didn't know at that time where she kept the knife, but it appeared with a magical swiftness, clicking, the blade lean, steady, pale as mercury, ten inches from Shack's thick throat.

"Hit me one time, Hernandez," she said, barely moving her heavy mouth as she spoke. "Just one time."

"Aw, for Chrissake, Nan," he said unhappily. "Put it away, huh. I haven't done nothing."

There were two customers at the bar. The bartender came around the end of the bar and over to the table. "No knives, hey," he said. "No knives. Don't give me trouble."

As Nan folded the knife and lowered it below the edge of the table, Shack stood up. There was a hell of a lot of him to come up so quickly and lightly. "You need trouble?" he asked.

"No. That's what I was saying, fella. I don't want trouble." He turned away. Shack caught him in one stride, caught him by the forearm and spun him around.

"I got mixed up," Shack said. "I thought you were asking for trouble."

The man was big and soft. I saw his face turn suddenly gray and sweaty. I didn't understand until I looked at Shack's hand on the man's arm. Shack seemed to be holding him casually. But his iron fingers were deep in the soft, round arm. The man's knees sagged and he forced himself erect with an effort.

"No . . . trouble," he said in a weak, gasping way.

"That's nice," Shack said. "Okay." For a moment his face was contorted with effort. The man gave a faraway bleating sound and closed his eyes and sagged down onto one knee. Shack hauled him up, gave him a gentle shove toward the bar and released him. The man tottered back to the bar. Shack sat down.

"The philosophy of aggression," Sandy said. "She got sore at me and took it out on Shack who took it out on fatso. Tonight, when he gets home, he beats up on his old lady. She kicks the kid. The kid kicks the dog. The dog kills a cat. End of the line. Aggression always ends up with something dead, Kirboo. Remember that. It's the only way to end the chain. She put the knife in Shack's throat, that would have ended it. We're all animals. Let's get out of here."

We went out into a low slant of sunlight. I had the cheap, shiny, Mexican suitcase. Sandy Golden had his rucksack slung over one shoulder. Nan carried a large, sleazy hatbox, a drum-like thing covered with red plastic stamped in an alligator pattern. Shack had his few possessions in a brown paper bag. The world was bright, aimless and indifferent. We hitched for an hour. There were too many of us. It didn't seem to matter. Nan sat on my upended suitcase. Sandy talked about the sexual implications of the design of the American automobile. In the last light of the day an old man in a stake truck stopped. He had the three of us get in back and he got Nan in front with him. He dumped us in Brackettville, thirty miles away. He had to turn north there. We ate questionable little hamburgers in a sour café.

I had been with them long enough to sense the undercurrents between them. Shack was stalking Nan with a relentless patience, with implacable purpose. When he moved near her, his neck looked swollen. She was aware of it, and so was Golden. But Shack was stopped just short of savage directness by his pathetic desire to please Sandy in all ways. It wasn't the knife stopping him. I'd seen him move. He could have cuffed it out of her hand before she could have used it. The focus of his desire was so strong it was like a musk in the air.

We found a place in Brackettville. A dollar and a half a bed. Moldering little eight-by-ten cabins faced in imitation yellow brick, each one with an iron double bed that sagged like a hammock, one forty-watt bulb, one stained sink with a single faucet, one chair, two narrow windows, one door. Cracked linoleum on the floor. Outhouse out back. Sheets like gray Kleenex. Nails in the studding for coat hangers. The Paradise Cabins.

There were six cabins and we were the only trade. We took three. Four and a half dollars for three beds. We sat around Sandy and Nan's cabin—Shack on the chair, Sandy and me on the bed, Nan on the floor. We talked. Sandy finally doled out pills.

"These all by themselves are death, man," he said. "You go down six feet under, where the worms talk to you."

We broke it up. I was in the middle cabin. I wasted no time piling into the sack, trying not to think about bugs. I fell away so fast I didn't even hear her come in. I woke up with a great start when she wound herself around me, saying in an irritable, conversational tone, "Hey! Hey, you! Hey!" She jostled me insistently.

I had fallen so deeply into sleep so quickly that time and place were out of joint, and with an almost unbearable joy I put my arms around Kathy Keats and found her mouth with mine. But the lips were wrong, and her textures were wrong, and her hair had a musty smell. Kathy was gray and dead, and as I remembered that, everything else clicked into place.

I took my mouth from hers and said, "Nan?"

"Do you think it's for Chrissake little Bo Peep," she said in a sleepy, sulky voice, administering a caress as mechanical as any song lyric.

"I didn't know you cared, kid."

"Shut up, will you? Sandy said pay you a visit. So here I am and so get it the hell over with, will you, without all the conversation."

Had I not awakened thinking she was Kathy, it would have been impossible. But it was not, and so we got it the hell over with because it seemed easier than sending her back with a no-thanks message for Sandy. With meaningless dexterity, she made it very quick indeed, and rolled out and, in the faint light, stepped into her slacks. She'd left her blouse on.

"Tell Sandy thanks," I said, with rancid amusement.

"Tell him yourself, sometime," she said, and the screen door creaked and banged shut as she left. Before I could enjoy my own bitterness, I fell back into sleep.

I learned Sandy's special motive on Monday when it was almost noon and we were a mile east of Brackettville on 90, swinging high and clear on Dr. Golden's encapsulated joy, thumbing the cars that whined by, trailing dust devils. Sandy reached over and patted Nan on the firm seat of her slacks in a proprietary way and said, "Did this chick do you right when I sent her to you last night, Kirboo, or did she drag?"

"She . . . she was fine," I lied, feeling uneasy.

And I had to turn and look at Shack. His face had turned a swollen red and he was staring at Sandy, and looking as if he had lost his last friend. He looked as though he would break into tears.

"Jeez-Chri, Sandy!" he said. "How come it's okay for him, but you never . . ."

"Don't we have to teach this upstanding young man all about life and reality, Shack? Would you deprive him of an education?"

"I figured you just didn't want to share, and that was okay, but if you're going to do like that, I'm going to . . ."

"You're going to what?" Sandy demanded, moving close to Shack.

"I just meant . . ."

"You want to go to New Orleans, or do you want to go back to Tucson, Hernandez?"

"I want to come along, Sandy, but . . ."

"Then shut up. Okay?"

Shack gave a long and weary sigh. "Okay. Anything you say, Sandy."

The scene had elements of the bull ring in it. Hernandez could have snapped Sandy's spine in his hands. The girl was the cape, spread in front of the black bull, then whipped gracefully away as he charged. I knew Sandy was testing his own strength and control. But when the scene was over, Shack looked at me in a way that made me feel entirely uncomfortable. Up until then he had been indifferent toward me. But now I could sense that he wanted to get those big hands on me.

We finally got another lift in a truck, this time a pickup, with two weathered men in the cab, and the four of us in the back. This time we made forty miles. To Uvalde. After food and cabins, slightly better than before, we didn't have much money left. We sat in Nan and Sandy's cabin and pooled all we had. Not quite nine dollars.

"Going along like this," Sandy said, "we'll have long beards the time we get to Burgundy Street, man. Or we'll starve."

"We can stop and work some," Shack said.

"Never use that word in front of me again, sir," Sandy told him.

"It's on account of we're too many," Nan said. "I've been telling you. We can split up and you and me, honey, we could make it all the way through in a day, honest to God. I know."

"We're all too happy together to break it up," Sandy said.

"This is happy?" she asked sullenly.

"Shut up," he said. "This is hilarious like. Anyhow, I've got an idea. For tomorrow. We've got to start being shrewd like. Use all assets and talents. We need a car of our own, children."

"Grand theft auto," Shack said darkly.

"Maybe we can just borrow one."

"How?" I asked.

"Watch and learn," he said. "Watch and learn, college boy."

The next day was Tuesday, the twenty-first of July. That's the day they say we started our "career." He slugged us so hard Monday night, we weren't stirring until noon, and then he hopped the three of us high and far, and got what was left of the tequila into Shack. He made us walk east on 90 until we were dragging. It was a blinding, dizzying day. The coaching didn't start until he found a place that suited him.

It went off exactly the way he planned it. Nan stood on the shoulder of the road with her hatbox. We lay flat behind rocks and brush. A man alone, in a blue-and-white Ford station wagon, a new one, came to a screaming stop fifty yards beyond her and backed up so hastily you could guess that he thought he'd better get her before the next guy stopped. She got into the front seat with her hatbox. She smiled at him and suggested he set the hatbox in back. He took it in both hands and strained around in the seat. While he was in that position she stuck the point of her little knife into the pit of his belly, puncturing the skin just enough, and told him that if he moved one little muscle, she'd open him up like a Christmas goose. She convinced him. He didn't even let go of the hatbox. She held him there until two cars went by. When the road was clear in both directions, she gave a yell and we scrambled up and hurried to the wagon and got in. Sandy and I got into the back. Shack went around and opened the door on the driver's side, took aim and chunked the man solidly under the ear with his big fist. The man sagged. Shack hunted him over with his hip and got behind the wheel and in a moment we were rolling along at a legal speed. Nan checked the glove compartment. She found a .32-caliber automatic and handed it back to Sandy. He shoved it into his rucksack.

"I *do* like station wagons!" Sandy said reverently, and suddenly we were all laughing. No reason.

I felt no slightest twinge of guilt or fear. It didn't seem to me then that we had done anything serious. It was all like a complicated joke.

The man stirred and groaned and lifted his head. "What are you people doing . . ."

Nan put the knife against his short ribs. "No questions now, Tex," Sandy said. "Later."

After we'd gone maybe five miles, Sandy told Shack to slow it down. The road was clear. We turned off onto a

sandy road that was hardly more than a trace. We crawled
and bumped over rocks until we had circled around behind a
barren hill, completely out of sight of the road. Sandy had
Shack turn it around so we were headed out. Shack took the
key out of the switch. We got out. In the sudden silence we
were a thousand years from civilization. A lizard stared at
us and ran. A buzzard circled against the blue, high as a jet.
You could hear the hard high whine of the cars, fading down
the scale as they went by on the invisible highway.

There was a pile of rocks twenty feet from the car. Nan
and Sandy sat on the rocks. I sat on my heels not far from
them. Shack took a half cigar from his pocket and lit it, and
stood leaning against the front fender. The man stood beside
the open door of the car. He rubbed his neck and winced.
He was maybe thirty-five, with blond hair cut short and a
bald spot. He had a round, earnest, open face, pale-blue
eyes, a fair complexion. His nose, forehead and bald spot
were red and peeling. He wore a light-blue sports shirt,
sweaty at the armpits, and gray slacks, and black-and-white
shoes. He had a long torso, short, bandy legs, and a
stomach that hung over a belt worn low. He wore a wide
gold wedding band and, on the little finger of his right hand,
a heavy lodge ring.

He tried to smile at all of us, and said, "I thought the
little lady was traveling alone. My mistake."

"What's your name, Tex?" Sandy asked.

"Becher. Horace Becher."

"What do you do, Horace?"

"I'm sales manager of the Blue Bonnet Tile Company
out of Houston. I've been making a swing around the
territory. Checking up."

"Checking up on girl hitchhikers, Horace?"

"Well, you know how it is."

"How is it, Horace?"

"I don't know. I just saw her there . . ." He visibly
pulled himself together. His smile became more ingratiat-
ing. You could almost hear him telling himself that he was a
salesman, so get in there and sell, boy. "I guess you folks
want money and I guess you want the car. Everything is
insured, so you go ahead and take it. I won't give you a bit

of trouble, folks. Not a bit. I'll wait just as long as you say before I report it, and I won't be able to remember the license number when I do. Is that a good deal?"

"Throw me your wallet, Horace," Sandy ordered.

"Sure. Sure thing." He took it out and threw it. It landed near me. I picked it up and flipped it to Sandy.

Sandy counted the money. "Two hundred and eighty-two bucks, Horace. That's very nice. That's decent of you, man."

"I like to carry a pretty good piece of cash on me," Horace said.

"Mm-m. Credit cards. Membership cards. You're all carded up, Horace. American Legion too?

"I got in just as the war ended. Had some occupation duty in Japan.

"That's nice. Belong to a lot of clubs, Horace?"

"Well, the Elks and the Masons and the Civitan."

"What's your golf handicap?'"

"Bowling's my game. Class A. One eighty-three average last year."

"Drink beer when you bowl?"

"Well, that's part of it, I guess."

"You're in lousy condition, Horace, with that big disgusting gut on you. You should cut down on the beer."

Horace slapped his stomach and laughed. It was a flat and lonely sound under the hot sun, and it didn't last long.

"Who's the fat broad in this picture, man?"

"That's my wife," Horace said rather stiffly.

"Better take her off the beer too. These your kids?"

"Two of them. That was taken three years ago. I got a boy eighteen months old now. Like I said, you people can take the car and the money, and no hard feelings."

"If we do, would you call it stealing, Horace?"

The man looked blankly at Sandy. "Wouldn't it be?"

"That's a raunchy attitude, man. You're a big successful clubman. And you get this chance to loan us a car and some money."

"A loan?"

"We're your new friends. Treat your friends right, Tex."

"Sure thing," he said brightly. "It can be a loan, if that's the way you want it."

He had been edging back toward the open door of the car. I had noticed it and I guessed Sandy had. Suddenly he whirled and plunged headlong into the car, yanking the glove compartment open. He scrabbled with both hands, releasing a gay rain of trading stamps, dislodging Kleenex, sun lotion, road maps. His hands moved more slowly and stopped. He lay half across the seat as though in exhaustion, and we heard the rasp of his breathing. He pushed himself slowly back out of the car and stood and smiled in a small sick way.

"Now that wasn't polite, man," Sandy said.

A faraway jet made a faint ripping sound. Becher stood in his own small black pool of shadow. He was sweating heavily. The situation was changing. He had triggered it. I could feel a coiling and turning in my stomach.

Shack walked slowly back to the tailgate, opened it, slid a heavy cardboard carton out onto the tailgate.

Horace turned and saw him and said, with automatic authority, "Careful with that! That's a special order. Imported Italian tile for a bar top."

Shack picked the box up in his arms. With a great effort so smoothly controlled that it looked effortless, he swung it up over his head and launched it in a high arc. It turned slowly in the hot, white sunlight and landed with a jangling smash on the rocks. The box ruptured. Bright shards of tile clattered on the stones.

That changed it, also. It was a symbol. Becher probably sensed the way things were changing and accelerating, and so he said, "I can write it out for you. The loan of the car and the money. You'll have something to show."

Nan yawned like a cat. Sandy picked up a few stones and threw them carefully, one at a time, until the fourth one struck and broke an undamaged tile which had slid out of the broken box.

It was all growing and changing. We were all getting closer to the edge of something. I can remember a time very much like that time with Becher. I was fourteen. There were five of us, all of an age. On a Saturday evening in August we went on our bikes out to the Crozier place and up the long drive to the dark empty house. They had gone to their place in Maine for the summer. Paul Beattie, my best friend at that time, had a hopeless crush on Marianne Crozier. Our idea, riciculous, mischievous and slightly romantic, was to break in and find which room was Marianne's, and leave there a mysterious message from an anonymous admirer.

We got in through a cellar window. It was scary work. We had come prepared, each of us with a flashlight. The electricity was turned off. We moved slowly in a taut group, whispering. From time to time we would stop and listen to the emptiness. It was a huge old place, full of ghosts and creakings. By the time we had located Marianne's room, we had become much bolder and had begun to show off, each in his own way, for the others in the group. Fats Carey bounced up and down on Marianne's bed, with obscene commentary. Gussy Ellison found out that the water was turned on, and hurried from one bathroom to the next, turning on every faucet, stoppering every sink and tub. The constant roar of water gave us courage instead of alarming us. Kip McAllen began to pile the bed of Paul's beloved with the contents of bottles he found in medicine cabinets and on dressing tables. For a time Paul bellowed his indignation at this violation of the shrine, and tried to put a halt to all disorder, but soon be caught the spirit of anarchy.

It grew and blossomed with us. We ranged through the house, clumping up and down stairs, trying to outdo each other in acts of outrage, each yelling to the others to come witness *this* particular violation of decent behavior. When, at least three hours later, we pedaled away, trembling with reaction, laughing annd hooting in a coarse way, each one trying to exaggerate his own guilt, we left the ruin behind us—precious things ripped, smashed, smeared and degraded, books, mirrors, draperies, lamps, statuary, clothing. It was reported later in the paper that the water overflow had caused structural damage to the extent of fifteen thousand dollars, and the other damage was estimated at twenty-five thousand. There were editorials about vandalism. We lived in terror for a month. We got together and devised an alibi so intricate that it could not have survived ten minutes of intensive questioning. But we were never questioned. We all came from substantial families. A few weeks later three of us went off to private schools. Had we all stayed in Huntstown High, we might have given ourselves away.

I am trying to make this point: we did not go to the Crozier place to do forty thousand dollars' worth of damage. We went on a romantic errand. We rode our sprocket-wheel steeds up there through the warm evening, noble as knights. When we left it was as though we had been through a brief and shocking illness. The violence was a cumulative thing, building upon itself.

I can remember the dreamlike way I climbed onto a chair and took down the saber hanging on Mr. Crozier's study wall. I slid it out of the scabbard. It made a hissing sound when I swung it. There was a marble bust on a low table, the head and shoulders of a bearded man. "Off with your head," I whispered and swung with all my strength. The blade snapped off at the hilt. My hands stung. The bust rocked and fell, and the head split on the hardwood floor. It was all a hot excitement, a roaring release.

Now, not quite a decade later, I sat on my heels in hot country and felt it all building again, toward the crazed release.

Becher could not quite believe what was happening to him. On one level I believe he felt that it would all come to an end, and it would be a story for him to tell in the home office and out on the road. But on a more primitive level there was a knowing dread inside him. His color was bad. His mouth kept working. A man could stand like that in a pit of snakes, wondering how to communicate, how to appease yearning for invisibility.

Shack pulled the salesman's suitcase out of the station wagon, dropped it on the ground, unzipped it. He pulled the clothing out, then stood up with a fifth of bourbon, half full. He uncapped it, took two long swallows, coughed and offered it to Sandy.

"Give it to Horace," Sandy said. "He's a nervous cat."

Shack gave Horace the bottle.

"Chug-a-lug," Sandy said.

"It's warm," Horace said faintly.

"Every drop, man. No stopping. Or you get some hard things to do. Drink it down, man."

He looked around at us, licked his mouth, then made his try. He tilted it up, squeezing his eyes shut against the sun. The soft throat worked. The level went down. He almost made it. But his stomach rebelled. He staggered and went down to his knees. The bottle dropped and broke. He spewed up the contents of his stomach onto the hot stones and sand. He got up slowly when it was over and leaned against the car. His face was yellow-gray.

"You're out of shape," Sandy said. "You need exercise. Anybody got any ideas?"

"Somersaults," Nan said. "They're nice."

"Somersaults—around the car," Sandy said.

"I don't think I . . ."

"You got some hard things to do, Horace. Come on!"

Shack drifted closer to him. Horace started. He found a soft place for his head. He went over sideways the first time. He did it right the second time. When he rolled into a sitting position, the stones bruised his back. He went slowly and laboriously around the car. He stopped, florid, shaking, gasping for breath. Sandy told him to go once around again. It took longer. As he was balancing, near Shack, to go over again, Shack booted him solidly in the rear and he went over very quickly, so quickly he rolled up onto his feet, staggering to find his balance. The back of his shirt was bloody.

"Do it every day and you'll live longer," Sandy told him. "Will you do it every day?"

"Yes, sir," Horace said. There was no resistance in him. He had accepted humiliation, and there wasn't much of him left, beyond a blind desire to please. His life had given him no tests of strength, no resource with which he could resist this nightmare in the high noon sun. He hoped to endure. That was all.

Nan was kneeling, pawing through the suitcase. She took out a toilet kit and opened it, took out a shaving bomb and pressed the button on top. A long worm of suds gouted onto the stones. She grinned at Sandy and at me.

"Bring me that yellow shirt there," Sandy said. She took it to him. He stood up and took his own shirt off. He was narrow and pallid, a spindly, rib-sharp whiteness in the sun, without a hair on his chest. He put the yellow shirt on and buttoned it. The shoulder seams came part way down his upper arms. It hung on his torso.

"It's a gone color," he said.

"It's too big," I told him.

"I can write it out, about the car," Horace said. It was a talisman phrase, repeated like a prayer without hope. His mind was dulled by illness, fear, pain and exhaustion. "I can write it out."

Sandy trotted to his rucksack and took out the automatic. His blue eyes were all a-dance behind the lenses of his glasses. The look of the gun in the sun changed it all again. I came slowly to my feet on cramped legs. Nan stood, her head tilted to the side. Shack was motionless, emotionless.

Sandy snatched up the shave bomb and flipped it underhand to Horace. It bounced off his chest onto the ground.

"Pick it up, Horace. That's just fine. I love you, Horace. You're the backbone of the new South. Move away from the pretty car. Further. That's my boy! You're a swingin' thing, man. This is the William Tell bit. Make like you can hear the drum roll, citizens. Balance the can on the head, Horace."

Horace's eyes seemed to actually bulge. "You can't . . ."

"Trust me, man. I'm a dead shot. Get it up there! I love *you*, Horace Becher, sales manager, bowler, family man."

Becher stood with his eyes shut and his hands at his sides. He swayed slightly. Sandy bit his lip. I saw the muzzle of the gun make small circles in the air. He held it at arm's length, sighting carefully.

The gun made a snapping sound, a sound hardly more impressive than that of a child's cap pistol. Horace flinched violently and the can fell to the ground. Sandy made him pick it up and put it back. He aimed again. The pistol made its little crack. A little black hole appeared high in Becher's forehead, slightly off center toward the left. His eyes came open as the can fell off. He took one step to spread his feet wide, as though to brace himself. And then he went down easily, breaking the fall. He was braced on one elbow for a moment, before he rolled onto his back. His chest lifted high, and then the air went out of him with a shallow, coughing, rattling sound.

Everything was changed forever. We all knew it. We had been walking back and forth through a big doorway, and suddenly it had been slammed, locked, bolted, while we were on the wrong side of it.

Nan made a soft, tremulous sound. I looked at her. She was standing bent forward from the waist, her fists pressed hard against her belly. Her underlip sagged and her expression was totally empty and slack, as though in sensual release. She made that sound again.

Sandy went darting over and looked down at Horace Becher. He laughed in a high, wild way. He whirled toward us and fired one shot straight up into the air and stuffed the gun in his pants pocket.

"A hundred thousand guys so like him you couldn't tell them apart with an electron microscope," he said breathlessly. "I love every square one of them. I dig all their dull little lives. It doesn't count, just one of them. You'd have to kill them all, digging them at the same time, and they're like the marching Chinese, so you can't."

I don't know if he aimed that shot to kill. It doesn't really matter. We were going to kill him. We'd begun to smell death. His helplessness kept pushing us further and further. My legs were trembling as I got into the car. It had happened. The sky would never look exactly the same again. Once it had happened, it was as though it was what we had been looking for. It mattered, and yet it didn't matter. I had helped soap a dirty word on the biggest window in the world. Yet nothing could ever be totally serious after that instant of looking at Kathy, bloodless gray on the blue tile floor.

We drove east. We made time. Sandy was behind the wheel, Nan beside him, Shack and me in back. Within five miles I knew Sandy was an expert. He held the wheel high and hard and sat with his chin thrust forward, and he was a part of the car.

"How are we swingin', college man?" he asked me with a hard gaiety in his voice.

"We're way out, Sandy."

"Break out the portable pharmacy, Nano," he told the girl. I swallowed my pills dry. The edges of the world had begun to blur. In fifteen minutes the D kick was reinforced, and reality was brilliant, steely and ludicrous. I thrummed like an open power line. We sped away from the sun that slid down the western sky, lengthening the shadows. We got right up there onto the curling edge of our big wave, and Sandy and I alternated making up verses to a requiem for Horace Becher, Sales Manager. We made Nan and Shack join in on the choruses. We bought gas boldly, and kidded around with the pump jockey, in the town of Segun, beyond San Antone. Ole Horace was daid on the lone prairie, and they wouldn't find him for a month, and we'd merely saved him from the coronary which would have gotten him anyway.

We had funds and a car which would float along at ninety, so that every minute brought us a mile and a half closer to New Orleans.

Shack went soundly asleep. We hammered an endless hole into the gathering dusk. Nan fooled with the car radio, changing stations with annoying frequency, keeping the volume high.

And, off the random dial, the name of Horace Becher roared out at us. The car swerved slightly as Sandy reached over, slapped the girl's hands away, and turned the dial back to the station.

We picked up pieces of the story here and there, all over the dial. A woman from Crystal City, Texas, loved animals and despised buzzards. She had a habit on trips of watching for their slow circling over animals near death. When their area of interest seemed accessible, she would park and hike into the barren land. She had rescued colts and calves and sheep and hurt dogs. She took a carbine along to put the hopeless ones out of their misery. She had seen the black birds circling low, had walked in and found the dead man, the broken tile, tire tracks, and spilled suitcase, the wallet, and the bolder carrion birds already tearing at his face. She had shooed the birds off, gotten a heavy tarp out of her truck and covered him and weighted the edges down with stones. She had driven to the nearest phone and called the Rangers and guided them to the body. In a very short time, aided by the information in the wallet, they had put the car description and the plate number on the air. An hour later a truck driver had reported seeing a blue-and-white station wagon turn out onto the highway where the man had been found. I remembered a truck in the distance when we had turned out. It had been far away, but it had passed us while we were picking up speed, and soon we had passed it. He reported that this had happened at about one o'clock or a little later, that the station wagon had turned east, and there had been two men and a woman in it. The woman had found the body at twenty of three. The truck driver had reported at quarter to six.

We had all of it, more than we could use. Shack was cursing in a heavy, monotonous way. Sandy pulled way over onto the shoulder, turned off the lights, punched the radio off.

"We've got a car we don't hardly need, man," he said.

"We walk?" Shack asked.

"We should split up," Nan said.

"We got the car and it's night and we can make time," Sandy said. "Getting far away is the deal. It's important to make these fine miles. But the vehicle is torrid."

"So?" I said.

"I don't like the going east," Sandy said. "Not enough roads through the swamp country. Too easy to check the cars. So let's get off these big fat main roads. Let's go to New York. It's a good town. When you're there, you're lost."

"In this car?" Nan asked.

"Who said in this car? Let's turn north on a nice little road, and we'll find a spot to trade cars, and we'll keep on rolling, on those nice little back roads."

We put the dome light on and checked the maps. We found a good place to turn, and we kept pushing. I spelled

Sandy for a while and he slept. I wanted to be rid of the Ford. Every pair of headlights in the night was potential danger.

By two in the morning we'd made over five hundred miles and we had come to a small place named Lufkin. A roadhouse beyond town was doing capacity business. A lot of banners were strung up, so I guess it was some kind of club affair. We parked a hundred yards beyond the place, and Sandy went back with Shack, after telling me this hadn't been in my course of study.

Nan and I waited in the dark car, ducking low when another car came by and the headlights swept across us.

"I keep telling him and telling him it's better we split up," she said indignantly. "No, he's got to have a crowd, an audience like."

"You can take off any time. Go ahead right now," I told her.

She told me what unmentionable thing I could do to myself. We waited there in unfriendly silence. I kept thinking of the magical way that black hole had appeared in the peeling, sunburned forehead, with a small frothy edge of blood around the bottom of the rim.

A car without lights suddenly drifted up beside us and pulled ahead of us. The brake lights glowed briefly. Sandy yanked the door open beside me and said, "Go get in the other car. Make it quick, man."

Nan and I got into the other car. Shack was behind the wheel. The Ford pulled around us, lights on. Shack turned the lights on and followed it. They'd picked up a weary old Olds that smelled like a farmyard and sagged low in the back left corner. We were on the road to Nacogdoches. Sandy, ahead of us, slowed way down as we crossed a small bridge over the Angelina River. No cars were coming in either direction. Beyond the bridge was a long slope covered with brush. Shack came to a stop as Sandy turned the Ford down the slope. He gunned it and went churning down through the brush, bounding recklessly, making a hell of a racket. He got a good long way from the highway. We could see only the reflected glow of his lights. They went off. In a few minutes Sandy appeared in the beam of our headlights, grinning toward us. Shack got out. They scuffed out the tracks of the Ford on the shoulder. They had also taken a spare plate from another car. With difficulty we got it onto the Olds and threw the Old's plate off into the brush.

Sandy took the wheel and we got back up to speed. The engine was noisy. Sandy laughed with delight. "Man, we lifted the plate first, and we moved around until a drunk came wobbling out. He stopped at this car and we came in behind him and soon as he had the keys in his hand— *pow!*—like a tree fell on him. Our luck, she is running good. The tank is full."

About a hundred and fifty miles later we crossed on over into Arkansas. The Olds was running hot. There was a line of gray along the horizon in the east.

Sandy checked the maps again and we headed more directly east. Somewhere west of Eldorado, Arkansas, with the misty sun high, we turned off on a dusty track that faded away in dense woodland. Sandy slept in the front seat, Nan in the rear seat. Shack and I stretched out on opposite sides of the car. Birds and insects made sleepy midday noises. The forest floor smelled sweet and loamy. I felt a thousand taut springs unwinding, felt the world fading. Just as I tilted down into sleep I wished that it was a sleep that would never end.

Sandy nudged me awake with his foot when the day was almost gone. There was an icy stream a hundred feet away. We used the cold water to freshen up and scrape the stubble off. Nan went a dozen feet downstream, stripped, soaped herself, squatted in a shallow pool and rinsed, not knowing or caring that Shack did not take his eyes off her for an instant. When she pulled her slacks on again he made a low moan, very deep in his throat, half growl and half moan.

I had glanced at her a few times as she bathed there. The tilted sunlight came between the trunks, dappling the grass, her haunches and the black pool. With that heavy crop of hair and the faint and dusky shadow of the pelt that ran down the cleft of her back, she could have been Prehistoric Woman, a diorama in a museum of natural history. Our modern culture had put red paint on her lips, metal in her mouth, and a puckered surgical scar on her belly. But all the rest—the slightly brutish cast of features, the S curve of waist into hip, the saffron nipples, the pubic pyramid, the elemental savageness—these were unchanged across fifty thousand years.

I could not want her. She had been tossed to me, the way you flip a pack of cigarettes to a friend, and it had been nothing. Once you have accustomed yourself to drinking acid, sour red wine is like stale water on the tongue. I sensed, however, how sublimely suited to each other were Nan and Hernanadez. Sandy called them the animals. They were displaced in time. They both belonged in prehistory, back in callous violence, roaming the raw land, mating with random fury, tearing at each other, charring the bloody meat of the latest kill in the fire in the mouth of the cave.

They were not for this time. But their inadequacy was not the same as Sandy's and mine. There are the constitutional inadequates, whose bodies have too frail a grasp on life. And the mental inadequates, trapped back in their dim minds. Sandy is a moral and social inadequate, unable to cope with the folkways and structures of his culture. I am an emotional and spiritual inadequate—but this can be said in a much simpler way: I have no capacity to love. A man who cannot love is like one of those machines that jokester mechanics build as a gag. Wheels go around and lights flash and plungers go up and down, and it makes a ratchety noise, but it has no purpose. A machine without a purpose, once it is out of control, is dangerous. Once I came very close to being able to love. But that, of course, was Kathy. After Kathy the pointless machine began to work with greater speed and fury. . . .

As we drove east into the Arkansas dusk, I felt dull, wooden, spiritless. I felt as if all the furniture of my mind had been reupholstered in dusty black velvet. I took a hundred small naps, and in the periods of going to sleep or awakening, their voices sounded metallic and unreal over the rolling thunder of the Olds.

I was asleep when they picked up a better car, a red-and-white Chevrolet, a new one, in some small city in Arkansas.

They picked it up in the parking lot of a private club. I vaguely remember transferring from the Olds to the newer car. And I can remember Sandy relating their adventure in his taut, tumbling voice.

He was calling Shack a monster. In sneaking through the dark and crowded parking lot of the club, hearing the music come from the club, they had come across a car where a couple was making love in the the back seat.

"Both of them bagged," Sandy said. "So before I can move a pinky, the monster opens the rear door, takes that stud by the nape of the neck, pulls him out, pops him one time, drops him and kicks him under the car. The woman is saying in a little whiny voice. "Wheresha go? Arthur! Arthur! Whereya, baby?' So the monster says, 'Here I am! and he dives in there like a fullback going over center. In about five seconds that broad realizes something brand-new had come into her life, and she didn't like any part of it, man. She starts yelping like she's being killed, so the monster thumps her one too. While this is going on, I'm pulling Arthur out from under the car and checking him over. Fifty-eight bucks, but no keys. When the monster got out, I had him pick Arthur up and cunk him back in there with her. When the lights come on for those love bugs, they're going to be confused like. The next car I checked was this one, and it had the keys in it."

So now, I thought, we add rape to the list. After Horace, it was about as serious as disorderly conduct. After Horace there was no worse place you could go.

I slept again. I remember waking up when Shack and Nan were sleeping. Sandy was pushing the Chev hard. I saw the glow of the dashlights against the small round knob of muscle at the corner of his jaw. The dark land wheeled by. He was singing. He sang that part that comes after you finish singing "I've been working on the railroad." But he sang only one part of the ending, over and over. "Fee fie fiddly-I-oh, fee fie fiddly-I-oh, oh, oh, oh. Fee fie fiddly-I-oh, fee fie fiddly-I-oh, oh, oh, oh." Over and over, endlessly. Listening, I realized I had heard him doing it before. Now it has become a part of all the memories of that time. The night and the running roar of the car, and Sandy's voice, like the sound track of an art movie.

Sandy shook me awake in the predawn light. We were parked outside the office of a motel near Tupelo, Mississippi. "We got to have the services of the clean American yout'," he said, "he who by virtue of his shining countenance is above suspicion. Rise and give me that scout master beam, Kirboo."

After I got out and yawned and rubbed my face and stretched, I was able to be the responsible errand boy. The red neon vacancy sign was lit, and a light over the night bell. After three long rings I heard somebody stirring. A very pregnant dough-faced blonde in a red satin housecoat opened the door, stared stupidly at me and said, "Yah?"

I signed us up. Mr. and Mrs. Ivan Sanderson, Mr. Kenneth Tynan and Mr. Theodore Sturgeon. It shows poverty of invention, but I plead sleepiness. Much later this gave the prosecuting attorney a wonderful opportunity to display his considerable talent for sarcasm.

I paid her eighteen dollars for two twin-bed doubles. It was a fraud motel, glossy and landscaped on the outside, full of borax furniture and junk plumbing on the inside. I almost fell asleep standing up in the cranky shower. By the time I got into bed, Hernandez was snoring like a snare drum. It didn't bother me a bit.

We were back on the road just as the sun went down. Sandy had doled out pills which lifted us up and out and away, glowing with induced joy, floating on numbered clouds, making bad jokes. Even that tension between Shack and Nan was gone, and they were unexpectedly animated. She sang some dirty little French songs a sculptor had taught her, her voice husky and untrue. Sandy did a long imitation of Mort Sahl.

But we were on our way through Nashville. I am not going to write the Nashville episode into this record. The newspaper did enough chop-licking over it. It was a sick, dirty business, pointless, cruel and bloody. This is, I suspect, as close as I can come to apology. I cannot say that the business of Horace Becher had any particular grace or style. But it had a flavor of some kind that the Nashville affair did not. The Nashville affair was symptomatic of sickness and desperation. I took part in it directly. From then on Sandy dropped the "college man" routine. He brought it up one more time after that, during the Helen Wister thing, but that was all. In Nashville I won my dirty spurs.

Also, in Nashville, I learned something about us, the four of us. I learned that we were going to be caught. I had been thinking that we might get away. We might get to New York and split up. But Nashville demonstrated that we weren't going to let ourselves get away. When things started looking to easy, we would compulsively compound our problem and intensify the search. Even if Sandy had not dropped and lost Horace Becher's pistol at the scene of the killing, I suspect the two would have been tied together. But he practically handed it to them, even though they took a long time to check it out. His losing it there was part of that same compulsiveness too, I believe.

Nashville was a pointless gesture of hostility, a dirty word yelled at the world. It was without style or meaning. Pigs are slaughtered with more dignity. After Nashville we were committed all the way. Even Sandy was slightly chastened. We discussed splitting up, and said it was a good idea, and we would split up later. But I think we all knew we'd never get the chance, and, in some obscure, perverse way, didn't want the chance.

Auto theft, rape, kidnap, murder. They were big words. I couldn't make them real in my head. They were things other people did. The things I did were different, because I was Kirby Palmer Stassen, unique. For me the words were different. I was not engaged in a career of crime; I had embarked on a program of social experimentation. After it was all over, I would lecture to thoughtful groups, electrifying them with my pertinent observations on the meaning of life and the meaning of death

When we had tumbled back into the car in such great haste, Nan and I had gotten into the back seat. I think we must have been twenty miles from Nashville when she did a curious thing. I think she knew from my silence that I was deeply troubled, and it is even possible that in the shadowy recesses of her spirit there was the dim urge to give comfort. She picked up my hand, my right hand, reaching across me to take me by the wrist, and she pulled my hand over and slipped it into the V of her blouse and pressed it tightly against her warm, scanty breast. The slight stir of the nipple against my palm was as distasteful as though I trapped some sluggish insect there and it moved slowly in panic. And then I remembered, too vividly, the fatal thing my hand had done. My window was halfway down. I pulled away from her, found the electric button that put it down the rest of the way, leaned far out and gouted vomit into the soft, warm night. The hard wind snapped at my croped hair and whipped the tears out of my eyes. When I sat back I was weak and dizzy. No one made any comment. Shack dug the final bottle of tequila out of Sandy's rucksack. Sandy didn't want any. Shack and Nan and I passed it back and forth until we had killed it. Nashville then was much more vague, but I knew it would be back, unbearably vivid. I knew that that final scream would sound forever in a closet in the back hall of my brain.

The reverend came again today. As time grows shorter they seem to be sicking him onto me with increasing frequency. The governor has signed the execution warrant. Today I told him I was far too busy to grant him the standard courtesy of ten minutes of my time. I said I wanted to be certain I would complete this journal. He looked at me severely and told me it would be more fitting if I devoted the time to the nurture of my immortal soul. I told him that I agreed heartily, and I was looking for my immortal soul in my own fashion, and half expected to find it somewhere on these pages, and it would probably be a gray, sly little fellow in a gnome hat, peering maliciously out from behind a bad word. He went away, shaking his ecclesiastical head.

T E N

Ｉᴛ is curious to note that during the weekend recess which was followed almost immediately by the summations of the prosecution and the defense and the judge's charge to the jury, Riker Deems Owen, the attorney for the defense, used precious time and energy in the preparation of his final informal memorandum on the Wolf Pack Case.

Certainly the same time devoted to his summation would have resulted in a more effective job, but it is possible that Owen realized by that time, as did most of the perceptive spectators and communications people, that he had already lost his case. Even with a lost case, however, it would seem more in keeping with Owen's evident egomania and distorted sense of history to have worked up a summation which he would hope would rank with the deathless ones of Darrow, one of his household gods.

There is the alternate assumption that Owen did give the preparation of his summation every morsel of time and energy he felt it required. Those of us who were present that icy day can be forgiven for believing that his final effort in the trial could have been improved upon, regardless of the outcome. His case was beyond saving. His professional reputation was not.

Though it is not pertinent, it is somehow touching to see how perfectly the Owen memoranda were typed by Miss Leah Slayter. They were without erasures, strikeovers. It is likely that whenever she made an error, she started the page over. Though this is prescribed procedure with legal documents, it could only be considered proper for informal memoranda when the typist has the feeling she is typing a work of great importance for a great man.

It is rather pleasant somehow to realize that this devoted employee was blind to the hapless performance of her boss in his most famous trial, and thought his rambling memoranda so precious as to deserve infinite care.

Certainly Riker Deems Owen's total performance in that trial can be considered of the second-rate. If we assume it was a case no man could have won, we can at least say that there are men who could have come closer. The electrocution of a female is a startling example of the ineptitude of any defense attorney.

It was the post-trial derision in the public press which reduced Riker Deems Owen to a shrunken and rather hesitant old man.

At the time he wrote this final memo on the case, he was not absolutely certain he would lose the case. Certainly he had no suspicion that his conduct of the defense would cause him to be jeered at. He had no idea of placing his professional reputation on the line when he took the case. But sometimes we gamble without knowing what the stakes are.

Long days of testimony, of exhibits, objections, cross examinations tend to focus the mind and the attention on trivia, so that the larger issues are forgotten. John Quain is a clever, dogged, tireless prosecutor. I cannot take the chance of giving him perfectly free rein to establish the State's case. I must protect my clients through emphasizing the chance of reasonable doubt in certain areas, in spite of my master plan of defense which borrows from certain interesting aspects of the Loeb-Leopold Case.

John Quain is perfectly aware of my obligation to weaken, insofar as is possible, his edifice of evidence, and thus I must be constantly alert to avoid the traps implicit in his presentation. This, despite the competent staff at my elbow, is an exhausting task.

I believe that I dug a few important holes in the testimony of the youngsters, Howard Craft and Ruth Meckler. The most significant one was Howard's admission that it is possible that Arnold Crown struck the first blow, and due to their angle of observation, they missed it.

Murder in the first degree implies motive, opportunity and prior intent. The priority of intent need be only a matter of a split second. If a murderer had adequate reason to have a rock in his hand, premeditation would be difficult to establish. But should he seek a rock and bend and pick it up, premeditation exists during that interval. However, should he be struck or injured in any way before picking up the rock, the chance of proving premeditation is weakened thereby.

Would that I were permitted to defend these people before a judge and jury and spectators who had never heard of their wicked exploits. Justice, in the circumstances I face, is a farce. A whole nation watches these four human beings. An outraged nation demands they be executed. You can feel the weight of all the pressure in that courtroom. It is a tangible heaviness. If Stassen, Golden, Hernandez and Koslov had come from the most remote planet of the galaxy, if they were creatures of slime and tentacles, they could not be watched with any more curiosity and revulsion.

They are being tried for what was done to the salesman, to the Nashville people, to Arnold Crown and to Helen Wister, not just for Crown alone. So this case is only symbolic, and hence my defense is the only possible one.

It is interesting to see the various ways the four of them accept their long hours on trial. Stassen, in his well-cut flannel suit, with his polite, attentive and somewhat detached manner, would look much more at home at the press table. He writes me short notes from time to time. Some of them have been mildly helpful. I have noticed that he often stares directly at his jurors. I sense that he seems to baffle them, that they cannot equate his demeanor with the evidence presented.

The idleness, the enforced spectator role is most difficult for Sander Golden to endure. He jitters and twitches endlessly, keeping a dozen mannerisms going at the same time. He whispers and mutters to the other defendants until he has to be silenced a half dozen times a day. He stares with bright mockery at every member of the jury in turn until they look away. He has written me foolish notes in an awkward hand, miserably spelled.

The girl sits placidly. She plays with her hair. She nibbles her nails. She yawns, and often, out of boredom, sighs audibly, recrosses her legs, scratches her thigh, yawns again. She cannot understand why she cannot have magazines to look at. Sometimes she draws the same face over and over again, the empty comic-book face of a pretty girl.

Robert Hernandez endures it with the silent, unmoving patience of an ox. His metabolism is low, his deep, slow breathing imperceptible. A bear in a cage, when it is not pacing, will endure in that same way. He stares at the floor fifteen feet in front of him. A hairy fist lies slack on the table. The jury regards him with more assurance. This is a criminal type. Can't you see it?

I have tried to analyze the tangible emanations of hate that come from the spectators. It is uncommon, even in murder trials. I believe I have the reason for it. They did not kill for profit. Their entire adventure netted them less than fifteen hundred dollars, and finding so much cash on Crown was an accident they could not have anticipated.

So because it was violence without meaning, they made a small, cheap thing of life. It is the instinct of man to consider life of greatest importance. If it is to be taken away the reason should be substantial. So he who denigrates the value of life, tries to give it a lower value in the market place, must be punished for the commission of great evil.

And they have made a small, cheap thing of love. That is

the second unforgivable. Reckless lust, if it should shake a man and overwhelm him and make him commit idiocies, can be partially understood and thus forgiven. But a casual code which makes of the act of sex a function barely more important than shaking hands invites hate and punishment.

By diminishing life and diminishing love, they have threatened to diminish every man and woman who learned of their acts. When anyone seeks to reduce you, in your own eyes, to unimportance, you fight.

So these hated four sit in a court and famous artists draw them for the big magazines. A journalist coins the name Handy Nan, and ten thousand dirty jokes are invented. A hundred thousand fathers give their wayward teen-age daughters overdue whippings, and a predictable number of them leave home as a result. Car thefts have increased greatly. There is a higher than normal incidence of rape. A few people have been kicked to death by vicious metropolitan youngsters.

And all of this, too, is a part of the circus in the courtroom. What we do each day affects a number of lives impossible to compute.

As the man who must defend them, I have made a special effort to avoid emotional prejudice toward these four distorted people. But in all honesty I must confess to a distaste which has been caused by the way they have cheapened the illusions man holds most dear.

They have made me feel less safe in the world. Deep in my heart is the wish they may come to great harm. But I cannot permit that emotion to affect the professional competence I am contributing to their defense.

These four I defend do not concern themselves with the slightest romantic rationalization in their personal relationships. And so their only differentiation from beasts of the field is that they stand on two legs rather than four. One hundred years ago animals were still tried for murder, condemned and executed.

I have discovered no exercise of logic which can soften my distaste for these defendants. That is one handicap I face. The second handicap is the lucidity and shrewdness of the prosecutor, John Quain. The third crucial factor is the impression these people make upon the jury—a thing now out of my control. Lastly, there is the philosophy of my defense. I keep stressing, at every opportunity, the accidental pattern of this whole thing.

In my summation I shall use an analogy which I hope will not be too crude. It should be effective. I have dismantled my hedge clippers and I shall take them into court. Two blades, two handles. One blade will represent the girl, the other one Hernandez. One handle will represent Stassen, the other Golden. I will assemble it before the jury and show them that any three parts, assembled together, can do no damage. It is only when the four parts are brought together that you have an instrument which can clip a hedge, or a throat. So does it make sense to take the four parts, now disassembled and hence of no danger, and destroy those parts separately? The thing responsible for the crime was these four, acting as a new entity, doing things which any three of them would not and could not have done. So is not society satisfied merely to make certain that these four pieces can never again be assembled into an instrument of destruction? If hedge clippers should destroy a beautiful shrub, can you blame one handle? Or one blade?

If I have any pride at all in this situation it is in my earnest desire not to try to use this case, as many men would, to further my own career. I was selected for it only because they happened to take a highway through this area, because they happened along when a lovely girl lay helpless on the road, and because two young lovers watched a murder take place. It was a web of accident.

My duty is to fight for life imprisonment for these people, for a verdict of guilty with a recommendation of mercy. That is the ultimate I can hope to attain. Had I cared to use this public exposure, indeed this national exposure, for my own purposes, I would have selected a line of defense with less chance of succeeding, but offering more range for me to display my competence at this sort of work.

It would help me in times such as these if I had one human being very close to me to whom I could talk with the utmost frankness, to whom I could reveal my hopes and fears, my joys and my sorrows. I cannot speak to my wife of such things. She has no training in, no knowledge of, and no curiosity about the law. I cannot talk fully and deeply to my associates in the office. This would have to be a special relationship, resolutely intimate, close and unafraid. Perhaps all troubled, lonely men have yearned for this difficult goal, and perhaps have had the good fortune to attain it.

I suspect that Dr. Paul Wister is one of those. In his hour of blackness I saw in him that kind of strength that cannot be maintained and sustained in the ways of loneliness.

I doubt that I could endure the blow that fell upon him. . . .

ELEVEN

By mid-afternoon on Monday the twenty-seventh, Herbert Dunnigan made the executive decision to pull his special group out of Monroe. All investigative possiblities had been exhausted. It was a valid assumption that the wanted ones had slipped through the net. He left one agent for administrative co-ordination and, after dismantling the emergency communications network, emplaned for Washington with the rest of his group. The death watch could be endured with more efficiency there, and the press kept under better control.

The important journalists and the roving tape crews and the few radio people also moved out on Monday. Monroe had lost its priority. After the wolf is long gone, the nervous flock can begin to feed again.

Both Dallas Kemp and the Wister family took this mass departure to mean the abandonment of hope for the life of Helen Wister. There had been a meager comfort in the presence of top authority—in much the same way that troops on a hopeless front will cherish the presence of the commander of an army. When he leaves they once again remember how easily they can be overwhelmed.

By three o'clock on Monday afternoon, Helen Wister had been captive over forty hours. Criminologically speaking, the prognosis was bad.

The departure of top authority left a hole. Sheriff Gus Kurby had an instinct about such things. There were times to keep your head down. There were other times when you could safely stomp and bellow. But you had to come up with something usable.

He sat in his big corner office on the second floor of the County Courthouse, in his big red leather swivel chair, his hat shoved back, his belt comfortably loosened over a late and heavy lunch. The day had turned humid. There was distant thunder, and a brassy quality to the afternoon sunlight.

On the pale-gray walls of his office were the framed evidences of many small triumphs. On the desk, mounted on a cherrywood base and a slender silver pedestal was the misshapen slug, .38 caliber, which, in 1949, had punched a raw hole under his collarbone, nicked the top of his right lung and cracked the shoulder blade and won an election. With the slug in him Gus had disarmed his assailant with such emphasis that he had snapped both the man's wrists.

Gus Kurby sighed mightily as he watched his favorite deputy, Rolly Spring, working on the map. Rolly was a spare little man, a crickety fellow with seven kids, a genius for loyalty, a sour outlook, and the single flaw of being entirely too quick and willing to put random patterns of hard knots on surly heads with his hickory nightstick.

The map was new and large. It was a map of the United States and it covered most of the big bulletin board. It was printed in black and white, so the track of red crayon being applied by Deputy Spring stood out vividly.

The work was also being watched by a local newspaperman named Mason Ives. Mase was, occupationally speaking, a displaced person. He was in the classic mold of the old-time reporter, lean, rumpled, bitter, iconoclastic, skeptical, imaginative and compulsively curious. Any alert producer would have cast him immediately as the reporter who beat the mob. But the reporting was all being done by wholesome tractable journalism graduates who drew Guild wages, kept regular hours and did exactly as they were told. And so Mase was relegated to doing an op. ed. column for the Monroe *Register*, rather weakly syndicated around the state, plus sporadic feature-story work. He had learned to so mask his corrosive irony that it delighted the bright reader without awakening the indignation of the dullard majority.

Mase Ives was the only newspaperman Gus Kurby trusted implicitly. Mase was the only man who had an understanding of what Gus was accomplishing, and Gus's way of accomplishing it. Mase, with tactical advice and some speech writing, had helped Gus win elections.

"You got to realize," Gus said, "I'm just a plain shurf."

"Sure, sure, sure," Mase said. He was sitting on a small table beside one of the large windows. "A plain little ole country sheriff, trying to get along. A simple graduate of the top police schools, with one of the biggest libraries on criminology in the state. Tell me more, simple man."

"Hell, Mase. Some very bright people are doing this same job of studing this thing out, maps and all."

"And any ideas they get, they got to go through channels and committees. They're big for staff work, Gus."

Gus sighed again. Spring had finished and checked his work. "I got me a couple of ideas. I could check 'em out with you, Mase."

"I'll listen and try to confuse you."

Gus got up and latched his belt and went over to the map. Rolly Spring had drawn a red line, following specific highways, from Uvalde to Monroe.

Gus studied it in silence for a few moments. "I'm just guessing, now. There's a make on one of them. Hernandez. From the record, he's got just enough upstairs so he can feed himself. And he isn't what you'd call a playful type. Those kids in the barn heard all that smart talk, that wise-guy talk from the one with glasses. He's bright. So let's say he's running things. And he's playful. He does things on impulse. He was driving when they stopped to kill Crown and take the Wister girl. There's something playful about killing the salesman, like they toyed around with him some.

I say they're using drugs. It smells that way. But not something to make them crazy enough and reckless enough to get caught easy. Okay so far?"

"You haven't said a hell of a lot yet."

"I'm guessing on some of these roads but from the places they hit, these roads are pretty good guesses. They were picked smart. They're fast secondary roads. All traffic patrol is spread so thin these days, about all they can cover is the main highways. You take the little roads, the only trouble you can have is in the towns and small cities. And if you take it easy in those places, you can stay safe, even with the hottest plate in the country."

"If you say so, Sheriff."

"What I'm doing out loud, Mase, is building up a half-ass M.O. on this bunch. What they've had luck with, they'll keep doing. Keep switching cars, keep taking secondary roads, hole up in the daytime. It's my guess they won't split up, and that's only a guess."

"I have that hunch too, Gus. Particularly hopped up. They won't want to change the dice."

"Now let's put some of this stuff together and see where we get. Extend the rough line and its aims at New York. We got to make some assumptions if we're going to come up with anything, so let's just say it's New York. Why the hell not? If you want to lose yourself, get in the middle of the biggest crowd you can find. Okay?"

"Unless one of them is from someplace else and they have a good place to hole up, and how the hell can you tell that?"

Kurby stepped over to his desk and picked up a soft pencil and a ruler. He went to the map, made a measurement against the scale, and then drew a black arc, one third of a circle, northeast by east of Monroe.

"That's four hundred miles," he said. "So let's say they went about that far and holed up Sunday morning. They could have dumped the girl, dead, or kept her with them. Last night they got on the road again. They'd be in Pennsylvania, the way it looks. They'd stick to the M.O. and change cars. So they've got Pennsylvania plates, and we don't know what kind of car, but it won't be a junker. They'd stick to secondary roads last night, heading across the state. And there's one thing that state hasn't got, it's a good fast way to get across it without you take the turnpike."

"I remember the days before the pike," Mase said. "It was a life work crossing that state."

"So let's say they got maybe to this area by daylight this morning, and holed up again." Gus Kurby drew an elongated oval on the map, the long dimension of the oval north and south, fairly close to the Jersey border. "Let's say they're somewhere inside this area right here, sacked out this minute."

"You make it sound real, Gus," Mase said with a grin that pulled the corners of his mouth down.

"Let's say they haven't pulled anything since killing Crown except one auto theft. We know they had the use of a car radio in the Buick. They know, even hopped up and crazy confident, they're the hottest thing in twenty years. What they don't know is they're so hot that it makes confusions that work to their advantage."

"Where is this heading, Gus?"

"Now I got to contradict myself. If they stick to the M.O., I'm licked. If they take secondary roads across Jersey, I'm in deep left field. They want to get to New York. They're close. They're hot. They're pooped. Three in the morning is no time to hit New York City. It stays light until damn near nine. They're close to the Pennsy Pike that feeds into the Jersey Pike. Evening traffic in the summer is heavy. Put yourself in their place, Mase. What would you do?"

Mase chewed his lip and then nodded. "I might chance it, Gus. I might get rolling earlier, take a chance on the pike, and get to the city before midnight. But, on the other hand, instead of holing up, once I got so close, I might have pushed all the way on through and be in New York already."

"There's that chance. But they've been a long, long way, and maybe the girl used up some time, and getting their hands on a car used up some time, and they had to fight

those Pennsylvania roads all night. Maybe they didn't make
it any further than the Harrisburg area."

"What we're talking about, Gus, is whether you're going
to stick your neck out, and how you're going to do it."

"You take those big pikes, you got a problem. You got
two places to check. One is from the entrance booths.
They've got phone communication to the control towers
where you've got the short wave to the cars on patrol. The
other place is the cars on patrol. You've got normal traffic
loads, plus the vacation load. At least it's not a weekend.
You get three abreast, bumper to bumper traffic, wheeling at
sixty-five—if you're looking for something, you got to be
looking for something simple."

"I can see that."

"So suppose the toll-booth boys in the twelve entrances
from Harrisburg to the Jersey Pike are alerted to watch for
three men and a woman in a pretty good car with Pennsylvania plates. Or, on the off chance, three men and two
women."

"Wouldn't there be hundreds of those?"

"A hell of a lot less than you'd think. It isn't a normal
traveling group. The cars with one, two and three people in
them account, I'd guess for ninety-nine out of a hundred
cars. When there's four, it's two couples or four women or
four men. I'm leaving kids out of this. I'd give orders to
suspend normal traffic control procedures so your road
patrols would be looking too, and I'd put the best guys
available on the logical exits from the Jersey Pike."

Mason Ives thought for a few moments. "Have you got
time to sell this?"

"Not direct. But I think Dunnigan would buy it, and he
could sure as hell sell it. Maybe it's all set up already."

"Somehow I doubt that, Gus. What worries you? You've
stuck your neck out further than this many times."

Gus sat down again and grinned like a pirate. "You got
this one backwards, Mase. If it doesn't work, who ever
knows or cares? But if it does work, there should be some
horn blowing going on."

Ives looked startled for a moment. He grinned. "Okay,

you big ambitious bastard. That's why you got me up here. I'll go over to the shop and set it up, all ready to file. Kurby devises traffic trap that tonight snapped shut on the Wolf Pack and so forth."

"And you could sort of set it up with Peterson over at the station?" Gus asked humbly.

"And make sure he gets a network tie-in too, for God's sake. I'll go pick fresh laurel and make a wreath. Now it's safe to call Dunnigan."

"I called him an hour ago," Sheriff Kurby said mildly. "He seemed to like it. I had to go through maybe nine people to get to him, but I finally did, and I kept getting that fifteen-second beep, so I knew they got a good record of it. And I got one too, Mase. I strictly don't know the law about using such a thing, but while I was talking to Dunnigan I was thinking that if it does work out, it might make a nice tape Peterson could play for the people, so I was careful, the things I said. I put in a part about how wonderful it is to live in a society where the world's greatest police department will listen to a plain county sheriff."

"Have you ever thought of being governor, Gus?"

"Only late at night when I can't get back to sleep. A man'll think of a lot of foolish things in the small hours."

On Route 30, between York and Lancaster, and not far from the Susquehanna River, on the north side of the road, on a wide curve, in rather pleasant rolling country, is the Shadyside Motor Hotel. Steam Heat, Tile Baths, Innerspring Mattresses, Home Cooking. The units are separate, small brick buildings, square and rather ugly. There are only six of them. They are set well back from the highway at the foot of an apple orchard hill. The highway sign is in front of a large white farmhouse set much closer to the road.

The brick cabins were constructed over twenty years ago by Ralph Weaver, then fifty-five, who had farmed those eighty acres all his life, as had his father and grandfather before him. When he became crippled by arthritis he put his savings into the construction of the six cabins, despite the continuous opposition of his wife, Pearl. He died of a stroke two years after he completed the final cabin. Neighbors expected her to sell out. There was nothing to hold her there. Pearl had had four children. Accident, disease and a war had taken all four of them before any of them had married. She could have lived on a tiny income, with great care, and that's what the neighborhood expected her to do.

But she sold of all but five acres, and she ran the small business. Had Ralph Weaver built less solidly, maintenance would have eaten up the marginal income. At seventy-two, Pearl Weaver was a tall, erect woman with a square powerful figure, and an alarmingly loud, shrill voice. A half-wit woman from over the hill came in once a week to help with the heavier cleaning. A neighbor boy helped with the big lawn. Once a week Pearl Weaver drove her ancient Dodge truck to York and did her marketing. Each year she planted a large kitchen garden, and canned what she could not use. For those who wanted it, she would provide a gargantuan country breakfast for sixty cents. The cabins rented for five dollars a couple, four dollars for a single, during the summer. In the last few years it had become a great rarity for them to be all filled—unlike the early days when sometimes all the cabins were filled and so were all the spare bedrooms in the main house. It had been three years since she had had anyone in the main house, but she kept the whole house just as spotless as the cabins.

Summer was the best time. In the winter a whole month might go by without a single customer. The summer money had to last out the winter, and each summer she took in a little less. She was realist enough to hope that she could survive in this fashion until she died. She did not want to give up the house. Her life was in that house, all the remembered voices and gestures of love. Her only concession to her loneliness was a six-year-old television set, and she felt guilty every time she sat and watched it.

Two cabins were occupied on Sunday night. She had hoped for more. The single said he would leave too early for breakfast. The young couple said they'd like breafast at eight. And that was another dollar twenty.

Though she had great need of every bit of income, she

was careful about the tourists to whom she rented her cabins. Each night before going to bed she would go out and turn on the floodlight that shone directly on her sign, and take down the board that masked the legend, "Ring Night Bell for Service." A fat, red arrow pointed at the bell button set into the sign itself.

Her bedroom was in the front, overlooking the sign. The night bell rang in her room. Whenever it would ring, she was up and out of bed in an instant, and she would look out the window at them. They would be illuminated by the floodlight. She would watch them carefully for the look of drink, the staggering and the loud voices. And she would be wary of the too-young giggling couples. When she did not like what she saw, she would fling open the window and yell down in that terrible voice that cut the night like a sword, "Closed. Go away. Go away." No one argued with a decision delivered with such finality.

On Monday morning, not long before dawn, the night bell awakened her. She stood at the window in her nightgown and looked down through the copper screening and saw a good-looking automobile parked near her sign, and a man standing quietly beside it. He turned and said something to someone in the car and she heard him answer, but could not hear what was said. He seemed respectably dressed, and she could read fatigue in his posture.

"Come to the front door of the house," she called. "I'll be down in one minute."

She put on her robe and went down. She turned on the bright overhead porch light and looked at him again before she unlatched the door. He was big young man, quite nice-looking.

She talked to him in the hall and he told her what he wanted and she named the price, and she took him into the parlor and had him sit at the old breakfront desk and write the names in the book. He did not want to look at the cabins first. She assured him they were cleaned and equipped. She told him to take the last two on the right as you stood facing the row of them, and please be careful about noise because folks were sleeping. She asked him when they'd be leaving, and he said he didn't know, but somewhere around the end of the day.

After she had walked him to the door and waited until the car drove out to the cabins, the lights touching the trunks of the big elms in the yard, she walked back into the parlor with the ten-dollar bill in her hand and looked at the names he had signed in the book, Mr. and Mrs. J. D. Smith. Mr. W. J. Thompson, Mr. H. Johnson. All of Pittsburg.

She stood with her lips compressed, sensing a wrongness that she could not identify. The young man had been very tired. And yet he had seemed to feel the need to force himself to be quite jolly. He had laughed a few times at nothing at all, an empty, social laugh. She remembered that it was exactly the way Ralph used to laugh when his conscience bothered him. The young man's hands had been quite dirty, and that did not fit the rest of his appearance, or the cultivated sound of his voice. And his hands had trembled as he had written in the book. The writing was shaky. And they were such terribly ordinary names. But lots of people had ordinary names. That's what made them ordinary, of course. And people with ordinary names could travel together. And it was a nice-looking car.

She shrugged away her feeling that something was wrong, and went back to her bed. She was up an hour later, and she was hanging the board that masked the night bell when the single drove out, a salesman who had stayed with her before. He waved and she waved back. The young couple appeared for breakfast at eight-thirty. She insisted they eat until they begged for mercy. She felt great satisfaction in sending them on their way with what probably the first decent breakfast they'd eaten in a year.

All the time she did her housework she was conscious of the car out there, the four people sleeping. They had parked the car between the two cabins, heading out. It was a brown-and-tan car, with double headlights, and the big front grill was a shiny frozen grin.

It always irritated her when people slept through the day, even when she was perfectly aware they had driven all night. There was something obscurely wicked about daytime sleep. A body should be up and doing under God's sun. Even though their money was in the old brown purse hung way up in the back of the upstairs hall closet, she couldn't stifle her resentment, and several times she caught herself mumbling to herself as she did the day's chores, and told herself that talking to yourself was a sign of senility. She had planned to drive into York, but she didn't want to leave the place untended with people there. Tomorrow would be soon enough. As was her habit, she worked off her irritation by finding something she had been putting off. After her meager lunch she went out and scrubbed the whole length of the front porch on her hands and knees, and then scrubbed the porch railing, posts and all.

She heard the old water pump start up at a little after four and it pleased her to know those people were finally getting up. She remembered she hadn't spoke to the young man about breakfast. It was a funny time of day for breakfast, but if they could eat it, she could cook it, and you couldn't sneeze at another two dollars and forty cents. Before going to ask them, she went to the kitchen to make certain she had enough to feed four of them. Just enough eggs and more than enough of the corn bread, but the bacon would be skimpy. Two good melons, and oatmeal for those as wanted it, and use the middle-size coffeepot. That should do it just fine.

She took off her apron and hung it on the back of the kitchen door, gave her hair a few pats and went out the back way to walk back to the cabins. When she was twenty feet from the back stoop she heard the slamming of car doors and heard the motor start. She was walking along the driveway, and she began to hurry, adjusting a social smile of invitation.

As the car came toward her she returned its wide smile and held up her hand for them to stop.

The car made a much greater sound and it suddenly seemed to leap upon her. The awareness of death flashed bright and hot in her mind. She had the feeling that she stood frozen by terror for a very long time. In actuality she moved almost as nimbly as an athlete. She whirled and plunged to her left, diving rather than making the mistake of trying to run, diving so that both feet left the ground, her arms reaching forward to break her fall. Even so, the wide right edge of the bumper cracked her painfully on the right ankle bone, turning her slightly so that she landed in the softness of the grass on her right arm and shoulder with a jarring thud and rolled up and over onto her back, legs high and kicking.

She sat up, dazed. Over the years she had had to purchase ever stronger reading glasses, testing them at the counter of the five-and-ten in Lancaster. But her distance vision would have gratified a hawk. In the moment before her eyes filled with tears, blurring everything, she saw the car a hundred feet away, slowing for the turn onto the highway. She was too dazed to think of license numbers. She looked at their faces. A raggedy-headed girl with a mean, pouty look. A man so ugly he could get work in a cage at the carnival. A man driving, going bald, wearing glasses. A pointy-faced one he was, like an egg-sucking fox. She saw them vividly for one instant and then her eyes filled. The car was a shiny blob, turning onto the highway, heading toward Lancaster.

Close at hand she heard a red squirrel scolding her. Her eyes cleared. She saw him on a low, fat limb, staring down at her.

"Tried to kill me!" she told him. "Sure as I live and breathe."

The squirrel survived the first two syllables, before the sheer volume drove him back up into his hole, high in the tree.

Pearl Weaver stood up very slowly, testing every muscle. Her shoulder was wrenched, her right arm numbed. Her right ankle was beginning to puff, and it hurt to put weight on it, but not too much. She hobbled toward the house, and her thinking was still not clear.

"Ready to say something about breakfast and they run you down," she grumbled.

She went into the palor and sat in the big leather chair. It had always been and would always be Ralph's chair, and she would never sit in it without feeling she used it on sufferance.

"Why?" she demanded of the fringed lamp, the pottery cats on the mantel, the floral wallpaper. "Why?" she asked the imitation Oriental rug, the Boston rocker, the cataract eye of the silent television set. She had heard a whoop of shrill derision after she had jumped out of the way. "For fun?" She kept looking at the television set. "Or . . . didn't they want to be seen?"

Something stirred in the back of her mind. She'd followed it on television. A terrible thing! That poor girl. And they matched the words said about them, the descriptions, every one of them.

"Lord God Almighty!" she said, and she said it very softly. "They missed me," she said, "and they can come back for me and finish it."

She moved with desperate haste. She did not feel partially safe until she had all doors locked, and had Ralph's shotgun that she had always meant to sell and somehow never had, with a dark-green-and-brass shell in the single chamber, and the hammer back.

She had had the phone taken out six years ago. She waited for them to come back for a full fifteen minutes before deciding they were gone for good. And then she walked down the highway to the Brumbarger place nearly a half mile away, carrying the shotgun just in case. She was limping very badly by the time she got there, and her shoulder had begun to ache.

Two minutes after Pearl Weaver entered the Brumbarger home, a sergeant in the Pennsylvania State Police sat with a comedy look of consternation on his face, holding a phone almost at arm's length, while two men in the office chuckled. But suddenly the words began to get through to him. The dispatcher nailed the car nearest the area and sent it to the Brumbarger house on the double.

Fifty long minutes later, every entrance booth previously alerted had a new and specific piece of information to put with their previous emergency instructions. Look for a '58 or '59 Mercury, brown and tan, two- or four-door sedan, fog lamps, radio aerial, Pennsylvania plates, three men and a woman.

The old lady had been observant, and she was pleasingly positive.

Laughlintown, Pennsylvania, is not a unpleasant small town in the Laurel Hill area of the state, not too far from the 2684-foot summit of that range of not-quite mountains. No resident of Laughlintown could approach in the intensity of his disgust and dismay at having to live there, the strong emotions of Michael Bruce Hallowell. That was not his official name. He was registered in the local high school as Carl Lartch. He was certain that this summer, between his sophomore and junior years, was fraught with more misery than one spirit could safely contain.

In the confidential records maintained on him in the high-school files he was recorded as being highly intelligent, imaginative, a poor organizer, poorly adjusted socially, no athletic ability, inclined to be argumentative and sarcastic. Dedicated teachers considered this limp, spindly, myopic gangling, acned, large-headed, unorganized child a challenge. The journeyman teacher was delighted to pass him through the course and be rid of him. His more muscular contemporaries believed they could make of him a more socially desirable citizen by beating him on the head at every opportunity. But they could never whip him past the point where he could still wipe his bloody mouth and in iciest contempt call them peasants.

His two sisters thought of him as an almost unendurable social handicap. His parents were baffled by him.

Carl Lartch was not confused at all. He had read his way through better than half the books in the Laughlintown library. The world of the books was infinitely more satisfying than the world around him. He kept a private secret journal and wrote his opinions and impressions in it, comfortably aware of the danger that, should it ever be made public in his home town, the reaction would be murderous. A recent exposure to early Mencken had solidified his contempt for the booboisie. His was total confidence that one day the people of Laughlintown would be astonished that such a man could have once lived among them, and so gratified even his continuing contempt for them would be a welcome recognition of the place of his birth.

On this particular summer Carl had learned that books could be made even more enjoyable if devoured far from the foolish clatter of mankind, and so on every day when the weather was favorable, he would load books, his private journal, his peanut butter sandwiches and his Thermos of milk into the basket on the front of his bike and pump his way up into the hills.

On Monday morning, the twenty-seventh day of July, Carl pedaled up the long slopes of highway, panting audibly by the time he came to his turnoff, a sandy road that was wide and clear for a hundred yards before it faded away to an impassable track. As he rested, before hiding his bike in the brush, he noted that a car had turned around with some difficulty and gone back out, leaving the only set of fresh tracks since the last rain. He also saw a jumble of footprints. Picnickers or neckers, he thought. It was correct to assume their activities were trivial, whatever they were.

He hid his bike and, clasping his packaged possessions, went down the short, steep slope from the road to a fast, wide, noisy brook, crossed by stepping from stone to stone, and climbed the long hill beyond the brook until, winded once more, he came to his favorite place, level, grassy, shaded by old trees. From there he could see for miles but it was a view undefiled by man, consisting of only the gentle contours of the uncontaminated hills.

He spent the long summer day in reading, writing and peaceful contemplation. When he was finally warned by the angle of the sun, he gathered up his things, took a look at his private landscape, and trudged back down to the creek. His view was obscured by the brush that grew on the hillside. Sometimes he angled to avoid especially steep places. Consequently he came out at the creek at least thirty yards downstream from where he had crossed in the morning.

As he crossed the creek he noticed something out of the

corner of his eye, not far away. He turned and saw, sprawled against the small round boulders at the water's edge, the silent, lovely symmetry of a woman's legs, a soiled white skirt wrenched upward to mid-thigh, a quiet curve of back in close-fitting green, a hand stubbed cruelly against a boulder, wedged there by her weight. The face was hidden, but the water, moving with chill insistence around a small pebbled curve, tugged with endless persistence at a floating strand of blond hair.

He stared, then burst up the abrupt bank in front of him, running wildly toward the hidden bicycle. But as he ran he began to realize that his reactions were not suitable to a Villon, a Mencken, a Christopher Fry. Detachment was the epic quality of his whole galaxy of heroes. And so he stopped and turned and went slowly back to the woman and knelt there for a moment, studying her closely. He then reclimbed the bank and began to saunter toward home. After he had reached the highway, he remembered his bicycle. Once he had retrieved the bicycle, the empty basket reminded him of his books. By retracing his steps he found them beside the creek.

He was able to coast a good part of the way to Laughlintown. He went directly to the police station and strolled in.

"I should like to report something," he said haughtily to a bored shirtsleeved man working at a scarred desk, typing a report with two fingers.

The officer looked at him with growing distaste. "Report what, kid?"

"Perhaps twenty minutes ago I found the body of a woman up in the hills. She's either dead or seriously injured. She's blond, barefoot, possibly in her twenties, wearing a white skirt and a green blouse. From tracks on a sand road near where she's lying, I'd say she's been there since last night."

After a few moments of astonishment, the officer jumped to his feet and said, "Tell me exactly where you saw this woman, kid!"

"We could be there before I could possibly explain to you

how to get there. So why don't you get a doctor and an ambulance and more officers if you need them, and I'll ride in the lead vehicle and show you the way."

"If this is some kind of a gag . . ."

Carl said icily, "If I enjoyed jokes, I'd think up better ones than this."

It went well because it was handled by experts, and because the plan was flexibile, imaginative and airtight. And there had been advance warning from so high a place that it was taken seriously.

The instructions from the control centers were monitored and recorded, and so this particular pickup was sufficiently well documented to become a classic—written up in the mass magazines, and used as a case study in the police schools.

When a pickup is badly handled, it becomes a bloody, dramatic, unorganized thing. Where it is done properly, it can happen so quietly that people ten feet away are unaware of it.

This pickup presented a unique problem. A high-speed, high-density, limited-access highway is no place for heroics with sirens. A car can't be forced over onto the shoulder without the risk of a gigantic pile-up. A chase could result in heavy casualties among the innocents on vacation. And so it was decided that it had to be a stalk, a stalk so discreet that the prey would be lulled into a place where they could be taken quietly. It could be assumed that if it was fumbled, their desperation could result in explosive violence. And it was assumed the vehicle was a rolling arsenal. There can be no room for optimism in such an operation.

At 5:22 the target car entered the Pennsylvania Turnpike at Station 22 at Morgantown. The attendant phoned the nearest control center immediately and reported the license number. It checked out as a car reported stolen in the Pittsburgh area Sunday night. As any law enforcement agency will confirm, plate numbers and descriptions of stolen cars are constantly circulated, but they are next to useless in apprehending car thieves. The volume is just too great. A very few patrol officers with excellent memories make a hobby of constantly checking for stolen vehicles as a way of combating the boredom of patrol, but generally speaking, if a stolen car is operated in a legal manner by a person who does not excite suspicion, apprehension is exceedingly rare. Routine checks of operators' licenses, arrest due to traffic violations, and abandonment of the vehicle are the usual channels through which recovery is made.

In this instance the check of the license against the latest theft list was an additional confirmation of the identity of the vehicle.

As soon as word was received that the vehicle was on the pike, an all-points alarm was sent, and the nearest vehicles were diverted to the priority target. During the twenty miles and twenty minutes it took the target vehicle to reach the Valley Forge area, the pattern of the stalk had been established. An unmarked vehicle containing two officers had caught up at high speed, slowed, and drifted close enough to confirm the identification, and had then dropped inconspicuously back into position four hundred yards behind the Mercury. A standard patrol car followed approximately a mile behind the unmarked car. As quickly as possible other patrol cars were stationed at the exits ahead, one at each exit, each one in contact with the unmarked car tailing the target vehicle.

The procedure to be followed should the target vehicle attempt to leave the turnpike had been established. It would move over to the exit lane. The unmarked car would increase speed so as to exit immediately behind it. The patrol car a mile back would be alerted and would increase speed also, so as to exit as close as possible without creating alarm. The patrol car waiting outside the gates would be alerted. As soon as the target car had committed itself to one particular exit, the waiting car would move across the front of it and block it. The attendant would drop to the floor of the booth. The unmarked car would block any attempt to back away. The rear car would plug traffic at the exit ramp to keep the public away from the party.

Though it was not anticipated that the target vehicle would leave the pike until much later, this eventuality had to be covered with great care.

Pursuers and pursued rolled at a steady sixty miles an hour through the hot late afternoon toward the shadows of dusk gathering far to the east. Other vehicles moved steadily along with them, vacationers, salesmen, people heading for an evening in Philadelphia. A few cars caught up with them and moved slowly by, made cautious by the patrol car to the rear which they had recently edged by, eyes flicking back and forth from the highway to the speedometer.

At Central Control men watched the big electric map and talked in low tones. It was particularly important that there should be no news break. The Mercury had a radio. So far the lid had been kept on. And any news break which hinted at what was going on would bring a thousand idiots in their cars onto the pike, hoping to see blood.

The tanned young man is driving. Eyeglasses is in front beside him. Hernandez and the girl are in back. The girl seems to be asleep. It is a four-door vehicle.

The group of men made an executive decision. They checked with the New Jersey Turnpike. The interchange between pikes was an inefficient and potentially dangerous place to try to take them. The same tail car would follow. The Jersey people said they would be all ready and waiting by the time the guest arrived. The tail car was informed.

At 6:35 the target vehicle transferred at the interchange to the New Jersey Turnpike. The remote tail dropped off and a new patrol car picked up its function. It contained three officers, and heavier armament.

The break came at 7:18 when the Mercury slowed, moved over to the exit lane and entered the service area. With the unmarked tail car a hundred feet behind, it moved past the parking lot and the Howard Johnson's to the banks of gas pumps.

The tail car reported. Control said, "Can you take them there?"

"It isn't too good. Lots of cars at the pumps. Kids running around, but . . . hold it! The driver got out and the one with glasses is behind the wheel. The one who got out is pointing over toward the waiting area beyond the pumps. Looks like they'll park it here. Now it looks good."

"You got Car 33 with you, and we can back you up with 17 in . . . four minutes, and 28 in six minutes."

"Put 17 down there ahead on the grass, ready to plug access back onto the pike just in case. We'll take the driver right now."

Kirby Stassen went first to the men's room, from there to the cigarette machine, from there to the crowded order counter for take-outs where, when his turn came, he ordered four hamburgers and four coffees to go. When they were ready, the girl put them on the cardboard tray and put it on the counter. As Stassen reached out with both hands to pick it up, a big hand reached from the left and another from the right, and the cuffs snapped down snugly, with metallic efficiency, onto his wrists. He tensed for a moment, looking neither to left nor to right, staring incredulously at his wrists, then let all the air out of his lungs in a long, gentle sigh. The men who held the ends of the two sets of cuffs yanked his arms down to his sides. The few people who saw it gasped and murmured.

They walked him to the manager's office, searched him roughly and thoroughly, handcuffed his wrists behind him and left him there under the cold eye of an enormous trooper in uniform.

When Nanette Koslov came clacking out of the women's room in her slacks and high heels, hips swinging loosely, sullen hair bouncing against the nape of her neck, two large men moved in from the side and grabbed her, each one clamping one hand on her wrist and the other on her upper arm. Her scream silenced all the clatter. With her eyes gone mad, with foam at the corners of her mouth, she bucked and spasmed with such strength that the two strong men could barely hold her, and one of them, twisted off balance, went down to one knee. But they gained control, and half ran her into the private office. They held her arms straight out while the dining-room hostess, agreeable to this extra duty, searched her, found the knife, placed it on the corner of the desk. Nanette Koslov was still taut, waiting, savage as an animal, so they cuffed her by wrists and ankles to a heavy office chair.

Hernandez and Golden waited in the car. It was too far away from the main building for them to have heard Nan's animal screamings. The long minutes passed. Golden got out of the car and stared toward the building. The dying sun glinted orange against the lenses of his glasses. He shrugged and started toward the building at a half trot. A man who had been stooped low, came angling out from behind a parked car at a dead run. Before joining the State Police he'd had three pro seasons with the Steelers. It was like hitting a rag doll with a hurtling sack of bricks. Golden went out and stayed out for twenty minutes. The glasses skittered forty feet across the asphalt without breaking. When the ex-defensive guard was halfway to his target, a man who had crawled into position suddenly rose up and filled the open window beside Hernandez with his big shoulders, his face wearing an expression of hard joy, rock-steady hand aiming the barrel of the .38 at the center of Hernandez' face.

"Just move a little bit," the officer pleaded in a half-whisper. "Move a finger, an eyeball. Move anything."

Hernandez sat like a statue. A man opened the other door and got in. The wrists were so large the handcuffs were set at the last notch. After they got him out of the car, lumbering, docile, dazed, they found, wedged into the seat, a .45 Colt automatic pistol, army issue, with a full clip and a round in the chamber. It later proved to have been in the glove compartment of the stolen vehicle.

They were loaded in patrol cars and taken off the turnpike, jailed on suspicion of murder, printed, photographed, identified, given prison issue denim, and locked in isolation cells.

The finding of Helen Wister had been on the radio and television newscasts since seven. That story was vastly fattened by news of the capture released in time to hit the nine o'clock news.

The Stassens would have had the news before nine, had they been home. They were at a large cocktail and buffet dinner party. At nine they were just beginning to eat. Somebody turned on the television set. It was ignored until somebody yelled, "Hey! *Listen* to this!"

They listened. Ernie Stassen had a five-martini edge. She put her plate down with great care and went over and turned the set off, and turned and looked at all the other guests. She wore a curious smile. The room was very silent. "That's all nonsense, of course," she said in a high, flat voice. She laughed like a windup machine. "It's a ridiculous mistake." Walter got his wife by the arm and got her out of there. All the way out she talked about the mistake in her high, wild voice. When they got home the reporters were there, waiting for them, and it had just started to rain.

Millions heard the news and were gratified the four had been taken. Thousands realized they had been on the turnpikes at the same time. They told their friends, and had a sense of having participated in something historic. After the detailed account was published, hundreds upon hundreds changed their stories, a little bit at a time, until at last they were able to convince others as well as themselves that they had seen it all, that they had been in grave danger, that they had held themselves in readiness to assist if there had been any slip. Every big news story creates throngs of imaginary heroes.

At Basset, Nebraska, reporters did not arrive at the Koslov farm until the following morning. Anton Koslov in his muddy barking accent had one statement to make. His daughter, Nanette, was dead. She had been dead long time. No more talk about Nanette. Go away.

One San Francisco reporter, familiar with the nether world where Nanette had lived, dug up a few anecdotes about her which he cleaned up enough to be usable, and tracked down some eight-by-ten glossies from her days of offhand modeling. One of those pictures, after the addition, by air brush, of halter and shorts, became the picture most often reproduced across the country.

In several score cellar apartments, cold-water flats and coffee houses, the acquaintances of Sander Golden gathered and marveled at his unexpected notoriety. They said it wasn't like him. They said he was a mild and amusing type, a no-talent type with an erratic intelligence.

One freckled little poet with red handlebar mustachios did remember a time in New Orleans when Sandy Golden had been less than mild. "He was splitting a back alley pad on Bourbon, way over, with Seffani, the bongo man that killed himself a year ago, remember? and one night they're like dead, man, and Seffani's chick, a large one with runty little brown teeth she felt were killing her career, she strips them clean of bread and goes has her teeth capped pearly white, so a month later she's in Kibby's back room, loaded with horse up to here, snoring a storm, and Sandy went out, came back with pliers from someplace and he uncapped that big chick. That Golden could come out mean, man. Bear it in mind."

The story had been sagging. The papers had been fighting to keep it alive. And suddenly they were rich. They'd had their fun with Hernandez, and now they had three new identities to pry apart. New backgrounds to search. They had a Rich Boy—Only Son, and they had a green-eyed Refugee—Ex-Model, and they had an honest-to-God Beatnik who was the Brains of the Wolf Pack Rampage.

They kept it dancing for a week, and then it finally died, falling off the bottom of page 16. But it wasn't death. Only a coma. The trial would play big, bigger than all that had gone before. When the trial came along, they were all ready. And it fed an estimated one million dollars into the economy of the city of Monroe.

T W E L V E

I DEATH HOUSE DIARY

have torn up too much of this. I become too mystic and esoteric. So I had to tear it up and I have lost too much time.

It is going to happen TOMORROW. That's the biggest word in the world. It's hung on the back wall of my mind, flashing off and on. I didn't sleep at all last night. If I can manage it, I'll stay awake all night tonight too. I sense exhaustion may have certain morale benefits.

The human brain, facing extinction, is an illogical organism. It goes around and around the cage, checking every crack and corner. It refuses on some very primitive level to accept tht fact that TOMORROW it is going to be turned off like a light in the attic. It is really and truly going to happen. Nothing can stop it. I must endure a brief ceremonial procession, seat myself in the ugly throne, suffer a few mechanical ministrations, then brace and wait for that special usage of what Mr. Franklin gathered on his kite string. Manmade lightning this time, focused for maximum efficiency. At times I can think of it as though I were going to be an observer, calm and curious about it all. The next moment I remember it will be Me, invaluable, irreplaceable Me, and the sour edge of nausea pushes upward into my throat. I flex my right hand and study it with great care. It is a wonderful, intricate tool, strong, flexible, healthy, self-mending. It has another fifty years of use in it. It seems an inconceivable madness, a grotesque waste, to turn it into cold, dead meat. My eyes move with oiled ease, focusing with an instantaneous precision. What is their guilt, that they should be glazed into eternal stillness?

Flaccid within the trousers of prison twill lies the reproductive sack, obscurely comic, no further anxious labors to perform. The sperm lie sleeping in hidden warmth, remote from any egg, unaware of the imminence of their death and mine. Where is their guilt? Who can tell that one of them might not have created greatness?

In some more sensible world all this innocence will be saved. There will be a table, I expect, and cleverly directed streams of electrons, and careful technicians at work. Guilt, identity, memory—all these will be destroyed. But the blameless body will be saved, and a new identity, a new memory, built into the brain. It will be a kind of death of course, but without all this clumsiness, which is like burning down a house where sickness has occurred.

I am very aware of another thing—and I suppose this is a very ordinary thing for all those condemned—and that is a kind of yearning for the things I will never do, a yearning with overtones of nostalgia. It is as though I can remember what it is like to be old and watch moonlight, and to hold children on my lap, and kiss the wife I have never met. It is a sadness in me. I want to apologize to her—I want to explain it to the children. I'm sorry. I'm never coming down the track of time to you. I was stopped along the way.

Yesterday I tore up page upon page of asinine generalizations about the condition of man. I know they are going to kill me TOMORROW.

I can say a few very obvious things, but I now know them

to be true. You cannot know yourself. No man can know himself. No man can detect or define the purpose of his own existence, but it is the dull man who ceases all conjecture.

And there is this, too. We all—every one of us—walk very close to the shadows, to strange dark places, every day of our lives. No man stands in a perfectly safe place. So it is dangerously smug to say, I am immune. No one can tell when some slight chance, some random thing, may turn him slightly, just enough so that he will find that he is no longer in a safe place, and he had begun to walk into the shadows, toward unknown things that are always there, waiting to eat him.

Sandy drove circumspectly through Monroe that long-ago night, and it wasn't until after he had turned off onto Route 813 that he began to make time again. Speed felt good. I wanted to get far away from many things. I wanted to put a lot of space and a lot of time between me and Kathy. And the salesman. And Nashville.

The world kept changing for us, moving faster toward some unknown climax. I kept trying not to think backward or forward, but to focus only on the moment after moment of actual existence. I could not think of what the end of it would be. It was too late to think of any return to normalcy. I begged more pills from Sandy. It put you way out where nothing bad could ever happen. All your senses were sharpened. You were with the best three people in the world, acquiring stories you could tell when you were an old, old man. It was like being fifteen again, after three cans of beer, eight of you in one car, rocketing home from the beach through the vacation night.

After Sandy banged the brakes on and we came swerving to a stop, the wonderful tableau in front of the headlights, centered in the white glare, was like outdoor theater.

At first the man thought we were going to help, and it is even possible we would have helped had he reacted differently. It was all balanced on the edge of impulse. We had no plan. Everything was improvised. The man—he was tough and husky and scared sick about the girl—pushed it just far enough in the wrong direction, and in a little while, as soon as he and Shack started belting each other, I knew we would kill him. That's the way things were moving for us. It had become, perhaps in the instant the salesman died, a twisted kind of togetherness. Nan had the greatest need of it. It was a kick that shook her, so that her need had become geometric in its increase, a savage and necessary release for her. Sandy had begun to go the same way, but he was not so far along as Nan. But there was that need in both of them, and suddenly you could sense it. I cannot make any guess about Hernandez. He had only his normal brutish violence, without the emotional-sexual implications. I am not certain about myself. I knew I was one of them. I knew we would kill him. I wanted to be a part of it, but I think that it was partially a desire to put something in on the stack of memory, on top of Nashville.

Had there been more of it later on, I could have gotten onto the same kick-track as Nan and Sandy, possibly. But my need was related all the way back to Kathy in some way that made killing symbolic. I needed to help this man become dead because Kathy was dead. It makes no sense. But it is as close as I can come.

After I had moved in on him, he hit me so solidly just under the ear that the sky spun, my eyes ran and my knees were jellied. It was good to be hit so hard. It called for extra effort. It provided a certain amount of excuse. And I was in it, a part of it, my identity, submerged into the group until, like awakening from a dream, I saw Nan working that knife into him, and saw her face, and it was like looking down into the lowest pit of hell. Blood looked black on her fist and wrist. I raised my foot, put it against his hip, and shoved the body off the back slant of the car into the ditch to get it away from her. She stood, shaking all over, the breath gasping out of her, then stooped to wipe the blade and her hand on the grass of the ditch bank.

The girl was sitting up. She was beautiful.

"The little lady has drawn the lucky number and won the moonlight tour. Bring her along," Sandy said.

I stepped in ahead of Shack. Nan and I got her onto her

feet. She was dazed and docile. In the headlights I saw a lump over her right ear, the blond hair bloody and matted. We got her into the back, in the middle, on my left, between Nan and me. Shack was in front, crouched over, counting the dead man's money by the light of the dash panel.

"We're rich!" Sandy crowed when Shack gave him the total.

My knees still felt trembly. The blow I had taken had given me a headache. The knuckles of my right fist were puffy and tender. I was very conscious of the girl beside me, sitting perfectly still.

"One less flannelhead in the world," Sandy said.

"I thought you loved them all, every one," I said.

"I do, I do, dear boy. God loves them too. He made so many of them. Nan, darling, turn around and keep your creepy little face in that back window. Our new lovely darling will be missed by somebody. I want to pile up those fine, fat miles tonight. Bleat if you see lights moving up on us, Nano."

"Why the hell did we bring her?" Nan demanded.

"Chivalry, dear. Old-fashioned, warmhearted chivalry. She had no transportation and no escort. What else could I do?"

"We need more women," Shack said.

The girl spoke then. "I want to go home, please," she said politely. It was a very small, clear, childish voice. I knew I had heard a voice just like that before, and it took me a few moments to remember that it had been at a party where one of those ubiquitous amateur hypnotists found that my date was a very good subject. So he had "regressed" her back to, I believe, the third grade in school. And she had spoken in this same childish voice.

A car passed us, going in the opposite direction, and for a moment I could see her face in the headlights. She was looking at me gravely and politely, but I had the impression she was close to little-girl tears.

"What's your name, dear?" I asked her.

"Helen Wister."

"How old are you, Helen?"

"What?"

"How old are you?"

"I'm—almost nine."

Sandy gave a whoop of laughter and Shack said, "That's the biggest goddam nine-year-old broad I ever . . ."

"Shut up!" I told them. "She's hurt. You can get one hell of a case of amnesia from a blow on the head."

"My head hurts and I want to go home, please," she said.

"This is spooky," Nan announced. "I don't like it."

"She could have a pretty bad brain injury, Sandy," I said.

"Now wouldn't *that* be a dirty shame!"

"Hell, what good is she to you? We could dump her in one of these small towns."

"Very interesting," Sandy said. "The stratification of society at work. She comes from his own class. He recognizes that at once. So all of a sudden she's a sister. What's she done, Kirboo? Touched your heart?"

"Well, what *are* you going to do with her?"

"I'll clue you, Samaritan. We keep her aboard. If she gets worse, we'll dump her, but not in any town, man. If she stays the same or gets better, she's for fun and games. Right Shack?"

"Fun and games, Sandy. You're the boss," Shack said.

"*Please* take me home!" Helen begged.

"We are taking you home, dear," I told her. "It's a long way."

"How long?"

"Oh, hours and hours. Why don't you take a nap, Helen? Here." I put my arm around her, pulled her head onto my shoulder.

"Jesus K. Christ!" Nan said.

"Jealous?" Sandy asked.

"Of a washed-out blonde with the crazies? Hell, no!"

The child-woman snuggled closer. She sighed heavily a few times. As quickly as any child, she slid away into sleep.

We moved swiftly through the night in a whirring silence and then Sandy began, "Fee fie fiddly-I-oh, fee fie fiddly-I-oh, oh, oh, oh."

She wore a woman's perfume. Her hair tickled my neck. My left arm went to sleep, but I did not want to disturb her. Shack got out the gin bottle. He and Nan were the only ones who wanted any.

We were trapped, all of us, in that small, drumming place. We were united, like survivors of catastrophe, floating down a river on a roof. No matter what happened, it was going to happen to all of us.

Nan suddenly said, "Remember Louie? Remember Louie, Sandy? In Dago?" There was a forced gaiety in her voice. It was a device she often used, this abrupt recollection of things shared, establishing hers as the closest relationship to Sandy.

"I remember that cat," he said.

"It was fun, Sandy."

"It was the greatest," he said in a tone of boredom.

The girl circled in my arm was clean and fresh, and her sleeping breath was humid against the base of my throat. Something stirred in me in response to her helplessness, and yet at the same time I resented her. I had seen too damn many of these brisk and shining girls, so lovely, so gracious, and so inflexibly ambitious. They had counted their stock in trade and burnished it and spread it right out there on the counter. It was all yours for the asking. All you had to do was give her all the rest of your life, and come through with the backyard pool, cookouts, Eames chairs, mortgage, picture windows, two cars, and all the rest of the setting they required for themselves. These gorgeous girls, with steel behind their eyes, were the highest paid whores in the history of the world. All they offered was their poised, half-educated selves, one hundred and twenty pounds of healthy, unblemished, arrogant meat, in return for the eventual occupational ulcer, the suburban coronary. Nor did they bother to sweeten the bargain with their virginity. Before you could, in your hypnoid state, slip the ring on her imperious finger, that old-fashioned prize was long gone, and even its departure celebrated many times, on house parties and ski weekends, in becalmed sailboats and on cruise ships. This acknowledged and excused promiscuity was, in fact, to her advantage. Having learned her way through the jungly province of sex, she was less likely to be bedazzled by body hunger to the extent that she might make a bad match with an unpromising young man. Her decks were efficiently cleared, guns rolled out, fuses alight, cannonballs stacked, all sails set. She stood on the bridge, braced and ready, scanning the horizon with eyes as cold as winter pebbles.

One of these invincible ones slept against me, all weapons discarded for a time. I found her left hand, found her ring finger, felt the small, cool angles of the engagement stone. I wondered about her prey. I sensed that it was not the husky type we'd left dead in the ditch. No, this was one of the very special ones, so she would have had a large choice of game like a hunter in a game preserve. So she had probably knocked down a trophy head, one who combined most of the advantages the girls of this station sought. He would be amiable, polite, well-educated, tall and "interesting-looking." He would be witty, but not in any acid way that might inhibit their social life. He would be gregarious without being a jolly-boy full of life-of-the-party routines, because that is in bad taste. He would have that quiet drive, that unobvious ambition, which would take him high and far. His occupation would give them good social status, so he would be in one of the professions most probably, or might be a junior executive type with a very reliable corporation. And, with all her tools and weapons, she would now have him noosed so firmly his eyes would be bulging. He would be so far gone he would be willing to trade his immortal soul for permanent legal uninterrupted access to her expensive panties.

Not for me, I thought. I shall never be suckered by that cold-hearted routine. And I suddenly realized that I had gone well beyond the point of choice. Even if I changed my mind and decided to fall in step with everybody else, it was now too late. Only in the animated cartoons could a small creature fall off a moutain, look down, register surprise, and climb back up through the empty air to safety.

She woke twice during the long night ride and each time

she complained in a sleepy child voice about wanting to be home in her own bed.

Sandy found the place we would stay, shabby dusty cottages at a resort area called Seven Mile Lake. He had a special genius for picking safe places. It was good to hole up. He'd had the radio on a few times, and it sounded as if the whole world was looking for us. The radio told us we had grabbed the daughter of a wealthy surgeon, and she had been planning to marry an architect. We learned for the first time how two witnesses had watched us kill the man. We found out his name was Arnold Crown, and that he had owned a service station. The world told us that we were despicable, heartless monsters, crazed by drugs, on a cross-country slay-fest.

We could not identify ourselves with the people they were describing. Sandy put it in words when he said. "They shouldn't oughta let people like that run around loose."

It broke us up.

I had no trouble with the slob woman who rented me the cottage. All she had eyes for was the twenty-five dollars. We got our stuff out of the car trunk and went in and turned some lights on. The bedrooms were off either side of the small sitting room. Nan escorted Helen to the bathroom, with Sandy warning her not to try anything cute with the blond. Sandy and I sat on a sagging couch, leaning back, our heels on a coffee table. Shack stood with the gin bottle and tilted it high, heavy throat pulsing. He lowered it and looked at Sandy. The tension was there, and it was building, and it made the pit of my stomach crawl. Shack's eyes were small, bright, hooded, vulgar—with long lashes, reminding me of the eyes of an elephant.

"How about it, Sandy? How about it?" he asked.

"Shut up a while," Sandy told him.

"Sure, Sandy. Sure thing."

Nan brought Helen back. Gray was coming in the windows, feebling the lights we'd turned on. There is a way a woman stands, and there is a way a child stands. Helen stood, toeing in slightly, chewing the first knuckle of her right hand, plucking at the side of her skirt with the other hand, regarding us solemnly. The look of her made the look of her breasts incongruous, so round against the green of her sleeveless blouse. Her diamond caught the light, refracting sharp glints of color. Her white skirt was of the material I believe is called dacron fleece. It had two high slash pockets, with a large green non-functional button on each pocket. Her green shoes were very pointed, with those tall, spidery heels, tipped with brass.

"Sit down, honey," Sandy told her. "Join the group." She sat in a wicker chair, plumping herself down as a child does.

"Be a good girl or you'll get a spanking," Sandy said.

Nan sat in another chair and pulled her legs up into the chair and watched the scene with a dark and sulky amusement.

Shack moved restlessly, nervously, lifting his knees curiously as he walked, fists balled, face dark and sweating, neck bowed. "How *about* it, Sandy?" he begged.

I suddenly remembered what he reminded me of. Long ago in a summer camp in Vermont, three of us sneaked away to watch a farmer breed a mare. When we got there, breathless after a long run down the country road, the stallion was in a corral beside the barn. The mare was in the barn, in a box stall. The stallion was pacing back and forth as close to the barn as he could get, ears back, nostrils distended, whinnying and blowing. From time to time he would trot in a curious compact way, lifting his knees high, bowing his neck. I learned much later that this is one of the basic steps of that art of horsemanship known as dressage.

They wouldn't let us into the barn. But we waited and we heard the stomping of hoofs and the men yelling excited instructions to each other, and the whistling, triumphant scream of the stallion.

"Jesus Christ, Sandy!" Shack said with growing indignation.

"Shut up, monster," Sandy said. He turned toward me, his blue eyes dancing bright with malicious curiosity. "You had a lot to say in Del Rio, boy. You said you'd come to the end of all crud. You said emotion was something you could do without from here on in. You said nothing meant a damn to you, and nothing ever would. Remember?"

"Certainly I remember."

"No sentiment, boy. But Nashville gave you the jumps."

"Did it?"

"Maybe you're a faker, college boy." It was the last time he ever called me that.

"How so?"

"You're just playing a game with yourself, maybe. And inside you're still loaded with crud."

"All this talk talk, for God's sake!" Shack said.

"I don't know what you're saying, Sandy," I said, but I knew which way he was going, and what he was doing, and I didn't know if I could take it. I just didn't know.

"Let's kick over a baby carriage, and see if you're kidding yourself. All you got to do is say the word, Kirboo, and we can stop it right there. Okay, Shack. Put the baby to bed."

Shack grinned like a shark and whirled toward the girl. "Come on, baby. Come *on!*" he said.

She looked at him with a childish dubiousness and distaste. He took her by the wrist and pulled her up out of the chair. She tried to pull away from him, her mouth beginning to make the shape of tears to come.

"Come *on,* doll," he said, his voice so thickened it was barely comprehensible, and spun her and got a thick arm around her waist, the heavy, hairy hand clamped on slenderness. He walked her with an almost grotesque tenderness toward the open door of the bedroom.

She tried to hang back, saying thinly, "I want to go home. Please, I want to go home."

I told myself that it didn't matter a damn to me. I told myself it was just an interesting play on beauty and the beast. I told myself that one more rape in the history of the world was hardly significant. I told myself that she was too dazed to have much knowledge of what was happening to her, and it was unlikely that she would remember any of it. I told myself that people were dying in agony as I sat there. I told myself that I had given up pity and sentiment and mercy. I'd stared at Kathy, gray and shrunken, pasted to the tile floor by her own cooling blood, and that had been the end of all mercy.

They had reached the doorway. Helen had begun to whine in the hopeless way of defeat and fear. Nan chuckled, and the sound of it sickened me.

"You win," I said to Sandy. "You win, brother."

He gave one yelping, derisive laugh and said, "No dice today, Shack. Break it off, monster. It's Kirboo's baby."

But, of course, it was too late. We should have known it was too late. Sandy had been testing that blind loyalty, putting an ever-increasing strain on it, always demanding, never giving. And so it snapped.

Shack thrust the girl into the room with such force that we saw her stumble, then heard her fall where we couldn't see her. He turned, filling the doorway, staring at Sander Golden and seeing a stranger.

"Go to hell!" he said thickly. "It's mine."

Sandy bounced to his feet and stepped over the coffee table. "You don't want me to be mad at you, Shack."

"Get back. Get back or I'll kill you, pal."

I got up and moved slowly, angling toward him, walking on the balls of my feet. He stood with his chin on his chest, eyes flicking back and forth from me to Sandy.

"You do what I tell you to do," Sandy said softly.

"That's over," Shack said. "No more of that."

And it was all going to blow up, right then and there, in ten thousand pieces. I edged toward the table lamp. The base looked heavy enough.

Nan said, "You damn fools!" and she went by me almost at a run, right at Shack, and for a moment I thought she had the knife in her hand, held low. But she flung her arms around his neck, pressing herself against him. "What do you want with somebody who don't know the score, honey?" she cooed at him.

He tried to pull her arms free, but they were strongly locked.

"Be nice to Nan cutie-pie," she murmured.

His face changed. She tugged him out of the doorway.

They went awkwardly across the room toward the other bedroom.

"What's going on here?" Sandy demanded.

"Close your face," Nan said sweetly, and they entered the other room and banged the door shut.

I went through the doorway. Helen was standing by the window staring at me, tears running down her face, shiny in the first pale light of day. As I closed the door from the inside, I looked out at Sandy. He spread his hands and shrugged as I closed the door and locked it. Nan had saved the group. I couldn't ask myself whether it was worth saving. Perhaps Helen was. You can go and go until you find the last limit of yourself, and there's no way to get beyond that.

I went toward her slowly, smiling to reassure her.

"He's gone, dear. He won't bother you any more."

"I'm scared of him. Why won't you take me home?"

"It's a long, long trip home, Helen. It's time to rest up now."

"Really?"

"Really and truly."

She tried a small smile, and wiped her eyes with the back of her hand. "All right, then."

"You better go to bed."

"I haven't got any nightie or anything."

"You better just stretch out, dear."

"Will you stay here?"

"I'll stay here. Yes."

"Okay, then." She crawled onto the bed closest to the window and stretched out and gave a great yawn and rubbed her eyes. "He knocked me down," she said in a little voice.

"It won't happen again. Go to sleep, honey."

I sat on the other bed, a few feet from her. She had turned toward me, her clasped palms under her cheek. I noticed something about her eyes. I knew that in the case of head injuries, one of the things they look at is the eyes. The pupil of her left eye was visibly larger than the pupil of the right one. I wondered what it meant, how dangerous a symptom it was.

Her eyes closed. Through the soles of my feet I could feel a faint vibration that shook the frame cottage. I could hear the muffled sounds of the mating of Shack Hernandez, a flapping, thudding sound as though some leathery animal had been caught in a trap and now, in a senseless panic, was killing itself with its struggles.

When her breathing was deeper and I knew she slept, I gently removed the woman-shoes from the tired, injured child. I sat near her and watched her sleep all that day, while the sun swung up and over us and down. I smoked cigarettes and dropped them on the cheap, shiny varnish and ground them out with the sole of my shoe. I had no desire for sleep. The stimulant drugs were making me use myself up.

Once, when she had turned, and one hand was free, I reached and took it on impulse, and her fingers tightened on mine. I wondered if sleep was good for a head injury. Several times I watched her closely to be certain she was breathing. Even with lipstick gone and her hair tousled, she was a beautiful woman, full of perfections that revealed themselves, one after another.

The long hours passed. Bright spots of sun came through the chinks of the blinds and moved across the floor, the bed, the girl. Outside the cottage I heard the sounds of summer vacation, the rasp of outboards on the lake, the squalling and shrieking of children, music too far away to be identified, men yelling commands, women yelping with jackal laughter. Serveral times people walked by, close to the window, and I heard mysterious pieces of conversation.

". . . so how d'ya like it, he comes back and he tells me it isn't twelve dollars any more, it's up to . . ."

". . . drawing forty a week from the union alla time he was on strike plus the unemployment . . ."

". . . I hope to hell she ain't gone already. Honest to Christ, Sammy, you never seen such a pair . . ."

And thrice more during the day the familiar animal was trapped and flapped its foolish life away.

I thought of my curious ambivalence, my schizoid attitude toward the sleeping girl, despising what she represented, yet feeling a protective tenderness which I would have thought impossible for me.

I did not want to think of what would happen to her.

I was standing purposelessly at the window, looking out through a crack in the blinds at a small slice of blue lake when I heard her make a slight sound, and heard the bed creak. I turned around. She was sitting up and looking at me. She had a puzzled look. Her eyes were clear and aware.

"Who are you?" she asked in a woman's voice.

I sat on the foot of the bed. She pulled her feet away and looked warily at me. "Back to arrogance," I said. "Back to imperious demands. Ring for the waiter, Helen."

"Are you trying to make sense?" she asked.

"You'd be very smart to keep your voice down, Helen. Very smart."

"But who are you? Where am I?" With gingerly fingertips she touched the place where her hair was black-matted with her blood. The swelling was not as great. "Was I in an accident?"

"Sort of an accident. You're somewhere in western Pennsylvania. Seven Mile Lake, if that means anything."

"It doesn't. Was I on a trip?"

"Keep the voice down, please."

"Why?"

"We'll get to that. Just accept the fact it's important."

She looked beyond me, frowning. "Wait a minute! They didn't want me to see Arnold, and I shouldn't have. He was completely mad. I couldn't communicate. When he started up, I jumped. I could feel myself falling . . ." She touched her head and winced again. "I did this then?"

"Yes."

She looked at a tiny gold watch. "Four in the afternoon?"

"Yes. You hit your head last night."

She stared at me with obvious anger. "My God, do I have to pry all this out of you bit by bit? What the hell am I doing in Pennsylvania?"

"You're kidnaped," I told her. It sounded ridiculously melo-dramatic.

"Do you mean that?" she asked me.

"Yes."

"You're asking my father for money?"

"No. It isn't that well organized, Helen. There aren't any special plans. You're just . . . kidnaped. We came along and you were knocked out, lying on the road. So we brought you along with us."

"You were drunk?"

"No."

"How many of you?"

"Four of us. One is a girl."

"What's your name, anyway?"

"That wouldn't be pertinent."

She sat, biting her lips, staring at me. I could tell that her mind was working, and I could sense that it was excellent equipment, agile and logical.

"Kidnaping is a very stupid idea. Don't you think you made a mistake?"

"It's possible."

"If it was just . . . a sort of joke, you could let me go, couldn't you? If you're not after money. I'd make sure you didn't get into any trouble. I'd say . . . I'd hitched a ride with you."

"The others wouldn't want to let you go, Helen."

"But they're not here. You could unhook the screen and let me out that window and tell them later that it was the smart thing to do. You do look and sound too bright for this sort of thing, really."

"You wheedle real well, Helen."

"Well, if you're not after money, what good has it done you to lug an unconscious girl around?"

"You weren't unconscious. You acted like a polite nine-year-old child."

"Are you telling me the truth?"

"It isn't the kind of thing you make up, is it?"

She stirred uneasily and her face got slightly red. "Did any of you do anything to me when I was like that?"

"Something came close to happening, but it didn't."

"Why can't you let me go?"

I looked directly into her eyes. "They wouldn't like it and it wouldn't be a good idea for me either. We killed Arnold Crown."

She closed her eyes. For long moments she had a pasty color. As the glow of health began to come back she opened her eyes again. "The way you said it, I believe you. But what a foul thing! Why did you do it?"

"That's a very good question."

She tensed suddenly and sucked her lips white, and her eyes went round. "Three men and a girl. Are you the ones . . ."

"We've had a lot of publicity lately, Helen."

That's when I expected her to fall apart, when the full realization of her situation became apparent to her.

To my surprise she forced a smile. "Then I'm in a hell of a spot. You people don't have anything to lose, do you?"

"That's the general idea."

"So it didn't make any difference whether you picked me up or left me on the road—whether you killed Arnold or didn't kill him."

"No difference at all."

"Is that what you're after? *That* kind of freedom?"

"Lectures I do not need, Miss Wister."

She frowned. "They know I'm missing?"

"I'd say eighty to a hundred million people know it."

"And they know . . . who has me?"

"Yes."

"What pure hell for my people. And Dal." She stared at me with obvious conjecture. "All right. I want to get out of this. Is there any chance at all?"

"Hardly any."

She closed her eyes again, but not for long. "So I'll be killed. For kicks. Isn't that the reason you people have?"

"We're expressing aggression and hostility, miss."

"What if it were up to you? You alone? It wouldn't happen then, would it?"

"You're judging a book by the cover."

"I'm asking you. Do you have any desire to help me? If you don't, I'll have to take any chance I can. It would be the same with me as it is with you—nothing to lose."

No tears, no begging, no hysterics. Yet a complete awareness of mortal danger. This was a woman. A woman in the same sense that the Spanish call a man *muy hombre*. A bright unquenchable spirit, the kind that won't break. Gallantry is a fitting word. You can't find many of those. I wondered if that architect knew what a wondrous thing he almost acquired.

I found another balk line across my soul, and knew I would help. I was becoming a veritable tower of virtue.

"Maybe I can help. *Maybe*. But you have to be a hell of an actress."

"I guess you can say I've got a hell of a motivation."

"We'll be leaving at dusk. You've got to be barely able to move. You've got to be semi-conscious. The head injury is getting worse. You're damn near in a coma, and going deeper all the time. You cannot let yourself respond to anything. Can you do that?"

"Yes, I can do that."

"When the time is right, I'll give you a signal of some kind, and then you have to start to die. We'll be rolling along in the car. I don't know how the hell to tell you to do it, but make it convincing. Then it'll be my problem to get you out of the car without injury. It's the only chance you have."

She thought it over. "Suppose, because of the way I act, they get careless and give me a good chance to make my run for it. Without high heels, I can run like the wind."

"It could be okay for you, but bad for them and bad for me. I'll watch so you don't get that chance to do it that way. It has to be my way."

"What if I started screaming this minute?"

"I'd knock you unconscious with my fist. And if you think you've picked a good time to start screaming when we're in the car the girl with us will have a knife into your heart at the first bleat."

"What are they like?" she asked me.

"You'll see."

"How did . . . someone like you get into such trouble?"

I smiled at her. "When I was a young girl I got raped by my uncle and ran away from home and I've been in this place ever since. You wanna buy me another drink before we go upstairs, Mr. Barlow?"

"You aren't what you look like, are you?"

"Not lately."

"But you were, once upon a time."

"I was?"

"Now it's the eyes, I think. That's the wrong part. They don't fit the rest. It's your eyes that give me . . . . a strange feeling."

"And your teeth are so big, Grandma."

"Please, please help me," she said.

"I told you I'm going to."

"It would be such a crummy stupid way to die."

I heard somebody stirring around at dusk. Then I heard Nan's voice. Somebody rapped on the door. I unlocked the door and opened it, after signaling Helen to lie back. Sandy looked in and said, "Kiss her awake, sweet prince."

"She doesn't seem to want to wake up."

"Get her up, man!" I looked at him in astonishment. He had snapped the order, but with an obvious uncertainty. He was a little man, posturing, posing, trying to regain lost authority. Last night he had been relieved of command. No matter how hard he strained, he couldn't get it back. And I suspected that the same thing had happened in all the other groups he had joined during his lifetime. With all his brisk energies Sandy would run things for a little while. Until finally he was pushed and he backed down. And then he would become the group clown. Good old Sandy. He's a gasser.

I shrugged and went over and shook Helen. She simulated a return of semi-consciousness. I got her up into a sitting position and slipped her shoes onto her slack feet. She mumbled incoherencies. I pulled her up onto her feet and, half supporting her, walked her out into the sitting room.

"Bad shape?" Sandy asked.

"She doesn't seem any better to me."

Nan took her and guided her into the bathroom. As they passed Shack he reached out and gave Helen a massive, fullhanded pinch on the buttock and winked at me with relaxed, expansive good cheer. "You made it good, doc?" he asked me. He had never been as friendly.

Nan, supporting Helen, looked back over her shoulder at him and pulled her lip up away from her teeth. "Good like you made it, you ox bastard?"

But there was no real rancor in her voice, and Sandy should have sensed that. He said, "I'll keep the monster tied up so he can't get to you again, darlin' Nano."

"Go chew a pill, you sick spook!" she snapped.

Shack gave a roar of laughter and clapped Sandy on the back. Sandy's glasses jumped off his nose and swung by one earpiece.

"She found herself a man," Shack said proudly. "She made a switch. You and Stassen split the blonde, Sandy."

"Don't bang my back, you goddam oaf!" Sandy yelled.

Shack banged him again and laughed. Sandy went over and sat down, brooding.

When Nan came out with Helen, the blond girl's eyes were almost closed, and her head lolled loosely. She was doing well, but she was almost overdoing it. We put the meager luggage in the trunk and got into the car, Nan in front between Sandy and Shack, with Sandy at the wheel.

Within a half hour the big jolt of dexedrine and the other wild range of happy pills had built Sandy back up to his usual level of joyous optimism. He wanted a new car, and he wanted to prove a theory of his. So we cruised a big residential area of Pittsburgh which seemed like damn foolishness to me. When he found what he wanted, he parked a block beyond and went back alone. He said he didn't need help. Within a shockingly short time he was back with a new Mercury. He said with roosterish pride that he had proved his theory that the last one to get to a private party doesn't want to block the cars in the drive, so he leaves his keys in the ignition like a good fellow. Hurray for the good fellow.

We brought both cars along. Sandy had another sparkling idea. We found a big auto dump, ran the Buick far back into the clatter, stripped off the plates and threw them into the night.

"Let them figure that the hell out. It's like confusion, man," he said. "How's baby doing, Kirboo?"

"I don't know. Maybe not so good."

We had another hot, fast car. We moved east, digging deeper into the night, never missing the little roads that Sandy had looked up and remembered. He had a complete map inside his head, and we were a little light moving along it.

I had to have a thoroughly empty road. If we were rushed by an oncoming car, it could go sour. And finally we were on a road that suited me. I took her hand and squeezed it hard. She squeezed back. And suddenly she began to breathe in a deep, rasping way, articulating each exhalation.

"What the hell?" Nan said, looking around.

"I don't know," I said. "I think she could be dying."

The great raw breathing went on, very audible over the sound of the motor and the tires and the night wind. It stopped abruptly.

"Is she dead?" Sandy asked.

Before I could answer, the breathing began again, slowly at first and then picking up the previous tempo.

"The next time," I said angrily, nervously, "it may stop for good, and the last thing I want back here with me is a dead blonde. Let's leave her the hell off, Sandy. This looks like a good place."

He slowed the car, then suddenly swung off into a wide and level dirt road. He deftly worked it around until we were heading out, and turned off the lights and the motor. The breathing seemed three times as loud.

"Jesus, that's a terrible noise," Shack said.

I got out quickly and went around the car and opened the door on her side and got her out. She was completely limp. I got her under the armpits and dragged her. Her shoes came off. I could see them, and the tracks her heels made by the light of a high half moon.

Sandy was beside me. "Where you taking her?"

"Off in the bushes."

We were talking in whispers. I heard Nan say, back in the car, "Hones' ta God, Shack, with you it's a disease."

And that cut the problem way down. I had been most nervous about Nan and her little knife, and her high delight in using the little knife.

I heard the sound of a brook as I pulled her into the bushes. And suddenly the ground dropped away and the girl and I went crashing and rolling down a short, steep bank into an icy stream. I cursed and hugged my elbow and got up onto my knees, in about five inches of water.

I suddenly realized that the harsh fake breathing had stopped. I got hold of the girl and wrestled her clumsily over to the muddy bank. There was an entirely new quality to her inertness, and I realized that this time it was genuine. She had gone headlong onto the rocks.

"You okay?" Sandy called in a hushed voice. He came cautiously down through the brush.

"Got wet and hit my elbow. Let's get out of here."

"Hold it," he said. He bent over the girl and put his ear on her back. "Heart's still thumping, man."

"So what?"

He found a rock the size of a softball and forced it into my hand. "Finish it up, man. Take it all the way."

I balanced the heavy stone in my hand. I touched the roundness of the back of her head with my hand, under the softness of her hair.

Sandy made a noise like a chicken.

I turned in a way that partially blocked his vision, and I struck down hard with the rock. I hit the hard mud close to her head. It made a convincing noise that would turn stomachs.

I stood up so abruptly I knocked him back against the slope. "Let's get the hell out of here."

"Is she . . ."

"Get moving!" I yelled at him. We scrambled up the bank. Sandy kicked her shoes into the brush. Shack and Nan had moved onto the back seat. They didn't know or care whether the car was moving or standing still. We got back on the highway, and soon we were keening down around the curves of a long and dangerous hill.

A long time later Nan asked, leaning over between us, "Is she dead?"

"Like stone cold," Sandy said.

"And I'm living," Nan said.

"She had better legs, man," Sandy said.

"So where is she? Walking, running?" Nan asked.

She leaned back. We rushed through the small hills, drifted through the silent, ugly, sleeping towns. Our headlights unraveled the patched roads.

"Fee fie fiddly-I-oh. Fee fie fiddly-I-oh, oh, oh, oh."

We were with it. We rode right out there on the forward edge of it, like a dog with his nose in the wind. The square world was noplace. We were a fly, and a blind man sought to catch us in his fist.

I have been asleep and I resent most bitterly the waste of the thin edge of time I have left. I would have told all of it, right up to the end, but I guess not much of it is pertinent, not after the time we drove away from the girl. I reached for a paper tray of hamburger and they snapped steel around my wrists. They were large, tough pros, and when they did look at me, it was the way a doctor might look at an abscess. Cool professional curiosity, plus the innate distaste of one who prefers to look at healthy tissue. Their stare turned me from a man into a thing. Put it another way. Maybe I had turned from a man into a thing, but had not known the transition was complete. Their eyes were cruel mirrors, so I soon learned to stop looking directly at anyone.

There was the temptation to drag this out. But I have said it all. TOMORROW has become TODAY and this is the end of me. This third day of April.

I'll try to get through what's left without slamming myself. I don't think I can. It must be a lot easier to die for something you believe in.

THIRTEEN

ON the fifteenth day of April, twelve days after the multiple execution, Dallas Kemp took an attractive couple in their late thirties out to see the hillside lot he owned. The man had that manner and assurance of money and success. A large corporation had recently transferred him to Monroe, and as he suspected he might spend many years in Monroe, he wanted to build the first house they had ever built. The wife was poised, and she had warmth and charm. When they talked together, there was about them that special aura only good marriages have.

They pulled the two cars over onto the shoulder of the country road and walked up and looked at the lot. Snow clung in a few long, shadowed places. The earth was moist, the first buds showing.

The couple was pleased with the land, with the privacy and the view. Dallas Kemp left them standing where the house would be, and went down to his car and brought back the blueprint of the floor plan and turned it so that it was in the same position the house would be, so they could see what the windows would look out upon.

The man said, "Isn't it a little unusual? An architect owning the land and selling it to his client?"

"It's getting hard to find land with an contour. I picked it up myself because it's such an attractive site. I had . . . a particular couple in mind, but they weren't able to use it."

"Then," the woman said, with a small frown, "if this house was designed for this site, then it was really designed for somebody else, not for us."

"Yes, it was. But the people I designed it for never even had a chance to see it. I like the house well enough so that . . . I would like to see it built. I could design one for you, but I don't know if it would be this good. I know it wouldn't be better."

"It's a beautiful house, Mr. Kemp. As we said in your office, it would have to be larger," the woman said. "We have four very active children."

"It was designed so that the new wing can go off the north side," Kemp said.

"This is sort of a package deal," the man said.

"I'll sell the land for exactly what I paid for it," Dallas Kemp said. "If the whole idea doesn't appeal to you, it will probably be a long time before anybody else comes along to whom I'd be willing to show it. I want the land and the house to go together, to the right people."

"Is this such an artistic compulsion with you that you'll resist any changes we may want to make before we ask for bids?" the man asked.

"I'll make all changes that do not disturb the basic design, the unity of the house. I do not make that sort of change for any client."

The woman turned to the husband and gently grasped the lapel of his tweed jacket. "I want the package deal, darling. Without ever knowing us, this very good and very honest young man made our house. I want this wonderful house and this wonderful hillside so badly my darn knees are weak and funny. If we don't have it, to live in, to be in love in— because it's the kind of a house that has to have love in it— I'll be wistful all the rest of my life."

The man flushed slightly and grinned at Dallas Kemp. "I guess there's only one answer to that. We'll go ahead with it."

"I'm glad," Kemp said. "I want to see the house built. It's too good a thing to be wasted."

After they talked for a time of arrangements, they walked back down to the automobiles. As they stood by the cars, the woman brought up Helen Wister. Dallas Kemp was sorry she had done so, because later she would learn more about the people living in Monroe, and she would remember being unconsiously tactless and it would bother her, because there was kindness in this woman. He knew it was only a product of coincidence and idle conversation when she said, "Isn't this the area where that terrible thing happened way last summer? Where that man was murdered and that doctor's daughter was kidnaped?"

"No. That happened out on the other side of the city."

"I read where they had electrocuted those horrors a couple of weeks ago. What was that girl's name, anyway?"

"Wister. Helen Wister."

"Did you know her, Mr. Kemp?"

"Yes, I knew her."

"It must have been such a terrible shock for everybody around here. I guess you people will always remember the details of a thing like that, I mean you'd be more likely to remember it than we would, living out in Seattle and just reading about it in the papers. Did they shoot her?"

Dallas Kemp was able to turn away from them by using the device of turning his back to the spring wind to light a cigarette. When he turned back he knew he was under control.

"As it was reconstructed, Mrs. Dennrig, and according to Stassen's story, she fell and hit her head when they abandoned her. The autopsy showed only minor head injuries. Death was by drowning. Apparently she came to in the night and perhaps tried to stand and fainted. You could call it murder, but they weren't tried for that."

"What . . . what horrible irony," the woman said. "It . . . almost makes it worse, somehow."

"Yes," Dallas Kemp said. "She was alone and they were gone. It almost makes it worse."

Dallas Kemp lied to them, told them he had some more measurements to take. They drove back to the city. He walked up the hill and leaned against the trunk of an old silver birch tree, his hands in his pockets, and looked at where the house would be.

He stood there and he wished he was old. He wished he had come back across time to look at one of the very early things he had designed, one of the good things. He had the feeling that when he had become old, thoughts of Helen would then have a nostalgic, drifting sweetness, like sachet and old love letters, and an old man could smile and remember the good parts.

But it was too close. He was trapped in this bitter segment of his life, and he could move away from it only with the agonizing slowness of the minute hand on the clock. Time pressed him close to all the vivid memories of her.

On the way back to town, during a time of inattention, he suddenly saw a brown puppy prancing out into the road directly in front of him, joyously ignoring the panic scream of children in the yard, ears flopping, too lost in his game to consider disaster.

Kemp wrenched the wheel, yelped the tires and awaited a soft small thud. It did not come. When he was well beyond that place, moving slowly, he looked in the rear-view mirror and saw a man pulling the craven puppy from the road by the scruff of its neck, whacking its stern with his hand.

Kemp drove on, but within a mile he was trembling so badly he turned onto a quieter street and let the car drift to a stop by the curbing. He did not believe he could have endured killing the dog. He felt he had been spared one final, unbearable thing.

He closed his eyes and rested his forehead against the top of the steering wheel. For a moment he felt on the very edge of perceiving and understanding some cosmic equation which balanced a logic of love, innocence, accident and death. But it was gone before he saw its shape.

Kemp straightened up, and, after a little while, he remembered how to start his car, and he drove the rest of the way back into the city.

About the Author

John D. MacDonald is a graduate of Syracuse University and has an MBA from Harvard Business School. He and his wife, Dorothy, have one son and several grandchildren. The MacDonalds spend most of the year in Sarasota, Florida. They summer in upstate New York near Piseco.